Portrait of Lydia
by
Hollie Van Horne

Grant Tyrell worked his whole life to attain fame, fortune, and power. When a Harvard professor did Grant's family tree, it didn't surprise the cool businessman that he had greatness within him. As a matter of fact, he was told that one of his ancestors had been Septimius Severus, warrior-emperor of the Roman Empire. So, when Grant saw Time Travelers, Inc.'s web site on the Internet, he decided to take a much needed vacation and travel from 2000 A.D. to 200 A.D.

Time Travelers, Inc. was offended by the fact that their client needed nothing from them but a portal, that he would have a Broadway costumer design his historic attire, that he had had the same professor do all the necessary research for him, that he didn't need Bruce Wainwright's help, and that he spoke fluent Latin. He didn't even mind it when they insisted that Bruce Wainwright accompany him on his trip to the past. Jim, Sam, and Bruce didn't want to take the man anywhere until he offered to triple their $150,000.00 fee.

What Grant Tyrell wanted was to experience total power. To decide the fate of millions! To own all the known world! And to experience the power and glory of the Roman Empire!

He never suspected that the time tunnel would have other plans for him. That he should have listened to Wainwright. Or that a young woman named Lydia of the house of Marcus Flavius Antonious of Rome would hold HIS fate in her pretty hands.

Prepare yourself!
Time Travelers, Inc. is about to take you to the Roman Empire of 200 A.D.

More than Grant expected!

The fighter was suddenly frightened and futilely lashed the sword left and right in the air. Grant used his round shield to move the slow lunges away from his body and pushed his advantage over the fighter who went down on one knee. The fighter's sword flew out of reach.

"Now's a good time to yield," said Grant in Latin.

The fighter shook the helmet in agreement, and Grant relaxed. Then the warrior grabbed Grant's leg and pulled him down to ground level. A push to knock Grant over only resulted in the new Thracian lying flat on the ground. Grant placed his sword to the youth's neck. The helmet shifted heavily across the larynx, and the New York businessman could hear the raspy sound of someone trying desperately to breathe. Hands reached out to Grant's arms. "Don't toy with me! Yield or die," said Grant not in the mood for play.

The fighter relaxed and shook the helmet up and down, showing that Grant had won.

"No hard feelings I hope," said Grant as he rose from the ground.

In muffled Latin a small voice said, "I've never felt anything like it before in my life!"

"Naturally. I am the student of Milos, the greatest gladiator in all Roman history."

The helmet was pulled from the head. Long sable-brown hair fell in curls from inside the visor. A perfect oval face. Two big brown eyes. Long dark lashes. Full, pouting, pink lips. Slender throat. Soft shoulders. Long fingers on graceful hands.

"A woman?" said Grant.

"It wasn't your fault," she said. "You had no way of knowing."

Grant removed his helmet and stared at the incredibly beautiful woman before him. Those soft but strong thighs should have given him some idea that the frame of the fighter was feminine. The uniform, with its covered midsection, should have told him something. He'd been in combat with a woman and was puzzled that he hadn't guessed it.

Portrait of Lydia
by
Hollie Van Horne

An original publication of Time Travelers, LLC

Time Travelers, LLC
Columbiana, Ohio
44408
www.timetravelersinc.org

For information about this as well as other Time Travelers titles address:
Time Travelers, LLC, Columbiana, Ohio 44408

ISBN: 0-9674552-2-7
Library of Congress Control number: 2002091676
First printing October 2002
Series book 6

Printed in the U.S.A.

Cover art: Lange Design
www.langedesign.org

Author's Note

<u>Portrait of Lydia</u> was written after a great deal of research into the lifestyle of gladiators, political figures, women, and slaves of the Roman Empire 200 A.D. Unlike nonfiction books, historic fiction does not afford the author the luxury of literary notations of sources. Many sources were used to help me write Lydia and Grant's story, but there were a few whose contributions inspired the direction and heart of this novel. With great respect to the authors of those books, I hereby note their contribution to this work of fiction:

<u>Cruelty and Civilization</u> by Roland Auguet, Barnes and Noble Books, New York, 1998, did more than help me describe the Circus Maximus, the Colosseum, the ludus environment, and the rules of the "games;" it inspired me and gave tone and depth to this novel.

<u>I Claudia Women in Ancient Rome</u> by Diana E. E. Kleiner and Susan B. Matheson, Yale University Art Gallery, New Haven, 1996, helped me create my heroine, Lydia, her lifestyle, and her father's home.

<u>Slaves and Masters in the Roman Empire: A Study in Social Control</u> by K. R. Bradley, New York, Oxford University Press, 1987, helped me understand the nature of slavery in the Roman Empire.

<u>Ancient Rome</u> by Simon James, Dorling Kindersley Eyewitness Books, 1990, added the touches I needed to describe the Roman Empire as well as giving me a very nice picture of Septimius Severus and his family.

This book is dedicated to

those men who died for the games

Portrait of Lydia

Hollie Van Horne

Chapter One

Grant Tyrell pressed the 250 pounds away from his body as forcefully as he thrust people from his life. The muscles in both arms moved under his suntanned skin the way pond water ripples when a school of fish swim far beneath its surface. His thighs tensed and then relaxed as he exercised. First tightening and then constraining, the strong muscles danced up and down his legs shaping his long limbs into perfect models of power and strength. Then he rested the free weight bar on the cradle above his workout bench. He shook his hands to relieve the ache. His bronzed, manicured fingers jiggled the blood back into them. His feet, which dangled from the black, Italian leather bench nudged the thick, burgundy carpet of his private exercise room. The sweat curled, rolled, and spilled from his lean and handsome face. His charcoal, black hair expensively shaped into a Roman style—with a straight bang across his broad forehead and the thick back section tapered at the neck and temples—by his private barber, was glued to his cheekbones by perspiration; the longer strands in the back hugged his neck.

He let his arms unwind and then set his hands just right on the bar, took a deep breath, strained again, and slowly blew the oxygen from his mouth. His abdomen flexed into layers of chiseled lines. His eyes, coal colored and cold, stared at the ceiling in abject concentration. His dark, heavy eyebrows suspended over those penetrating eyes which could, on occasion, give the appearance of an eagle surveying his territory for prey. That look had sent shivers up and down an employee's back. His lips compressed, one against the other, signaling his total determination in finishing this last, difficult rep.

This was his final set—the last unit of his daily exercise regime. Afterwards, he would step into the tanning booth for a quick ten minutes, then relax in the dry sauna for another ten and think about his forthcoming time travel vacation and today's agenda.

Grant arrived at his office at seven in the morning so that he could work out undisturbed, enjoy the sauna, the suntan booth, and take a long, leisurely, steamy hot shower before his barber came in at eight. His manicurist came in once every week on Wednesday but at twelve o'clock in the afternoon so that he never wasted time while he ate his lunch. At eight-forty-five in the morning, the barber left, and Grant ate one, toasted, sesame seed bagel with light cream cheese, one glass of freshly squeezed grapefruit juice, two boiled eggs, one medium sliced piece of Canadian bacon, and one cup of Colombian, just ground, coffee all of which were delivered from the gourmet restaurant in the lobby of his office building. He did this five days a week. The routine never varied. On the weekends, if he had no social events planned, he left the chaos of the city for a small cottage he had in upper state New York. He would fish, boat, or hike...alone.

A man of business, who amassed billions in one year, needed these stress relieving moments if he were to remain healthy and successful. This was why he needed the vacation. He hadn't had a real getaway for years. His barber had spotted a gray hair. His doctor, though pleased with the results of his physical, had suggested a peaceful retreat from work.

He wasn't sure if he could afford a three-month holiday the way his people loafed so. His employees were getting on his nerves. Childish idiots who expected to be paid a huge fee but did virtually nothing to earn it. There were some he respected and trusted but not many. He would just have to fire the dead weight if they didn't come through for him while he was gone.

He was thirty and not getting any younger. He was the right weight of 200 pounds for his six-foot-one inch frame. He was rich and handsome and any woman he wanted followed him to bed only to be dispatched the next morning with a curt comment that he had to get to the office early.

He didn't need anyone he couldn't buy. And he could buy anyone and anything he wanted.

His intellect was equal to his temper. A short fuse had to be extinguished constantly with wisdom and a bright, flawless smile he used sparingly. Grant reminded himself to never vent his ire on people who mattered—who could make or break him. And there weren't too many around who could hurt him now. So, anyone who irritated him in the slightest might incur his wrath. And with one command, one phone call, one flash of his pen on a piece of personalized stationery, they'd be out of a job. It was total power. And he loved it.

"That Bruce Wainwright is a fool if he thinks he can keep me from my trip," he thought to himself as the pain in his chest muscles surrendered to the sauna's dry heat.

"After all," he said to himself, "they advertised it on the Net. They should be glad to get that much money for one trip. I had Professor Timmiri do all the legwork for them. It doesn't surprise me in the least that he uncovered the truth about my Roman heritage. Sheldon's coming at two today for the final fitting—provided Sandra rearranged that appointment for me. So those time travelers have nothing to do but get me to the portal. I've done all the work for them."

He squeezed his lips together and smiled with genuine satisfaction, then pressed a button and a CD player hidden inside the wall by the door began conjugating Latin verbs. He followed the woman's voice. Such a soft voice. Pretty. He closed his eyes. His lips moved as he mumbled the sentences. Course three. He had two more to finish before the end of the month. Advanced Latin. And why not?

Grant graduated magna cum laud at Harvard business school. On a scholarship. He'd been the consummate student all through high school. Competed in football and track, played a mean trumpet for the stage band, was in the bridge, hearts, and chess club, the science club, single-handedly organized three years of Earth Day activities, won the state science fair two years in a row, was first at the flag for every Prayer Day, performed in the school's yearly musical obtaining the lead role in *How to Succeed in Business Without Really Trying* his senior year, won his National Honor Society seat the first year he applied, helped the speech and debate coach his junior year when one of her Lincoln/Douglas debaters got pneumonia and couldn't make the state qualifier thereby bluffing his way into becoming a state qualifier, earned straight A's in all the most advanced subjects, took photos for the yearbook staff, wrote a column for the school newspaper's sports page, did volunteer work in the community, gave blood during the school's blood drive, was student advisor to the board of education, named number one of the top ten students in his class, worked at the golf course at the local country club, caddied for the richest man in town, and went steady with the head cheerleader until the day they graduated. She was every boy's nighttime fantasy. Blonde, buxom, blue eyed, pink lipped, friendly in so many ways, and obviously in love with him. Condoms were a must for the lady had marriage on her mind.

As soon as he was free from high school, he started to charm that rich man's daughter, Constance, who was no match for the cheerleader: dull, squinty-eyed, flat chested, limp black hair, pale skin, skinny legs, and a dedicated virgin. He pronounced faithfully to dear old dad that he could settle down with a girl like Constance. The scholarship came; the student moved to this new college dorm; the town completely forgotten; the rich man left to his golf game; and Constance tossed aside. After all, they were going to different colleges now he told her. She should realize that long-distance romances never worked. How could he be expected to keep their love alive when he had to concentrate on his studies? Besides, the business he really loved was owned by a man with no son to follow in his footsteps.

Grant idolized Thomas Tyler who took him on as vice-president as soon as Grant graduated from Harvard. No moving up the ranks for young Tyrell. He devoured the man's wisdom, learning when to buy, when to sell, how to hire good people, how to fire loafers; and when the man started to lose capital and needed a helping hand, Grant bought him out and suggested that it was time for Mr. Tyler to take an early retirement.

Not bad for a kid whose father, a well-paid construction worker, who had left Grant's mother flat broke when the boy was only two-years-old, forcing her to work out of the home five and a half days a week as a secretary to the man who had the ugly daughter and who liked golf so much.

His mother had warned him that he would have to be the best, that there was no room for failure, that she was doing all she could to make a life for the both of them, that she was sacrificing her own happiness to raise him with no father, that if he were smart he'd forget about his deadbeat dad who didn't love his son enough to stay with the family, and that anything worth getting was worth anything you had to do to get it. She cautioned that he would have to work harder than the rest of the boys; the subtext being that it was because he lacked real talent.

Grant spent his whole life wondering about why his father had left them. He grew up assuming that his dad was disappointed with him. There was nothing that mattered more to the child than proving the man wrong. And no matter how hard he tried, how many prizes he accumulated, and how much money and fame he acquired, his mother always found him lacking—his father disassociated himself with them even more. He had to hide the tears when his father did not show for special holidays. Time and time again he was rejected. Disappointment and abandonment eventually turned into pain. Pain manifested bitterness. Bitterness produced anger. Anger became coldness. Coldness enjoyed control. Success, winning, being better than anyone else around him and taking all he could from everyone he knew was the soothing balm that healed the outer skin of the deeper wound. And, in the end, a heart was lost. And a soul was locked away in a dark, chilly cell covered by a perfect exterior.

Now he had proof that he was someone—or rather that he had

been someone powerful at one time. The Harvard professor had done the genealogical research for Grant and uncovered positive proof that Grant Tyrell had been Emperor Septimius Severus of Rome. Warrior. Husband. Father. General. Why he even resembled what was left of the man's statue. Now all Time Travelers, Inc. had to do was transport him to A.D. 200. He had chosen the date whimsically as it was in the middle of his former life's reign, and because, if you added another zero, you had the date of his departure, 2000 A.D. From A.D. 2000 to A.D. 200 and back.

Sheldon, the Broadway costumer, had created a wonderful traveling costume for him: an embroidered purple toga that would be worn over a gold-embroidered tunica, leather boot like sandals, and an actual antique fibula from 192 A.D. that cost a fortune but added just the right authentic touch. Of course, his thick, dark hair had been cut months ago to make him look like his ancient ancestor. He privately reveled in the idea that only a rich man could have managed this incredible transformation, and when Time Travelers, Inc. bulked at his request after the initial interview; he simply doubled their price. They would never pass up $300, 000 dollars. And they had virtually nothing to do for him save point the way. He had received a message from Wainwright that the time travelers had accepted his application with the proviso that Bruce Wainwright accompany him to Rome. He had agreed immediately because he liked the man and thought it might be nice to have someone from his own time period around in case of an emergency. He'd even had a simple toga made for Wainwright as a gesture of good faith. The man would be a good second lieutenant to an "emperor" trying to get his bearings in a strange era.

The flight would take place Wednesday night in Cooperstown—exact location kept a secret—and he couldn't wait. He had spent months preparing his business for this vacation. They'd not be able to call him on his cell phone. No way to ask him for help. He'd held a meeting Friday morning and explained to his people what they had to do while he was gone, reminding them that sales better be much improved by the time he returned. He worried about leaving his vice-president in charge. After all, he knew how deceitful such determined men in subservient positions can be.

Seven forty-five. Time for a shower and a fresh robe. He planned to install a Jacuzzi while he was on his trip. He'd even designed one himself and sent the sketch to a reputable firm. It would cost a fortune to put it into an office such as this, but they promised to have it done during the three months he was gone. They'd have to minimize his secretary's office space a bit, but, a proper, tiled Roman bath would be necessary to remind him of his time traveling vacation and his greatness as Emperor of Rome. He'd chosen a contractor whose specialty was Roman baths.

Grant fantasized about what it would be like as emperor of the entire Roman Empire. Servants offering him the finest foods and wine. Music. Baths. Women who would adore him. The wife would be inspected and accepted or rejected as he desired. Two sons to deal with. Who cared? He was emperor and he could do whatever he wanted. He'd have a different slave girl every night of the three-month stay if he wished. And a faithful wife to sleep with when he was in the mood for domesticity. An occasional chariot ride through Rome. Take in some theater and a game or two. But, what he was truly interested in was the day- to-day decision making that came with being emperor—with being the omnipotent judge and jury in Rome. Total power. More than he had now. Firing people wasn't the same as choosing who would succeed or fail by his order. Of course, he would be fair. He would listen to their pleas and determine their fate. Wainwright would be there to assist him.

Wainwright was obviously the most intelligent one in the time traveling business, and had had more experience traveling than the brothers Jim and Sam Cooper. Wainwright even spoke Latin which would be a boon in itself. And he liked the fact that Wainwright looked the part. The man had dark hair cut a little like his own rather than the long haired, colonial fashion of the Cooper brothers. In what century were those two living? Grant also liked the fact that Wainwright seemed resourceful and showed signs of being a good man of business. They were about the same age too. And Grant had learned that Wainwright's ancestors had been aristocrats in the Middle Ages and on down through time. Impressive. Sam Cooper was wildly unpredictable, and his brother too quiet and pensive. The brothers appeared to have moral and ethical issues that he just couldn't handle. Besides, he had a feeling that the Cooper brothers were very popular with the ladies, and Wainwright sent this vibe that he was no competition for Grant in the love arena. So, he had agreed with their plans to send one of their own as security for their client: their CYA in case something went wrong. But it wouldn't.

The barber was one minute late and Grant pointed it out to him. Just as the linen cloth was placed around his shoulders, Sandra interrupted the process.

"Haven't I told you to never break into this room while my barber has a razor at my throat?" he said.

"Yes, sir, but I'm afraid it's an emergency."

"Yours or mine?" Grant asked.

"Mine, sir," she said, placing her shaking hands behind her back to hide them.

"It's my sister. She's been diagnosed with cancer and has to start chemo next week. The prognosis is very good for her because they caught it right away, and she's only twenty-seven. Since I'm her closest relative, I was wondering if I could take a few days off to help her out—maybe move her into my apartment in New York to facilitate nursing her while I'm working here. It's too hard to travel back and forth from Pittsburgh to New York City to see her though this. I've even managed to get her doctor to recommend another clinic closer to my job so that she can continue her therapy near my work. It'll only take a few days—say three and then the weekend—to move her items to my apartment so that she can start her treatments on Monday."

"But I'm going away Wednesday and will be gone for three

months. I can't have you leaving the office now when I need you most. I'm sure you can catch a commuter flight down to Pittsburgh Friday after work, gather her things on Saturday and Sunday, fly back with her Sunday night, and settle her in before treatments and work on Monday. After all, how much would she have to move? She'll be in bed most of the time, right?"

Sandra bit her lower lip. "Yes, but...I haven't taken any time off in two years. Not even for the flu. I can stay a little longer tonight and Monday to make it work."

"It's just a really bad time for you to take off right now, Sandra. You understand. Mind that blade, Mitchell," he said to the barber.

"Yes, sir," Sandra said softly.

"Bring me my agenda book, and we'll sit down and discuss the day while I eat breakfast. Order yourself a bagel when you call down to Antoine's if you wish."

"No thanks, Mr. Tyrell, I'm not very hungry."

"Suit yourself," he called to her. "By the way, you did remember to change that fitting to today, didn't you?"

"Oh, ah, you mean Sheldon?"

"Yes," he said irritated in having to repeat himself.

"I'm not sure. I'll have to look. When did you tell me that, Mr. Tyrell?"

"Friday afternoon."

"Oh, yes, I called and left a message on his machine. He was gone for the day. It was almost five when I called."

"Well, get on it. Call him at nine and make sure he changed his plans. I'm leaving Wednesday, and it's the final fitting for Christ sake. I have to have those togas."

Sandra hurried from his office.

The barber smiled and said, "Togas? Going to a singles' island, Mr. Tyrell?"

"Is it any of your business?"

The barber fell silent.

"Wednesday is my last appointment with you," he reminded the barber.

Grant paused while the man shaved his neck then added, "Sandra will call you in September to set up an appointment, and take some clippers to the back of my neck, won't you?"

Grant knew that the emperor would have servants to do this for him when he joined bodies with his ancestor in what was outlined to him by the time travelers as the Gemini effect; but, it was a good idea to feel comfortable just in case.

"I need to get dressed quickly this morning. Didn't expect Sandra in so early. Can't start the business of the day in a terry robe."

"Yes, sir—I mean, no sir. I'll be done in a minute."

Grant relaxed and closed his eyes while his barber shaved the dark, curly hair at the nap of his neck. Soon, very soon, he would be master of the known world of 200 A.D. and basking in the glorious sunshine of Imperial Rome.

Chapter Two

Grant said, "I'm not putting that toga thing on until we're at the cabin."

They were at the Trudy/Wainwright house in Cooperstown. Sam, Jim, Grant, and Wainwright had eaten dinner in Tunniclif's pit, sampled a bit of gourmet coffee at The Stagecoach, and were now sipping Wainwright's imported sherry back at the house. Grant mentioned that it was a satisfying way to start a vacation.

Sam said, "It's getting late, and Jim needs to get back to Milford. I'll drive you up to the cabins. We have a slew of guests right now. One of our better summers. The usual customers and a few new faces. I was in the cabin earlier tonight and left the light on for you, and the door open. It's better I don't go inside. Don't need to accidentally travel tonight."

"I must admit that this whole time travel business is thoroughly astonishing. It's difficult for me to believe that by tomorrow morning I shall be Emperor of Rome. The omnipotent ruler of all around me."

Sam winced. "Just make sure you have the research tucked away in your travel bag just in case you get into any trouble."

"He doesn't need a travel bag, he has me to guide him," said Wainwright, swallowing his final taste of the sherry.

"I know," mumbled Jim, "that's why Sam's worried."

"And we'll return to the cabin in September? Correct?" asked Grant.

"Now I warned you that I did my best on estimating the calendar. There are so many changes in the Roman calendar throughout its vast history, but, basically, the days in their month are close enough to ours. So, my guess is that we'll be home on or around the 2000 autumn equinox. The time tunnel will know when it's time anyway, and that's all we really need to know."

Grant looked away as if he were lost in deep thought.

"Getting a little worried?" said Sam.

"Not at all. Three months just isn't enough."

"You can always go back there," said Wainwright. "I mean, later, if you decide to return that is."

Grant's smile was painfully perfect even though it was one hundred percent fake. His teeth were pure white pearls, and his lips curled in such a charming, almost boyish manner, that the sweetness of the expression simply dazzled you. It was something he wore to impress people like a tailored suit or a designer tie. He didn't smile much so the contrast forced you to notice how attractive it was.

"I intend to. Often. I plan to reap all the inherent benefits of being the man who holds the power of the known world in his hands. Septimius Severus."

"Are you sure you know everything about the warrior emperor?" asked Wainwright.

"Why would you ask such a thing?" he answered with a controlled tightness in his voice.

"Oh," said Wainwright turning away from the man and grinning, "just wondering that's all."

Sam and Jim gave Wainwright a sharp look. Then all three smiled. Whatever Wainwright knew, he was keeping it to himself. Considering how arrogant Grant had been with them the last few weeks, it was good to know that Wainwright had the intellectual upper hand. You could always count on him to have the answer no matter how long it took for him to uncover it.

"Right now I think you and Wainwright better get a move on if you want to hit the solstice by two. My chariot," Sam pointed to the old, worn truck that sat by the curb in front of the funeral home, "awaits. Night, Jim."

Jim watched as the three men left the house. Then he locked Trudy's house, found his car parked on the next side street, and headed for his home in Milford.

"I wasn't sure if a soldier would wear the royal purple robe," Grant said. "I mean, being that he was so rugged and completely interested in his military. His wife ruled while he was away fighting, but I'll take control when I get there. I'm not too sure how I should approach Rome? Where do you think we'll end up when we go through the tunnel? Hopefully in camp just outside the city."

Wainwright said, "I checked some records on my own. He might have been further from home than you think. What if it takes us three months just to get to the city?"

"I'll see to it that we break records getting home. March all night if we have to."

Sam said, "Wouldn't a Roman general's uniform have been more appropriate?"

Grant wasn't offended by Sam's question. "I thought about that, but I figured that I'd be wearing this so much in Rome, and I'm positive the other man's clothes won't fit me. I'm probably triple his size, and how we'll explain that I can't guess."

"You do know how to ride a horse like a Roman leader?"

"I should hope I do."

Sam smiled and steered the truck up the curvy, rocky roads to the cabins. "Looks as though you have your research down for the trip. The explanations as to your height difference will have to come from Wainwright. That's why we're sending him with you. Ah, here we are."

The three men hurried into the cabin and Wainwright and Grant slipped into their new clothes.

Sam looked at an oddly wrapped gift on the center of the kitchen table. "A gift from Celeste," he said to Wainwright. "Wonder how that got here?"

"Remember, you must be thinking about the time period to land there. Are there any last minute instructions you want to give Sam?" Wainwright asked.

"I've taken care of all that by giving my secretary a three-month agenda book. She'll know what to do. Thanks anyway."

"Very well, gentlemen. Have a safe trip, and I'll see you in September," said Sam. He was about to walk to the door when he thought of something. "Take care, Wainwright."

The sudden show of concern surprised Bruce. He paused, cleared his throat, and said, "Certainly. Thanks, Sam."

"Are you sure there isn't someone in this cabin?" asked Grant.

"No, Jim's 'guest' is only up here on the weekends," said Sam as he shut the door behind him.

Grant was flushed with excitement. "So, this is it. I'm both exhilarated and apprehensive although I can't imagine why."

"You don't want to take anything with you?"

"What do I need? You have all our maps, first-aid kit, et. al. in that satchel."

Wainwright gave the contents of his satchel another look. "I brought along a journal to write down my daily activities. Never done that before, but the Cooper relatives did it, and those diaries have proven to be most useful. Should be interesting to find out where a general transfer to 200 A.D. Rome will get me."

Wainwright noticed his reflection in the wall mirror. "It's a good thing no one can see us in these. We look like we're going to some party at a fraternity house."

"It'll probably be best if you stay behind me when we meet the troops."

Wainwright smirked. "Of course."

They sat at the table quietly and waited. The time tunnel opened at two in the morning. Grant felt the swish of air, the twirling and dizzying effects of the spiral, and the disconcerting feeling of being thrown into complete darkness and tossed up and down like lettuce in a salad.

When Grant opened his eyes, he was in the middle of a dirt road with his fine clothes getting filthy by the mud and dust. He looked around for the troops. There were none. He looked for the seven hills of Rome; there were none.

"Hold there. You! How came you upon us so suddenly? Are you a thief? Answer me," screamed a man who spoke in crude Latin.

Grant quickly interpreted what the man said, adjusted his thoughts to speak Latin, and wondered at how quickly the time tunnel expected him to make the living transition to 200 A.D. There wasn't a moment to think, get in character, focus on the sun, smell the sea, notice the birds flying above him in the clear blue sky, or feel the mud crawling into his beautiful leather sandals. It was all so fast. He'd expected to awaken slowly, in the early morning hours, perhaps in a bed or a cot, be able to shake the dizziness from his head, and peruse his surroundings before entering this new world.

Now this man was expecting something from him. Yelling at him rather. Not the way a man should speak with his emperor. For a brief moment Grant was frightened and disoriented. So this is it. Move. Talk. Do it. Now! You're here, and you better not slip up. Get all that research going and talk the talk...walk the walk. You're a Roman now.

He should be angry with this man for speaking in such a disrespectful manner to his sovereign. Grant looked left and right to see to whom the man was truly addressing and then pointed at his chest with his index finger. "Are you talking to me?" he asked in Latin, displaying his best New Yorker attitude to this insolent commoner.

The man with the grotesque face looked at the chained men and said, "Deranged madman. Thief. Beggar." Then he squinted his eyes half closed to look back at Grant. "How do you come by those fine clothes? Did you steal them?"

"I ...ah...well I'm the emperor. Show some respect."

Several men in a long line of prisoners chained at the foot laughed so hard some actually fell into the ditch. By the look of it, this was obviously the best laugh they'd had in years.

The six-toothed man in brown leather who sported a bushy, unkempt hairstyle cackled loudly, smirked—which was not a pretty sight by any stretch of the imagination—and said, "And I'm his precious wife, Julia."

The prisoners laughed even more robustly.

Then this man, who was obviously in charge for he carried a whip, told another man to bind Grant's feet with chains.

"Hey, you can't do that to me! Don't you know who I am?" said Grant in amazement.

"Do you have a name?"

"Ah..." Grant thought better than to try the Emperor of Rome line again after watching the mirth his last comment had aroused.

"Oh, I don't care if you think you're the Queen of Sheba; you're mine now, slave."

"Slave?" Grant said softly. The man's comment had the same calculated effect as a kick to the jaw

"You're on the Via Papilia, slave, heading to Capua. You're a good sized one, a real giant. And stronger than any man I've ever seen in my life even if you are a bit old. You'll make a good pupil. Anyway, coming with us will get you out of the sun which has obviously burned your head."

Grant's feet were tethered with the same chain that linked the other men. "Pupil? For what?"

"The games. Who do you think we are, slave?"

"Games? As in Colosseum like games?"

Grant winced with the pain of being pulled into the footsteps of the man in front of him. He searched the horizon for a sign of Wainwright, but the time traveler was nowhere.

Chapter Three

It seemed as if they had walked for years instead of days. Unaccustomed to the heat, exposure, and lack of food and water, Grant thought that the small trip to Capua seemed like an eternity. If he slacked at all in his march, he felt the sting of the whip across his back. The long line of doomed men, who would be educated in the fine art of fighting only to die in the arena, had been given rest periods along the route. Hastily offered water and thrown slices of stale bread were given to the men who ate and drank along the roadside while the sun baked their skin.

So many thoughts swam in Grant Tyrell's overheated mind as

he trudged along the path the Roman lanista/trainer called the Via Papilia. Would he just die here? Was it even 200 A.D.? Maybe he'd slipped further back because his mind's vision was incorrect for the time period? Maybe that was where Bruce Wainwright was—in 200 A.D— with the Romans wondering what on earth had happened to his client.

Grant needed a bath, a private toilet, a barber, a sauna, a seven course gourmet meal, a cold beer, a pair of shorts, a T-shirt, and an aspirin. Every part of his body ached including his head and shoulders. His skin burned despite the pre-tan he'd had before he left New York. His lips were parched and cracked. His shackled foot was cut, bleeding, and numb from pain. Everything smelled of fish, urine, mud, the sea, and sweat. He had lifted weights at home, but his cardiovascular system was far too weak to handle this daily tramping on hard, flat ground.

There had been one salvation on his three-day march to Capua. A Greek named Theodosus, who was ahead of him in the long line, tried to befriend him. The man was obviously a military prisoner—a soldier—and would have been excellent domestic slave material if it had not been for several distinguishing features. He was handsome, strong, well-built, an athlete, and seemed intelligent by the varied facial expressions he made to Grant. His eyes, however, burned with a mighty anger and passion for revenge. Unfortunately, Grant could not speak Greek, and whenever the man tried to say something, Grant was completely baffled.

Theodosus tried to communicate with the new "lunatic" repeating his name repeatedly, pointing to his chest as Grant had done with the slave driver until it was understood that he was referring to his name. So, Grant pointed to himself and said that his name was Grant Tyrell. The Greek soldier tried to say 'Tyrell' but it came out Tyrellius. Grantus Tyrellius was as close as he got. It wasn't his fault that Grant's 2000 A.D. name didn't match the Roman Empire of 200 A.D., if that was where he was. From that moment on, the two communicated with hand movements and gestures—and grins.

Theodosus was younger than Grant but not by much. He had a ready smile, his hair was light caramel colored, and his eyes were bright, azure blue. This man didn't belong with the slaves. Riding his horse along the coastline while the wind combed his hair away from his noble, high forehead, standing guard beside an emperor, preparing for battle with a courageous general, or charming a beautiful woman into his bed, would have been the proper life for this man. He was far too intelligent for gladiator school. On the other hand, a quick mind might prove to be a lifesaving attribute where they were headed. At any rate, Grant was glad to have him as a friend—something he needed more than he wanted to admit.

Despite his new friendship with Theodosus, Wainwright's disappearance still puzzled Grant. Would he ever find him or was he doomed to be separated for three months from his 'own-time-period pal'?

Grant had always been a survivor, and though he had initially been thrown off balance by the odd turn of events, everything he had read about slaves and gladiators made him confident that he could succeed in this realm. He had played sports in school, after all. He was in shape. But, if he didn't get some better food, the emptiness in his stomach would make him far too weak for combat. If he'd only thought to bring sun block!

Once they arrived at the ludus, his expensive, accurately designed costume was rudely stripped from his torso and replaced with a humiliating, athletic miniskirt that made him glad in one respect he'd pumped some iron before his trip. He cut a formidable half-naked figure of physical prowess wearing it. His antique fibula had been stolen by the slave driver, and his fine, but now torn, leather foot gear was replaced by heavier military sandals—caligae—that were stronger and cooler than his original ones. They laced around his ankles with leather straps and had iron hobnails in the soles.

The first idea that crossed Grant's mind, as he was being

unchained and locked into his tiny cell, was to ask for his money back from the Harvard professor. The time travel experiment had worked, but his role in the Roman Empire was not linked to the Emperor Septimius Severus. He hadn't genealogically transferred. Apparently, he didn't even bear any resemblance to the man by the way the slaves had carried on.

They gave him a crust of bread, a bowl of 'something' that was hot, and a cup of water. He ate the food gratefully and tried to lie down in the cell. That was almost an impossibility, but he managed to curl his body into a fetal position on a piece of soft, woolly cloth. He could see the sky from his small cubicle. The stars were shining down through the grill above his head. Dark sky. Tiny, bright stars cut into the black velvet cloth of the night. Same sky as in New York. He used to stare at the sky every evening by way of the sky light above his bed. He'd always had trouble sleeping, and so he hired a contractor to put the open roof above his bed so that he would be able to see the moon, clouds, stars, and passing planes. It calmed him to look up at the darkness. He lulled himself to sleep every evening by searching heaven for the answers to vacuous question he was afraid to ask himself in the light of day. It was all right to show weakness to the moon. To show his other side. The one that was afraid to see who he'd become. But he knew. Yes. He knew that he'd been unkind to his high school girlfriend, that he'd been cold to the rich man's daughter, cruel to the older businessman, indignant to his mother, and proven a bastard to the people who worked for him. And by the looks of his future right now, he'd say he was about to pay for those sins. But, what could he have done differently, after all. You were supposed to be clever and witty, bold and bright, lucky and fated. But never wrong. God no, Grant couldn't be wrong about anything. There was no weak spot in him. None that had ever been found by the numbers of women and men whose lives he held in the palm of his hand. His heart was locked in a cubicle, much like this one, and there was no one who owned the key to open it.

He looked at his cut, swollen ankles, torn feet, bruised hands, and then stretched his aching, sunburned back while crying out in pain like a hurt animal. They all had laughed at him—even the slaves. He was nothing more than a common slave and a crazy one at that.

He was in for the time travel trip of a lifetime by the looks of the training camp. He felt utterly, hopelessly alone. The only one who could keep him alive in the next two weeks was the young man he'd left back at high school—on the football field and the track. The boy who had never allowed pain or disappointment to stop him from attaining his goal. "Keep going," he told himself. "Use all you have and then some to stay alive. You can do this."

Grant Tyrell *would* succeed. He would make it to the equinox if he had to kill anyone who crossed him. It was this sort of mindset that had always made him victorious in the past, and he saw no earthly reason for it failing him now.

Chapter Four

Grant didn't know it at the time, but he happened to be staying at one of the finest ludus in all Capua if not in all the Roman Empire. That thought might have given him comfort in the weeks ahead, but presently it was not making him feel any better as he lay crumbled in a mass of flesh and arms on the floor of his 'cell'. He could see above him with the aid of the skylight. He was awakened by the sound of sandaled feet hurrying on the grid above him.

Life at most camps was brutal. The food was disgusting, and the men were beaten and treated worse than the animals captured for the arena's 'hunts'. Grant's training camp was built in the shape of a picture frame with the work area filled with palus—wooden stakes or posts—two yards high. The cells surrounded this fighting area and made the yard similar to the real arena except for the fact that it was rectangular instead of oval or bowl shaped. At one end was a small but high area for the spectators. The barracks were on two levels and four yards long. At one end was a huge kitchen with a wall long cooking range. There were rooms used for the armory at the corners of the frame. These rooms held the rudis—wooden swords—wicker bucklers, and other equipment such as helmets that the tiro—novice gladiators—would use to learn how to fight and die in the arena.

The doctores—specialists or trainers who comprised the familia quadrigaria or staff—would encourage the men who were criminals and war prisoners, or had otherwise been dubbed damnatio ad ludum, to learn a particular style of fighting. These men had the unique honor of being doomed to the training camps and to a performance style death by combat with another one also doomed. In a grotesquely bizarre way, this might have been considered a blessing.

There was always the chance of survival and fame as a gladiator so being sent to this training camp was preferable to being executed in a cruel but crowd pleasing show of butchery in the arena; or, if there were many animals and the owners were low on food, being used as a source of nutrition for the lions.

Being a gladiator meant one had a chance for obtaining many enviable items. If he showed promise in the arena, and survived his first combat, the gladiator could become a star. His name might be advertised on the walls of the Colosseum, women might swoon and call to him in the street as he passed on his way to his daily exercises. The emperor might award him some money above and beyond his normal pay. He might earn a home in the city, bed many wealthy women, dine with the rich, and receive the ultimate prize—freedom and retirement after three years.

If, however, he lacked skill, poor footwork, and was not clever in battle, he died. He would toss away his shield, which indicated to the crowd that he could fight no longer, and raise one finger of the left hand towards the spectators. He was no longer to move his arms to ward off a blow or make a surprise attack. If he'd shown some degree of excellence with his sword, or appeared brave, he might hear the crowd chant, "Habet! Hoc habet! Mitte!" — "He's had it. Send him back!" If the combat were early in the day, however, and the crowd was anxious to see blood; they would turn their thumbs to the ground—pollice verso—and demand his death. Others would raise their hands, palms upwards, and beg for clemency. Later in the day, after much fighting and killing, the crowd might be more generous. At any rate, it was never a unanimous decision, and the least little thing could change their allegiance to the supplicant man. The crowd never really determined the fate of the warrior anyway. Though their cries helped determine the ultimate decision, it was the president of the games, or editor, who made the final judgment. If the gladiator showed promise, he would allow the combatant to fight another day. What was the point in wasting all that expensive training, after all? If the man had fought like an oaf or a coward, he was executed on the spot. Further work on this fighter was a waste of food, clothing, and shelter.

When it came time to die, the gladiator was expected to receive the final blow with his whole body—accepting his death valiantly. Without removing his helmet, the victim threw himself down on the ground and sat back on his heel with his head bowed awaiting the editor's decision. He remained passive in his defeat, and when he realized that he was to die, drew himself up into a half-seated position, lowered one knee to the ground, took hold of his executioner's thigh just above the knee, so that he would not shake or move when he received the fatal blow.

The victor would pull back his own free arm, put his other hand on the victim's helmet so that he would not miss or be clumsy, and push the tip of his sword below the victim's vizor, then pushed it into the gladiator's neck thus cutting the unprotected throat. To die in this manner—without flinching the head away or allowing the hand or arm to tremble—was an honorable death; and, with the other less glamourous ways of dying from any number of offenses from adultery to sacrilege, arson, petty theft, military disobedience—a list that could be added to if the Empire was low on gladiators—death by combat could be considered...a chance to live and be a star, a suspirium puellarum—heartthrob to the women, and to be viewed as something other than a "non-citizen of Rome," or slave.

A gladiator would only fight an opponent he considered worthy. There was a sort of esprit de corps among the fighters. Private, unspoken, secret, the condemned men had a variety of unspoken rules about honor. The winner did not flinch or show mercy when the fight was finished. There had been stories told of fighters who had shown sentiment and not cut the throat of their opponent, giving them a second chance. The end of the tale was that when the tables were turned, the opponent did not show the same pity and killed the softhearted victor. "No pity for the vanquished!" was the credo in the barracks of the ludus. No exceptions. That made the blood sport more exciting for the audience, and fighting in the Colosseum was meant for the entertainment of the *true* Roman citizens.

Grant was dragged from his cell and pushed, unchained, to a line moving slowly towards a row of tables and long benches. He could smell the bread and just washed fruit and figs. He couldn't remember what the professor had told him about food, and what did it matter after all, he wasn't going to be eating like an emperor now.

Just before he was given a plate to serve himself, he was motioned, with the others, to a bucket where he was to wash his dirty hands and filthy face. The water felt wonderfully cold and refreshing. After the long march to Capua, this small comfort was a delight. He splashed the water over his forehead, neck, and chest. He wasn't sure he could manage the morning without coffee, but he did notice his usual early-riser energy flood through his muscles. They ached for him to exercise, and after breakfast, he would have a full workout by the looks of the makeshift arena.

He placed some figs, grapes, olives, and a small loaf of hot bread on his plate. Then he was given a brown wooden cup that he was to dunk into another bucket of water. This was to be his beverage. He saw Theodosus, smiled, and went to sit next to him. As soon as he sat down, a bowl of hot oat like mush was placed before him. A wooden spoon was dropped into the middle of it.

"Well, at least the food is superior," said Theodosus in Greek.

Grant smiled and said nothing. It looked as if his friend was pleased with breakfast. Grant could not speak his friend's language.

"Fattened for the kill, I guess," Theodosus continued.

Grant shook his head to remind his friend that he didn't speak Greek. Then he tasted the mush. It had no sugar or spices and tasted just awful, but his stomach was so hungry right now that such minor details seemed insignificant.

"Maybe we'll rate some meat for dinner," the new friend continued and patted his stomach to indicate more filling food might come.

Theodosus looked at Grant, cocked his head to the side, and smiled. Then he began pointing to various objects on the table and sounding out the Greek name for them. Grant caught onto the game and did the same but with Latin words. They taught each other while they ate.

A pretty girl came by and offered them some water from a pitcher. When she had filled their cups, she moved onto the next man. Theodosus was impressed with her figure and made exaggerated facial expressions to show that he thought her breasts and posterior quite pleasing. His focus moved up and down her slender but curvaceous body. She looked his way as if she sensed his gaze. He gave a low whistle and smiled. The girl was embarrassed but looked at Theodosus for a moment longer than she should have. "Back in high school again," thought Grant. "Lunchroom, girls, and practice."

"She's got some body," said Theodosus. Grant knew what Theodosus meant by his friend's body language, so he repeated the Greek words a bit too loudly.

The girl turned towards both of them and said in Greek, "Keep your thoughts to yourself, tiro."

"Ah," said Theodosus, "she speaks Greek. I'm in love!" He touched his chest near enough to his heart for Grant to understand.

The sun must have baked all Grant's brains away because he chuckled and said in English, "Yeah, she's hot all right!" Then he wiggled his fingers limply at the wrist, pressed them together, and quickly pulled them back apart while making a hissing sound of steam heat.

Theodosus laughed.

"No way you understand that, man," said Grant grinning.

Theodosus held up two fingers. "You speak two languages?" He motioned to his mouth while he spoke and motioned with his hand that he meant speech.

"Yes," Grant said in Latin. "Latin and New York!"

"Noo Yauk," repeated Theodosus in English. Then he tried the new phrase. "Yeuhsheushaut!"

"Close enough," said Grant smiling. "Sweet ass. Angel face. Nice tits."

Theodosus was alive with curiosity. His eyes sparkled with merriment as he perceived the discussion was about sex. He leaned closer to Grant. "Tuhts?"

Grant motioned with two hands to the orbs in front of a woman's chest.

"Ah, tits," said Theodosus doing the same movement and saying the word perfectly.

That did it. The girl came back to the two men, tossed the pitcher of water all over Theodosus, and sulked away angrily mumbling something neither man understood.

The other convicts looked up from the food to notice what had happened and laughed. Theodosus shook the water from his hair and spoke a word.

Grant raised an eyebrow, and swiveled his head back and forth to tell Theodosus that he didn't understand what was meant.

The Greek looked to the blue sky for help but could think of no way to explain. "Sheuss haut!" he said pointing to his head.

Grant then realized that his new companion in 200 A.D. liked a woman with a temper and a great body.

"Tiro! Come to the center of the arena and line up!" cried the instructor.

Grant sighed and said, "So much for breakfast. Coach calls." He motioned to Theodosus that they were to get in line.

There were twenty men of various sizes and shapes in the lineup. None of them were very old, and each one looked powerful for one reason or another. One man, who seemed round and physically unfit, had the most powerful arms Grant had ever seen. He looked as if he could crush a man with one massive bear hug. Another was slender but had solid legs and muscular thighs and appeared to be quick witted and intelligent. One had a serious attitude problem and seemed the most dangerous of them all. This man wanted to fight, wanted to kill. The man was bitter about something and looked like the type who might take out his anger on anyone who crossed his path. Theodosus was the most handsome, intelligent, and well-built rookie there next to Grant who was a giant in comparison with all of them. Grant and Theodosus were the only Thracian material there.

"You are low-life scum and don't forget that. Criminals, thieves, treasonous dung of Rome!" said the master who introduced himself as Gino. "You now have a chance to better yourselves if you are smart, strong, and obey my every command. Here, I will train you to fight in the grand arenas of the Roman Empire. Some may fight before the emperor himself if they show promise. You were all sentenced to death, but I took you because you showed promise as fighters. I prolonged your miserable lives so don't forget that. You will have a roof over your head, clothing on your back, food to eat, cool water, exercise to give you strength and agility. Most importantly, we," and here he motioned to the other men standing beside him, "will teach you the talents you will need for combat against another such as yourself. If you lack agility and are a poor fighter, you will die on your first match. If you are good, you might make a career of this, earn some money, and win your freedom from the emperor. That's up to you. If you do as I instruct, there are perks. An occasional feast and a woman once in a while. If you are lazy, there's always the whip. You are now a tiro, but someday you will be a gladiator of Rome. Men, and even women, yearn to wear the helmet and fight with the sword. Commodus, and other emperors of Rome, were so envious of the gladiators, they insisted on fighting in the arena. And every man and woman sitting in the gallery will watch you. Will want to *be* you. Women might even want to mate with you. Have your child. It is something to be proud of. You came from nothing," he said as he stared each man down, "but I will turn you into the stars of the Roman Colosseum."

Gino turned to the men behind him, the doctores, and said, "Choose from them."

The man who must have been the 'doctores thracicum' moved towards Grant and Theodosus. "These two are mine," he said.

Milos, who was known as the finest trainer in Rome and had earned his freedom as a retirement gift, took Theodosus and Grant aside.

His voice sounded like gravel being crunched under a truck tire. He said, "Listen, I don't care what your name is; you will be called tiro from now on. Some day you may be called gladiator. If you are skillful, lucky, and win; you may earn your name back then. That name will be known all over Rome. They like the Thracians. Very popular with the emperors and the ladies. But for now, know this. I'm life and death for you now. Obey me completely, and you will have all you can imagine; disobey me and you will die in the arena; run from me, and I will hunt you down and kill you. Swear to endure the whip, the branding iron, and death by the sword if you try running or revolt. Swear!"

The two rookies mumbled and shook their heads agreeing with the terms.

Milos said, "You are mine now. You don't even own your soul."

Grant thought, "Well, that's plain enough."

"We begin by running."

Grant thought, "You've got to be kidding. In this heat?" but said nothing.

Theodosus looked down at the earth.

"Are you Greek?" said Milos to Grant's friend.

Theodosus looked up on the word 'Greek'. He knew that one word in Latin.

"Very well, I will talk with my hands, and you will learn words from that."

Then he looked at Grant. Grant said, "I will cause you no problem, coach."

Milos looked quizzically at Grant, not knowing the word 'coach', and said, "Ah," and laughed, "you're the crazy one who thinks he's Septimius. Well, a little craziness is just what I want for a fighter. Start running."

The three of them exited the prison. Was Milos mad to free them like this? Grant remembered the man's threat that he would hunt them down and kill them if they ran away and then saw the hill. There was a trodden-down path that ran up the hill that was to be their course.

"Fifty times up and down. I'm keeping track. Now move it."

Chapter Five

Grant made ten laps before his throat was parched. The water girl came running with a bucket and ladle for the two men, and Milos allowed them to take a two-minute break because of the intense heat. Then back up the hill trudged the two rookies. The run took most of the morning and all their energy. There was a small recess for lunch—half a loaf of bread and two or three cups of water, then Milos switched his pupils' routine to skill work. He showed them the foot work needed to attack and parry during a fight. Theodosus took to this training quickly as he had learned it in Greece; but Grant looked awkward, constantly stumbling or shifting his weight incorrectly.

"You've much to learn, tiro, if you are to survive the games," Milos said to Grant before he sent them to dinner.

Theodosus chuckled while they ate.

Grant said, "Oh, sure, laugh now, just give me time."

Theodosus laughed at the remark having no idea what Grant had just said. He motioned to Grant's feet, covered his eyes with his hands, and then wiggled his fingers and waved his hands over one another as if to say that Grant was clumsy beyond salvation.

Grant grinned. "Oh, yeah? You think so. Well, I wonder how you'd fair in a football game with boulders trying to knock you over for the ball."

For some reason, exhaustion-heat, these words only made Theodosus laugh harder. He was showing no signs of fatigue from the day's workout, but Grant was obviously exhausted. The girl with the water walked by them again and looked at Theodosus.

"I think she's hot for you, man," said Grant.

"Sheus *haut*?" he queried.

Grant had the upper hand now as far as he was concerned. "No, I mean she wants you. Sex. Ah, Eros, erotica," and then he took the finger of his right hand and placed it into his clenched left hand and moved it in and out to suggest sex and tilted his head towards the girl.

Theodosus understood immediately and pointed to himself. "Sheus haut *for* Theodosus?"

"Yes, you primitive Grecian stud, I think she likes you. Women! One minute they drown you with a pitcher of water, and the next minute they give you the eye."

The Greek stared at his food, shook his head, smiled, and launched into dialogue. Grant wanted so to understand his new friend. What was he telling him about his life, his loves, his desires? He wanted to communicate and couldn't. Theodosus was the only salvation, the only human contact, who could keep Grant from losing his mind. He would have three months in this hell hole, but at least he had one friend.

They were taken to their cells after dinner. Peace could come even in this tiny room. He knew his body would hurt like hell the next morning, and that he would have to make it respond to all that he'd learned today. Back in his time period, people would pay a lot of money for this training. If he looked at it that way, he could handle it. He was at a camp—a spa; he told himself. This would be good for him. He'd learn something. Just as he was about to fall asleep, the cell door opened, and the little water girl was pushed inside. He heard laughter from the hallway.

The girl was frightened, physically trembling and covering herself. So, she was his prize. He wondered who Theodosus had if this one was his. Too bad, he thought, Theodosus wanted this one. She held a bottle of something in her hand, but there was obvious fear in her eyes. She was a virgin and given to the tiro for the purposes of mating. He wasn't going to take her for many reasons. First, they wanted him to, and he hated the idea of them counting on it. Secondly, he would never take a woman who didn't want him. It amounted to little more than rape, and he would never do that to a lady. Thirdly, his new friend liked her and wanted her for himself. He couldn't do that to Theodosus or to the girl because she seemed to want the other man too. And lastly, he could never make love to a woman in this tiny cell? He was hungry for sex, however, so the fact that he did not take what was offered was a victory in itself.

"Hey, come here," he said to her softly.

She gave a small squeal of terror. Men outside the cell laughed.

"No, no, I'm not going to hurt you," he said. He took the jar from her hands. "Is this oil for my muscles?" He made a motion of rubbing the oil onto his sore muscles.

Her face brightened.

"Please?" He pointed to the jar, the girl, and his back. She shook her head that she understood. He kissed her lightly on the top of her head and then looked into her eyes. "I won't hurt you."

She was Greek, and though she didn't understand his words, she sensed their meaning. He turned from her and lifted his hands to press against the wall so that she could rub the strong smelling liquid onto his back. It penetrated his skin, eased the sunburn and muscle tightness, and he sighed loudly.

The men outside laughed again. Obviously, they thought he was having sex with the girl, and they were enjoying that thought. Though he felt sorry for the slave girl's reputation, he had a hunch that his was on the line tonight, so he groaned again to ease their fears that their Thracian rookie might not like women. And, of course, the object was to impregnate the girl for the purpose of breeding strong, beautiful, salable slave children. Though he couldn't see any other cell but his, he could hear the screaming and the laughter from the men's apartments and knew that he was probably the only one who wasn't enjoying his woman. Except for, perhaps, Theodosus.

When his back felt better, he motioned to his thighs, and she massaged them as well. Her manner lightened due undoubtedly to the thought that he would not take advantage of his obvious right to have her. She smiled, and her eyes twinkled even in the dimness of the night. Grant wondered what Theodosus was doing with his prize.

"What's your name?" he asked her.

She tilted her head as if she didn't understand.

He pointed to himself and said, "Grant."

She pointed to herself and said, "Diana." She was quick on the uptake.

"Don't take offense, Diana, I think you're cute, but I just have real issues with people telling me what to do—especially when it comes to women. There's no challenge here, and it would be like rape."

Grant shook his head. How could anyone have sex like that—with someone listening to every sound? Then he remembered how he used to make love to girls while staying in the dorm at college and mused that if a man wants it, he'll take it no matter what the situation. The girl massaged his legs and feet, and he felt himself gaining an erection. With a small pair of 'trunks' covering it, he knew that she had to have noticed.

"Don't worry, I'm not that kind of guy. Sex with a frightened virgin isn't my idea of a good time."

She carefully placed the bottle on the ground and opened her arms to him. Reassurance—affection. That was all she wanted from him. He held her close to his body. "It's okay." He touched her hair gently. "You just go to sleep now. Here on my chest." He felt her body relax against his, and soon she was asleep.

The next day began in much the same manner as the first. Theodosus made the same motion Grant had made the day before and then placed his hands palm upwards and raised his shoulders. Grant pointed to the slave girl, Diana. Theodosus shook his head in disgust. Then Grant touched his shoulder and shook his head that he hadn't touched her. Theodosus smiled and pointed to a buxom lady who had a heart-stopping figure but a face like a horse. He imitated Grant's body language that he hadn't taken her either. Crossing his hands one over the other he said, "Haut?"

"Not hot!" corrected Grant.

"Nowt haut," said Theodosus and both men laughed. When Diana came close to them, she smiled at Grant, opened the shawl of her gown, and gave him some fruit that she had pilfered from the doctores' table.

"Graci," said Grant and smiled at her.

Theodosus looked concerned.

"Don't worry, she still likes you."

They laughed until Milos called to them.

"Oh, well, back to the salt mines," said Grant.

"Sawlt meynz?" said Theodosus. "Bak too de sawlt meynz," he imitated.

Grant smiled and patted Theodosus on the shoulder and said, "Not bad."

It was more difficult to run up and down the hill on the second day. The only blessing for the weary warriors was that the weather was cooler and clouds covered the sun at random intervals. Grant's muscles ached from yesterday's trial, but he could make the fifty laps just the same. He was rewarded with a better lesson in the afternoon. He moved with more agility, twice swishing away from Milos when he maneuvered near him. His legs were strong enough to move quickly, and he had learned to shift his weight from one thigh to another without losing his balance. He held his body at an angle and gained complete control of jockeying from side to side while keeping one foot in the same place. If he did have to move further from his starting place, he put the weight of his body on the other leg and shifted to the new spot. He never moved far from the pretended opponent so that he could conserve his energy for a counter attack. It gave him the appearance of being a courageous fighter because he never ran from the enemy's sword.

Milos yelled at them to shift, hold, lunge, shift again, attack, parry, stand, crouch, lift, lunge. Theodosus was agile, but Grant was gaining on him by bettering his own technique. Grant always kept an eye on Theodosus, mentally deliberating his talent against his friend's. It wasn't an avenue to gain superiority over the Greek fighter, nor an attempt on his part to pull Milo's interest away from the better tiro, but simply a way to make sure he was not far behind the Greek in skill. He had a feeling that he would practice with Theodosus once they learned the basics, and he had no intention of looking weak in front of his new 'coach'.

For some reason that Grant hadn't the time to think about, Milos's approval was crucial to him.

The master was pleased with his pupils' progress and changed the lesson plan to hand-to-hand combat using small wooden swords known as rudis. They learned five parries and practiced them against the palus—a wooden stake that was chipped and notched from many clubbings by other tiro.

Grant liked this exercise because Milos actually softened his voice and instructed, gave praise, and took hold of their hands and arms to reposition them when they were wrong. Grant sensed that he had to learn the parries perfectly; today they were being treated civilly because it was a new lesson—tomorrow they would be in trouble if they faltered.

That evening they were given cheap wine, fruit, bread, and one fried fish. Theodosus smiled happily and made numerous comments accompanied with body language about the feast this ludus prepared for its tiro. Grant wanted a huge pizza with mushrooms, extra cheese, and pepperoni followed by a nice cold tankard of beer.

"Well, he said to himself, "if you wanted brew, you should have time traveled to the Viking time period. That tenet gave way to an evening of thought about Wainwright's location. Would he meet up with him or was the time traveler gone for good? Maybe Wainwright hadn't flown at all. Maybe he was still back home in the Cooper's cabin.

His cell door was opened again, and Diana moved in with less fear. She smiled and offered the oil from her bottle.

"Absolutely, sweetheart. I'm all yours."

She took her time with him and moved the warmed oil over his skin, massaging his legs, arms, and back with the invigorating oil that smelled a bit like eucalyptus. She was wearing a new aroma, as well. The perspiration had been washed from her skin, her hair had been washed and laced with perfume, and her limbs had been lubricated with a floral cream. In a relaxed manner that indicated that she knew he would not hurt her, she placed her head on his chest, and the two slept in a semi-upright, semi-crouching position until the stars were no longer visible in the sky.

Chapter Six

The next morning brought a bright dawn and a hot day with a restorative cool breeze. Grant seemed refreshed, and a new sense of vigor took hold of him. His mind had a new challenge—to learn all that he could about combat in the Roman Empire. It was an education that he hadn't planned on gaining but, in retrospect, was worth more than Time Travelers, Inc.'s fee.

The air shot spasms of new life into his body. The workout was grueling and strengthening his body to its fullest potential. He no longer worried about his business; it was out of his control now. The only thing that mattered was surviving Milos's agonizing schedule.

Grant enjoyed learning the art of sword play. He guessed that Milos was a well of information and would teach it all to them. Grant had always pumped iron to stay in shape, but that paled in comparison with the ludus's rituals. The simplistic dishes and general lack of fattening foods was cleansing the impurities from his system. He was losing fat, gaining muscle, and turning into a lean, tanned Roman god.

Grant was inherently aware of the fact that he was completely alone with his own thoughts—no one knew English, and his closest companions spoke Greek. It was so freeing. Nothing to think about but physical conditioning, nothing to worry about but whether they would get meat for dinner, nothing but the hill to contend with in the morning. No business calls, no secretary to plan his day, no e-mails to answer, no meetings to manage, no deadlines to match, no problems in production to solve. Free in the most wonderful fashion. Free to confront himself on every level. Strengthen his legs to meet the fifty laps. Work his upper body to swing the sword with a swift and solid slice of the air. Focus his mind on his body's graceful movements. Cold water became more important than the finest wines in New York's upper class restaurants. Fruit and bread filled his stomach three times a day until his anatomy accepted the smaller amount and realized that there would be no evening snack, no gourmet dinner, no bagel breakfast. Fresh air replaced the aroma of air conditioning that permeated his office. The smell of the sea awakened him; the warmth of the sun penetrated his sore muscles; the teacher's voice became his lifeline to sanity.

Grant appreciated Milos in some bizarre way. The doctores reminded him of all the coaches he'd had in school, and the thought brought comfort. The man was trying to save their lives.

And finally, saying no to the beauty who cuddled next to him each evening because he knew she was Theodosus's heart was teaching him some integrity, discipline, self-control, and self-respect. He now knew that there was a part of him that could deny basic needs because of friendship. He had no desire to anger his one friend, and, in looking back on his life, realized that he had tossed aside all the people who had mattered to him for gain until there was no one left who really cared about him. Theodosus and Diana did. They liked him for whom he was not what he was. Despite the unnerving business of not being Emperor of Rome and losing Wainwright, he was not having such a bad vacation after all.

Those thoughts helped gain the fifty laps up and down the hill with Theodosus. He had always lagged behind, but today he was right beside the Greek warrior. Diana gave a secret smile to him as she ladled water from her bucket. Then she smiled at Theodosus who flirted in his own way. Milos seemed oblivious to everything that was going on between the three comrades.

After lunch, they perfected their footwork and practiced the parries while adding a few more lunges to their list of skills. They mixed the lunges and the parries, again, only challenging the stakes.

Grant taught Theodosus Latin and New York during every meal, and, in the evening, Diana practiced her new language while she anointed his aching muscles with oil. While she cuddled in his arms, he sensed her life softly slumbering close to his body. Her breathing, her heartbeat, her dreams that came to her in the middle of the night and seemed so troubling, all swirled in his head in a whirlpool of emotion. He felt strong and protective towards her. He had no intention of using her for anything but friendship and the oil she used to relax him. She trusted him just as others had in the past. He touched her hair. What would become of her? They'd never allow her to love Theodosus. His life would end in the arena, perhaps, and Diana would become pregnant with some slave's child so that she could bear children for her master. This was raw history. No one could change the facts established for this time period. This was no movie where you could alter the fiction to make a happy ending. But could a time traveler?

Grant eased Theodosus's mind the next morning by reminding him that he was not having sex with the girl because he knew his friend had an eye for her. Theodosus seemed to understand and by the look in Diana's eyes when she saw Theodosus at breakfast, something was going on between them. The poor girl who had been Theodosus's mate each evening—who had had no luck with him—thudded a hot oat dish in a wooden bowl in front of them and then huffed away.

Grant passed Theodosus on the hill.

Milos had plans to teach them by using himself as an opponent today. He showed them how to setup an opponent so that they would open themselves up for a strike. Theodosus had been trained for warfare but obviously lacked conditioning in hand-to-hand combat because Milos tripped him immediately and reminded him of his footwork. Then, Grant parried Milos's first thrust only to be backsided immediately. They had much to learn and now Milos had two men who yearned to be as artistic as their teacher. Milos had gained their complete allegiance, and there would be no more need for chains or ties. These skills would take months of steady practice to learn. The two slaves weren't ready to fight each other, but that was coming.

It stormed that night and Grant suffered for it. He had forgotten Wainwright's comment that storms brought on malaise, but tonight he was getting first hand experience. Diana never left his side as he groaned in agony. Each bolt of lightening compounded Grant's headache that rivaled a migraine in intensity.

Her eyes filled with concern, and she called to one of the guards who brought an herbal drink for her to give him. It worked. "What is that stuff?" he asked her.

She shook her head.

"Hey, come here, let's talk."

She moved close to him. "Thanks for the aspirin."

"As...per...sin?" she asked

"Close enough." Then he tried to look like Theodosus and imitated his voice and how she'd thrown water on him that first day. She giggled with recognition and delight. It was like playing charades.

"Theodosus."

"Theo...do..sis?"

"Yeah, that's right. He likes you, you know."

She didn't act as if she understood his meaning.

"Okay then, ah..." He crossed his arms around his body and made kissing sounds.

She giggled.

"Theodosus wants you. He's hot for you. What are his chances?" he asked.

"The...oh...do..sis hot for Diana?"

"Incredible! You are clever. Yeah, do you," he said pointing to her, "like him?" he finished by pointing to the cell next to his.

She blushed and grinned coquettishly.

"We got to get you two together."

"Together," she said and rested her head against his chest and closed her eyes. The juxtaposition of that word with the action of cuddling hit a nerve.

"Yeah. Together." He touched her head gently, and his eyes filled with tears. He shook them away. "Weird," he thought. "Why am I so moved to help two people I don't even know, and who will be gone from my life come October?"

Then the answer to his question shot through to his mind like a lightening bolt. "Because they like me for whom I am. I don't have to be anyone special; I don't have to perform. With unquestioned loyalty, Theodosus took the new 'crazy' slave on as a friend when everyone else cast me aside and laughed at me. And asking nothing from me but a little respect, this girl has carefully ministered to my every need with a sweet smile on her face not because she was told to—which she would have responded to anyway—but because she took pleasure in it. These two can't even understand my language, but they like me. I can't destroy their trust, or I'm a goner in this time period."

He smiled. It was difficult at first because it was a real smile, not a smirk or a grin, and not an artificial one intended to make a sale or butter-up an important client. It came from the heart. Something in his very soul tickled, went heavy then lightened, and then turned as golden as the rays of the sun that bathed Capua's finest ludus each morning. In an odd turn of events, Grant was happier now than if he had been the Emperor of Rome.

Chapter Seven

In the next few days, Grant and Theodosus learned every conceivable trick of the Thracian trade. Bobbing and weaving to avoid Milos's lunges, they learned to err on a move meant a crack of the wooden rudis on the back or the head.

"Remember, if you feel my sword now, you'll feel the real one in the arena."

The thought encouraged the two men to dart, shift weight, and rearrange their footwork to best maneuver offensively and defensively. The new strength they forged through their morning ritual of running up and down the hill gave them a solid base for agility and quick recovery from blows.

"You're ready," Milos said. "I have something special for you after lunch."

Theodosus and Grant could communicate better now that the Greek had learned an interesting combination of Latin, New York, and charades. Grant enjoyed teaching him English as well as Latin because it was the secret language only the two of them knew.

"I haven't really noticed the others much since we started working with Milos," said Grant, waving his hands towards the others and shaking his head.

Theodosus moved his arms to mimic the other fighters' techniques.

"Yes, different, and I think we have the best of it. Hey, there's your girl." Grant pointed to Diana. "I had a talk with her last night about you," he said, pointing to the Greek and then to Diana and smiling.

Theodosus turned into a schoolboy and dropped his focus to his empty plate. Diana came over to their table with her bucket and ladle and a small cache of figs she'd swiped from the headmaster's table. She placed them in front of them and smiled at Theodosus. Her eyes met his, and they just stared at one another for a few minutes.

"Well, if you don't want the figs," said Grant as he took two and ate them hastily before anyone noticed.

Milos called to them to come to one of the supply rooms at the corner of the training arena.

"All right, let's get you suited up," he said and tossed a leather and metal vest to each of them.

They needed help getting the straps to fit and be comfortable at the same time. They were given longer skirts to place around their hips. Then Milos gave them small round shields.

"This will help you deflect your opponent's thrusts. They aren't very big, because they aren't meant to protect your body. We don't want you looking like a coward, shrinking behind a huge shield. They are used to ward off blows, to push the sword away from you so that you don't get cut, and are small enough to not get in the way of your returning lunge."

He gave them new sandals and a brace that covered the front of the calf. Then he handed them the helmet.

Just before he placed the wide brimmed, finned helmet with the cage like face mask on his head, and locked it in place thus covering his eyes with metal, he caught Diana watching them. She was utterly transfixed with both men's appearance. Obviously, Thracians and their garb were very sexy to women in this century.

"Football helmet," laughed Grant as he adjusted it to his head. He had to admit the clothing was very flashy, the heavy metal and leather biker look, but he could see major problems with the whole costume. He couldn't see much with the helmet locked on his head. It was like looking out of a curtain full of holes. The leather breast plate didn't cover his stomach, and there was nothing protecting his shoulders or neck, thus leaving the upper part of his chest very vulnerable. His thighs had no pads to keep someone from slashing his legs right out from under him. The calf brace didn't protect that part of the leg at all and was meant for show or to aid if the fighter went down on his knees to fight. Grant was reminded of the knights in the Middle Ages. Leather was a poor covering compared to chain mail and metal. Though the helmet protected his head, he felt suffocated and trapped inside it; but by the look on Diana's face, he and Theodosus were major studs, and there was some consolation in that.

"Now let's see how you fight in this gear," said Milos.

He came at them now with fierce aggressive blows, and they tried to move as fast as they could in the new uniform. It was if they had to relearn everything.

Milos's wooden sword still hurt when it smacked his shoulders and thighs so that by the end of the day, Grant and Theodosus had burning red welts over the exposed skin. Then he handed them a different sword that was very heavy but still relatively harmless.

"You need to feel as much weight as possible. If you can maneuver with all this weighing you down, the real situation will seem easier," said the coach.

They practiced for about a half an hour and moved like apes while doing it. Every time Milos hit one of the bruises, the two men slowed their attack.

"You must not give up. We must build up your tolerance and strength. Don't be surprised if you feel as if you have weights attached to your feet."

He cut their workout down by an hour.

"See what areas on your body hurt tonight. Those are the places you need to protect," Milos stated pleased that he had abused his students so well. "Rest now. Eat. The women will be given soothing ointment to put on those bruises. Tomorrow we run with the leather on your body."

Grant hurt so much that he forgot his manners. "In the heat! God help us!" he exclaimed loudly.

Milos stopped, turned, and stared at him but seemed to not take offense at his student's outburst. "It's *all* about heat, tiro. Muscle and heat. Intelligence over emotion. Skill over fear. It will be like a fire in that arena. Your body will be full of excitement and hotter still. During combat, you will find yourself out of breath because of the sun's intensity. The sweat that will fall from your brow that will get trapped under that hot, suffocating helmet, will get in your eyes, and you won't be able to see a damn thing. Physical exertion and the high sun of midmorning make a tough combination. Yes, in the heat, tiro. So that you can see how the leather straps tighten on your chest when they get hot and saturated with sweat. Remember, tiro, you fight first, in the morning when the sun is rising, when they want to see men die."

Grant was quiet for a moment and then said, "You've been there?"

Milos shook his head and looked to the ground. "One of the best. You should always remember that. I survived. Will you?"

Grant smirked. "Have I got what it takes, coach?"

Milos smiled. "Against another Thracian, maybe. Against the retiarius, you'll be lion meat. You can't move fast enough, tiro. You're slow. Your friend over there may be the finest fighter I have ever seen. Try to keep up with him. You do have size, I'll give you that, and strength. All in your favor. If I were you, I'd try to learn to dart like a fish in the sea. Keep that thought. When you see a fish in a stream, it never is exactly where you think it is when you go to catch it. Reach your hand into the water to grab it, and you will find it isn't where your eyes tell you it is. But, if you grab a bit off the center of your focus, the fish is caught. Be like that, tiro. Move before they strike, put them off center of your true location, and just before they grab for the second time, when they are off balance with surprise and shifting weight, strike. Never count on your eyes in the arena. Let the sensation under your skin that feeling that someone is coming up behind you or near enough to hurt you, tell you where they are. Your instincts will be your guide in the arena not your vision. The helmet will prevent head and neck movements completely."

Grant felt humbled by the man's words. This man had no stake in his survival but had just told him how to live to fight another day. He had also told him that he would never be the best. The words were hard for Grant to digest. Coach didn't understand. He had to be the best at everything. Nothing mattered but to be the winner. It was starting to dawn on Grant that there might be some things in life...in other time periods perhaps...that just couldn't be yours. There were some skills you couldn't learn in a three-month stay in 200 A.D. So, Grant made up his mind right then to be the best sparing partner Theodosus could have. This Greek warrior would still be around come November. He'd be the one to fight in the arena. If Grant could become strong enough to give him some decent practice sessions, Theodosus might have a chance to retire like Milos, earn his freedom, and maybe buy Diana's as well. Grant looked at his friend.

"You ready for this?" asked Grant.

Theodosus paused, looked Grant dead in the eye, seemed to understand, and shook his head. He took the wooden sword and smacked it fiercely against his left palm. He was ready all right. With some burning hunger for revenge against the entire known world, Theodosus had his own plan for survival; and he would never hesitate to kill anyone who got in his way.

That night Grant was in complete agony. Diana did her best to saturate the bruises with a cooling, pungent balm, but Grant still couldn't sleep. Too much to think about. Too much pain.

Diana said, "Theodosus?"

"Yeah. That's his name," he said.

She pointed to Theodosus's cell and then placed her hands palm against palm and rested her fingers against her cheek and then tilted her head. Her eyes glowed.

"You want to sleep with him instead of me? Oh well, I can understand that, but I'm not sure what I can do about it. Not exactly in control here."

He lifted his hands and shrugged his shoulders then shook his head as if to say he couldn't do anything about it. "You're stuck with me. But, if it's any consolation to you, he's got to be hurting too and won't be touching the she-horse on account of pain and the thought of you. No one gets laid!"

She didn't sleep either but rested her head against the wall next to his head. They both stared at the stars and the clear Roman sky.

Chapter Eight

If Grant thought that Milos would appreciate their sore bodies and lighten up on the workout the next day, he was fooling himself. Not only did Milos make them run fifty laps in their new uniforms, but actually used the bruises as a teaching aid.

"Now, I'm going to come for you. You know where I hit you yesterday because you can still feel the pain. Don't let me near those wounds. Sense where I am and try to keep up."

Grant did very well because he just hated the thought of Milos striking the healing welts. He screamed on the first strike against a bruise, pulled back, and used his shield to deflect Milos's lunges. He didn't miss an opportunity to keep that wooden rudis away from his aching torso. Then he lashed back at his opponent when he felt there was a chance. He weaved and bobbed correctly, and his coach was pleased.

When Milos took after Theodosus—who had patiently watched the teacher's skill against Grant—the Greek seemed to wake from a coma.

Theodosus didn't just wince away from the blows, he made a

vicious attempt to obliterate the coach from the ludus. His eyes closed into cruel slits, his teeth gnashed against each other with solid determination, his attacks were calculated to cause the greatest pain with the least amount of his own energy wasted, his attitude and technique turned to that of a killer's.

Milos seemed stunned at first, and then began a real battle with the impassioned Greek. The fight went on for five minutes, and, then, with one weary movement, Milos tripped Theodosus who landed face down in the dirt.

"Never! Do you understand me? *Never* attack out of anger." He smacked Theodosus's rudis away from his hand. "You will be killed! Are you a lyre player, tiro? No wonder we conquered you if that's the best you can do. Come at me with *skill*. I'm a lot older than you; you should have murdered me on your first three strikes."

Theodosus moved slowly as he stood in an attempt to understand what the Roman was saying to him. Milos's mood and body language said more than his words.

"Use your head like your friend here. He knew he was wounded and fought defensively waiting for me to tire so that he could fight again when I had used all my energy. Your wounds are keeping you from moving. Your body may think it can overcome that fact, but your brain knows differently. I showed no anger and used your emotion against you. You forgot your footwork. You forgot everything. Stupid! Very stupid. Take a break. Get some water. Think about what I said and come back here when you are truly ready to fight me."

They didn't actually enjoy lunch, but they did rest and talk.

"He's right, Theodosus. You have to listen to him. You have a chance."

The Greek understood thirty percent of the words and one hundred percent of the hand gestures. The Greek smacked his forehead. "Stupid."

"No, you aren't. You've just got some chip on your shoulder. Lose the attitude, pal. Now," he looked at the clear blue sky, "how do I convey that?" He thought for a moment and then crossed his hands over one another to mean no, and then said, "Hot," and touched his head as Theodosus had done when he had first commented on Diana's pleasing display of temper.

If one can believe that women are placed on this earth to be a helpmate for a man, then Diana's sudden appearance at their table just then was meant to be the support the Greek needed at that precise moment. She ladled more water into their cups, placed some figs on their plates, and smiled at both of them.

She said as serenely as a kitten's purr, "Theodosus?"

The Greek was startled beyond words.

"Diana..." Grant prompted his friend to speak.

Theodosus said, "Diana?"

"I ahm haute, yes? Theodosus is haute?" The girl meant a whole lot in that one line. To all the others she might have just been asking whether he'd like more water on such a hot day, but the look in those blue eyes meant a totally different thing.

Again, the Greek acted with emotion. He stood up, tossed his cup aside, reached for the girl's arm, thereby making the bucket and ladle fall to the ground, pulled her into his body, and kissed her hard on the lips.

Grant smiled. "When in Rome..."

Milos and the other instructors watched while the whole ludus screamed with laughter and delight and whistled their approval.

"Or should I say, 'When in Capua'. Looks like I'm with the she-horse tonight," mused Grant.

The high moment during lunch changed Theodosus's attitude completely. Grant guessed that his friend must be thinking that his sudden attack of Eros might get Diana into trouble so he did everything Milos told him to do.

"Now you look like a gladiator. Don't get me wrong, you still have much to learn before you can fight anyone with real skill, but, I think you've done well enough to enjoy a change in the evening's entertainment."

By that Milos meant that Theodosus would be allowed to have Diana for the evening, and Grant would have another girl or no one. He would miss Diana's special care and sisterly affection as well as the comfort of sleeping with someone, but he didn't mind if it brought the two lovers together. "Lucky, Theodosus," Grant said aloud, remembering how sweet Diana's massages were.

He later found out that they had sold the she-horse to a trader right after the Greek had embraced the slave girl. The middle-aged fig grower had come by to sell them produce. He'd just lost his wife the week before and needed someone to help him pick figs. So, Grant slept alone that night, and it was the first deep rest he'd had since the first day he'd arrived in the ludus.

Theodosus was in love. It was difficult for Grant to make conversation with his friend who kept staring at his darling all through breakfast. Grant grinned at the thought that he would be able to beat him today at practice because his friend's mind was elsewhere. That wasn't the case. Theodosus was ready to perform in all ways. He ran up and down the hill easily. The heavy uniform did not diminish his strength. He listened attentively to his instructor, and did as he was told. He fought brilliantly against Milos who decided to challenge him first saving Grant for later.

"That's okay, coach, I'm the one with the good night's sleep," Grant said to himself. And then he proved it.

Grant was agile, clever, focused, unemotional, and ended the battle by tripping Milos with the exact same move that the doctores had used against Theodosus. Then he placed the rudis at the retired gladiator's throat. "Yield, goodly knight," he said for his own amusement.

Milos beamed. "Well, done, tiro! Well done. You've shown that first impressions are not always the best. You're a better man that I thought."

Grant pulled the wooden sword away and just stared at the man in the dust. "What?" he said in Latin.

"When I told you that you were slow and no match for the Greek, I was trying to get you angry enough to prove me wrong. You have."

"Are you saying that I'm actually good at this?"

"One of the best. I'd wager money on you any day."

Grant dropped the sword in the dirt. "I'm good?" he repeated, fearing that he hadn't heard correctly.

"Why are you so surprised?" asked the trainer.

"I thought I sucked," he said and then changed the descriptive phrase to one meaning horse dung.

"You're every bit as good as the Greek. Maybe better in one way. You aren't fighting with your emotions; you're using your head. You are a very intelligent student; I must say."

Grant turned to Theodosus, opened his arms wide, and said, "Hey! I'm good."

Just then Milos pulled Grant to the ground by grabbing his legs out from under him and then landing his great body weight on top of the rookie.

"But don't let it swell your head, tiro," Milos hissed. "I'm still better than you."

Grant laughed. He couldn't help himself. He just burst into a peel of laughter, grabbed the man around the chest, and tried to pull him over onto his other side. Milos had a good, hearty laugh and yelled threats and Latin curse words into the air. The other men in the camp just stared and grumbled something about how nice it must be to be a Thracian. The noise could probably be heard halfway to Rome.

Theodosus who had been tilting his head—wondering about the sanity of his friend and his coach—decided to jump the both of them. The three men wrestled each other in the dirt of the ludus's arena much to the bewilderment of everyone practicing nearby. The other doctores shook their heads and chorused something about the heat of the day having an odd effect on Milos.

When the play was over, and all three men were standing again, Milos said, "You've earned a feast on me tonight. I'll order it right now. Real food. Fried fish, maybe quail, grapes, figs, and the best wine I can find in this small village. Follow me."

They discarded their uniforms in the supply room and followed him to the other side—the forbidden outer shell—of the ludus. Just behind the prison was another building attached to the frame—one the 'prisoners' would never have known existed. "Coaches' locker room," said Grant to himself.

The doctores' bath was in this building. A large cool water-filled man's fantasy of heaven.

"Help yourself," said Milos.

The two rookies striped naked and dropped into the water like schoolboys after summer session's let out.

"There is a God!" mumbled Grant, splashing the semi-cool water into his hair and over his bruises and aching muscles.

When he was refreshed, Theodosus sat on one of the steps leading into the bath and said, "Diana!"

"She's good, huh?" Grant said, splashing the water playfully at his friend and grinning.

Theodosus touched his heart and looked at his friend.

"You're welcome, pal. What are friends for if not to hook up their best bud to an awesome babe? Yeah, I know. You got it bad. But not me," Grant said as he paddled on his back and then floated. He stared at the ceiling that had a fresco of some naked male god with his genitals exposed reaching out to a few naked virgins who wore perplexed expressions on their faces. The god's intent was obviously lecherous. After all, it was a men's lounge.

Grant let his body droop in the water so that his feet touched the bottom of the bath. "I wouldn't know about that," he said and then tossed the thought of companionship away and envisioned what Milos meant by the word feast.

"Man, being a Thracian sure is sweet! Studly clothes that attract the babes, cool coach, Roman baths, and better food. Bet the guys out there are jealous."

There was no point in talking to Theodosus because his mind was on his woman. Grant let his body relax on the step, closed his eyes, and slept half in and half out of the water.

Chapter Nine

After Theodosus had spent a few more nights with his lady love, he showed more fire in the practice sessions. During the next few weeks, the two men battled the stakes and Milos until they were ready to fight one another. The wooden swords were now weighted to make sure they felt as heavy as a real sword would in combat. No real weaponry was used. You didn't risk the student's physical strength now when he had just started to understand. One could parallel the winner of the afternoon practice fight with the heat of the day and how difficult the run up the hill was that morning.

They bathed in the 'pool' after their midday practice session, and ate their evening meal with their doctores, Milos. Obviously, sensing the great romance between Diana and Theodosus, Milos purchased her to be his servant so that she would only be serving their meals instead of being left in the heat of the arena to ladle water to the leering men and running exhausting errands for the lanista of the Capuan ludus. He ordered her to massage and minister to both of his students—which she didn't mind in the least. Of course, she stayed with Theodosus in the evening.

"Can't I get you another woman, tiro? asked Milos during one of their evening meals.

"You know what? I'd just as soon have no one right now and concentrate on my workout. I mean, I know what you people have in mind, but I have no real interest in the women around here. Except for Diana, I think they all look like cows."

Milos was drunk on wine and laughed at his 'crazy' student's words.

"It shows discrimination," Milos said. "I like that. But, wait until we go to the big city. These country girls cannot match the fine ladies of Rome."

He paused for a moment, as if pondering whether to reveal something about his own life. "I had a rich woman once who lavished money on me as long as I bedded her. She smelled like the flowers of summer. Her body was soft and oiled, and she wore a modest amount of makeup. Her hair was done up like our Empress Julia, and she wore gold around her neck and wrists and bobs of gold and gemstones in her earlobes. Face like a goddess; eyes like stars. She never walked out of the house without showing off her wealth and her beauty. She was a widow after only being married one year and had inherited real estate and a small business from her late husband."

"Were you in love with her?" asked Theodosus.

"I think I was," said Milos smiling. "Yes, I think I was."

"What happened, if you don't mind my asking?" said Grant.

"She remarried and her new husband took hold of everything she had, so I was forced out of her life. She gave me a ring of hers to remember her by."

He was wearing the ring and showed it proudly to his two

rookies. It was a plain gold band with one indistinguishable blue-green gemstone at its center. What it lacked in extravagance, it more than made up for in sentimentality. The look on Milos's face told the whole story. This was his one moment of happiness in a lifetime of pain. It meant a great deal judging by the lifestyle of the slaves and gladiators of Rome and since one's life could be extinguished at the age of twenty with one blow from a better fighter.

"When she gave it to me she told me how happy I had made her. More happiness than she had ever known in her whole life and cried a bit. I think I did mean something to her after all."

"But, if she were in love with you, why did she remarry?" asked Theodosus.

Milos gave the Greek a weak smile. "Social standing primarily. I was a slave, a gladiator, and hadn't earned my freedom yet. The rich man had prestige, a booming business in the heart of Rome, two fine houses, many important friends, and she was still young enough to give him children. The man had known her first husband and had always wanted her. He let her go on her own for a while to try her luck at her husband's business, but when he saw how interested she was in me; he made her a deal she just had to accept."

"Goodbye Milos," Grant said.

Milos smiled. "It's all right. I have my own revenge." He stared at the ring.

"Because she will never love him the way she loved you?" asked Theodosus.

"Of course, but more than that. She had just become pregnant before she married him. Too soon to show. The marriage came just in time to make it look as if the pregnancy were his doing. It was a son. In fact," he laughed again, "*twin* boys. I found out later. She told me when we met accidentally in the marketplace. I swore to keep her secret, and I have. She asked me to leave Rome, so I came to work here in Capua. I haven't seen her in a few years, but I will always remember the time we spent together." He swallowed more wine and grinned. "She was incredibly sexy."

Grant smiled at how much this conversation sounded like his own time period's chatter. It was wonderful to listen to Milos. It contrasted mightily with the fact that he could not communicate with Theodosus on any sort of important level. "She was good, huh?"

Milos stared at the virgins on the ceiling and then at the god's outstretched hand. "Unbelievable. A man's dream. She had a body like Venus, hair as shiny and black as a panther's, lips the color of a rose in full bloom." His focus shifted to Grant's reactions to his words. "I loved her night and day. There was no end to her lust. Very imaginative. She would do anything for me and I for her."

"So, you have two boys some rich guy thinks are his sons?" asked Grant.

"And it makes me happy to know that I gave her something she wanted more than money. More than me. More than him. I gave her an honored place in Roman society. Motherhood is so precious to these noble Romans. She may even have had her third child by now. Hope it was a son too. He looked like the sort of man who would kill daughters."

Grant stared at him as if he might not have heard him correctly. "What do you mean 'kill daughters'?"

"If her husband wants to, he can drown the girl baby if he doesn't want to raise her. Standard practice in Rome."

"Would you have done that?"

"Me? No. Any child that comes from these loins has a right to life. A poor man doesn't throw anything away that he has a right to. Besides, if she were as pretty as her mother, I wouldn't have the heart to destroy her."

"So, you're telling me that Roman fathers kill their daughters," Grant mumbled in astonishment.

Milos looked quizzically at Grant. "Of course. Don't misunderstand me, not all Roman men agree on this. I'm afraid he'll kill my lady if he finds out those boys aren't his. That is why I stay here for as long as I can. I'll have to take you to Rome; eventually, but she'll stay clear of me, I'm sure."

"Kill her?" repeated Grant.

Milos frowned. "Why do you seem so bewildered? Perhaps a thief such as yourself doesn't understand the ways of the aristocracy."

"How long ago was this?" asked Theodosus.

"Oh, it must have been twelve years ago. I'm not so good at remembering the time."

Diana had heard every word. She was learning Latin fast from hearing the men around her all day long. She'd been listening to the conversation from a distance and apparently catching the gist of Milos's words. Grant caught a glimpse of her peeking around a corner to watch and listen to Milos's love story.

"So, I *do* understand how you feel about Diana," Milos said apparently sensing that Diana was eavesdropping. "I don't know how you'll manage it, but there's always hope that you two can stay together. You'll have a year or two at least now that I'm her owner." Theodosus did not understand all the words but seemed to pick up the meaning.

"A year?" said Grant.

He looked at Grant. "It takes a few years of training to make you good enough to fight in Rome. Change your mind about having a lady?"

Grant went silent. He would never find Wainwright now. He would spend his whole vacation here in the ludus. What would these newfound friends think when he suddenly disappeared in September? That he'd run? Well, it wasn't his fault now was it? He hadn't asked to be transported to Capua. It bothered him just the same.

Chapter Ten

     The days in Capua 200 A.D. were sunny, and the skies were clear for the entire month of July. Grant's body stiffened with renewed vigor and prowess. He developed the muscles in his thighs to the point where they were almost too big, turned his tight stomach muscles into firm, flat rows of chiseled perfection, and created a wall of pure power across his chest and shoulders. His hands were strong and steady. In this one way, he was superior to other tiro. He was clearly bigger in height than any of them, and, since he'd worked out back home in his office, he'd had a jump on them in the ludus Mr. Universe contest.

Theodosus had a stronger cardiovascular system and was better able to contend with the heat than Grant, but once the New York businessman's metabolism became accustomed to that, Grant overshadowed him in many ways. Theodosus knew how to use weapons and fight from his years of being a Greek warrior, but Grant was a quick learner and soon conquered Theodosus handily in practice combat.

"I never thought you'd make it, tiro. When I saw you die running up that hill the first day and realized how much older you were than the Greek, I was sure he'd be the superior fighter."

Milos tossed his shield and sword to the ground as he spoke. "I don't know what crime you committed to get yourself into this prison, but I'd say you have a good chance of surviving the games in Rome. I don't see how they can beat you. Tomorrow I'll show both of you some of the techniques the other fighters are learning so, should they match you with another style of fighter, you will understand how to be victorious over them as well."

They had fought Milos that day, and Theodosus had done well, but Grant had been impassioned with cunning, courage, focus, and fire. He'd had many nights of solid sleep and was getting used to the food. The 2000 time period poison of calories and caffeine was gone from his blood system. If he could just remember how good this felt when he went home.

He'd learned how to adjust his fighting style to the moment and the helmet, evaluating each thrust and conserving his energy by using minimal footwork. Milos's style of fighting and his philosophy of combat worked perfectly. Theodosus had spent so many hours making love to his lady that he'd lost some of his superiority. Grant never thought that he'd see the day when he could fight and win against both men.

They had their training sessions in the morning now as it took less time to run the hill, and, after a small break, the two men appeared ready to fight. This gave them the afternoon to work on advanced skills—some of Milos's specialized tricks of the trade.

There was no one waiting for them when they returned to their private corner of the ludus after lunch. They put on their fighting gear and waited. Milos was nowhere to be seen.

Finally, Gino appeared. "You both suited up to fight?" Grant and Theodosus nodded their heads and put on their helmets. "A rich Roman citizen, who shall remain nameless, and who is watching in that balcony behind that veil," he motioned over his shoulder and behind him, "wants to see what you're made of. It could be a break for you if they sponsor you in the games. Milos told them that you're the best, so you'd better look good against their fighters."

"They brought their own?" asked Grant.

Gino smiled which was not a pretty sight. "Try not to kill them. I made them promise to use weighted wooden swords even though they think they can handle the real thing. Sorry to say that you won't get a chance to show your best skills." He laughed and walked away.

"We fight as a team?" said Theodosus.

From one corner of the training arena emerged three small, thin, and moderately built 'warriors'. They thought they were warriors, but they were the size and graceful build of young teenage boys. Their legs had a bit of muscle to them, but their arms looked painfully small, almost puny. Against men such as Grant and Theodosus, they would be pulp in a matter of minutes.

"Sure, friend. Look at this. What a joke."

Theodosus pointed to the boy who would be his adversary and motioned to the one Grant should take. They raised their shields, balanced their weight, and pointed their swords to their opponents indicating that it was time to begin. The midget fighters came at the two fighters with wild, uncontrolled lunges and swings that proved that they had no education in this art form at all. In a matter of minutes, two of the amateurs were down in the dirt and wounded.

The other warrior, who appeared taller, more in control, and more mature than the two youths, waited in the wings. Theodosus and Grant moved stealthily towards the one fighter. A shake of the helmet and a thrust of the rudis told them that the last fighter wanted Grant only and had no intention of fighting both men.

Diana was standing on the sidelines with her bucket of water and ladle. The concerned expression on her face puzzled Grant. Surely, she had to know that this scrawny youth was no match for Grant or Theodosus.

Theodosus acquiesced gallantly and moved aside, took off his helmet, and crossed his arms over his chest while he rested his body against one wall. "Haute now, eh, Grantus. Sawlt minz here, yes?"

2000 A.D. English interpretation: "What a joke this is, eh, Grant? What a complete and total waste of time, huh? Try not to hurt him too bad."

The fighter pointed to Grant with the sword indicating that Grant should make the first move, placed the shield in front of the body, and slashed the sword to the left and right above the helmet and away from the body to show off and to tell Grant to attack.

"Where'd you learn to be such a showoff? Hey, Theodosus," Grant called to his friend, "this won't take long." Then he turned his attention to the Thracian rookie. "Okay, kid, I'll play nice with you," said Grant aloud and in English. "Don't want Daddy to get mad at me."

Grant made a lunge to his adversary's stomach. The 'kid' parried with no movement of the feet. "Not bad," said Grant.

Then the 'kid' thrust the sword to Grant's middle section. Grant parried and made one backward step. "Cute!" said Grant.

Grant lunged to the opponent's left side. The 'kid' parried. Grant swirled his body around and a gave a backward kick to trip the fighter. His opponent twirled to move away from the kick. Grant stabbed his 'blade' into the attacker's arms. The 'kid' parried and returned with a thrust of the wooden sword to Grant's groin. "Ow!" said Grant. "Now that was *not* very nice. Okay, kid, no more Mr. Nice Guy. You want to play with the big boys, play with this."

The warrior was alerted to the oncoming lunges by the speed and sudden energy in Grant's rapid and nonstop movements: one to the left side, two to the right side, and three between the legs.

"Pay backs are a bitch," said Grant, flicking the sword upwards first before sliding it from between the bewildered youth's legs.

"That was just to introduce myself, kid," said Grant, hurling his next assault to the fighter's helmet. The warrior moved three awkward steps in retreat. Only two thrusts out of twelve went without contact to the young fighter's exposed flesh, and every time the wooden sword hit that soft skin, the novice faltered and seemed confused on what to do next.

"So, we think we're Thracian material, do we? Go back home and play with your toy gladiators. You don't belong here," Grant said in English.

Grant smacked the shield from his opponent's hand, and it flew far from the battle. Then he swatted his opponent's naked arms and thighs leaving welts to prove where his sword had made contact. Because the fighter's rich uniform was so extensive—covering the whole chest and stomach area— as well as being expensively decorated with silver rivets and the finest leather, rapid movement was difficult. The helmet also was far too flashy and heavy to protect the head, and stopped all shoulder movements. Grant saw that as an advantage and played on it. The fighter was suddenly frightened and futilely lashed the sword left and right in the air. Grant used his round shield to move the slow lunges away from his body and pushed his advantage over the fighter who went down on one knee. The fighter's sword flew out of reach.

"Now's a good time to yield," said Grant in Latin.

The fighter shook the helmet in agreement, and Grant relaxed. Then the warrior grabbed Grant's leg and pulled him down to ground level. A push to knock Grant over only resulted in the new Thracian lying flat on the ground. Grant placed his sword to the youth's neck. The helmet shifted heavily across the larynx, and the New York businessman could hear the raspy sound of someone trying desperately to breathe. Hands reached out to Grant's arms. "Don't toy with me! Yield or die," said Grant not in the mood for play.

The fighter relaxed and shook the helmet up and down, showing that Grant had won.

"No hard feelings I hope," said Grant as he rose from the ground.

Theodosus applauded and laughed. "Ees good now, eh?" he said.

2000 A.D. English interpretation: "I'm getting bored and hot. Let's get some food and water."

Grant turned his back on the fighter who no longer wanted to show any signs of assault. Grant heard a moan and a few sputters and gasps from the downed fighter. Out of curiosity, he turned to look at his opponent. Perhaps it was a sentimental reaction to a small pang of sympathy he felt knowing that the rich brat would be hurting tomorrow; or it might have been a sudden feeling of regret that he'd been so hard on the frightened youth.

In muffled Latin a small voice said, "I've never felt anything like it before in my life!"

"Naturally. I am the student of Milos, the greatest gladiator in all Roman history."

The helmet was pulled from the head. Long sable-brown hair fell in curls from inside the visor. A perfect oval face. Two big brown eyes. Long dark lashes. Full, pouting, pink lips. Slender throat. Soft shoulders. Long fingers on graceful hands.

"A woman?" said Grant.

"Oh, yez," laughed Theodosus. "One hot, yez? Nice swult minz now."

2000 A.D. English interpretation: "Whoa! All right! You got your work cut out for you now! My kind of lady! Wait until her father sees those welts. You'll be running one hundred laps tomorrow. Hoo ha!"

"It wasn't your fault," she said. "You had no way of knowing."

Grant removed his helmet and stared at the incredibly beautiful woman before him. Those soft but strong thighs should have given him some idea that the frame of the fighter was feminine. The uniform, with its covered midsection, should have told him something. He'd been in combat with a woman and was puzzled that he hadn't guessed it.

She seemed transfixed with him as well. "What's your name, Thracian?" said the fallen warrior.

"Grant, uh, I mean Grantus Tyrellius. Look, I didn't know. I'm really sorry. I'd never hurt a woman."

"I didn't want you to know," she said, positioning herself in a more comfortable spot on the dirt. She rubbed her sore arms and legs as she spoke. "You wouldn't have given me a workout. I would never have known how bad I truly am."

The other two youths, who had been watching but staying out of the action, took off their helmets. They were handsome young men of about twelve with a highly distinguishable feature—they were twins.

Grant looked back at the lady who needed help in standing. He offered her his hand. She grabbed his forearm and pulled herself up. They were very close to each other now, and Grant marveled at her beauty. He took a fast and thorough inspection of her body. She was shorter than he was by a foot or so. The leather stopped any examination of her figure , however.

"Are you allowed to tell me your name, lady?" he said softly into her ear.

Her smile could melt gold. "Lydia of the house of Marcus Flavius Antonious. Those boys are my nephews: Lucius and Marcus. We've been practicing back home with one of our slaves, but we need a real teacher. We encouraged my father, their grandfather, to allow my sister, Helena, to bring us to Capua in search of a teacher for the boys. My father doesn't approve of me fighting, but he isn't home right now." The twinkle in her eyes showed that the lady knew why her sister wanted Milos, and that she—like her sister—enjoyed disobeying her father. No secrets between these sisters.

"If Milos agrees, he will leave Capua and come home with us. By the display of skill you both have shown us today, I think the decision will be an easy one."

"Why do noble Romans, such as yourself, want to learn to be gladiators?" he asked.

She tilted her head. "Boredom, I guess. The boys want to be fighters and to drive like charioteers around the city. I decided to join in. Not a very feminine thing for a Roman lady to do, I suppose, but then I've never been one to follow convention."

"You mean to take Milos from us?" Grant felt a small panic attack at her words. He had grown to respect and trust Milos; the man had become his lifeline in this new world.

Lydia smiled. "Of course."

Milos's tale at dinner the night before came back to his mind in a rush. The two boys were his sons.

Lydia brought him out of his trance. "Thanks for the workout, Grantus," she said, picking up her sword and shield from the ground.

Theodosus gave a low whistle.

Chapter Eleven

The woman rearranged her outfit, touched her throat, and walked away. Grant knew she was hurting and trying to be brave about it.

Grant thought about how he'd had the warrior down and his sword at her throat, drawing the very life from her. He understood why she had disguised herself; he would have been gentle with her. Until, perhaps, her strike between his legs. But, why *would* he have thought he was fighting a woman? This was Rome 200 A.D. and women didn't suit up in Thracian garb and try to compete against a trained gladiator. He wasn't about to forget her name though: Lydia. Or those eyes. He stood silent and immobile, thinking about what he wanted to do next. He smiled at his thoughts. "Ask her out for dinner."

"Hey, *tiro*, food good, yes?" said Theodosus,

2000 A.D. English interpretation: "Are you going to stand there in a trance over some spoiled rich girl, or are we going to eat?"

Just then Milos came into view.

"Nice work, both of you," said Milos.

"If I'd known, I wouldn't have..."

"Don't worry about it."

"The boys. Who are they?"

"My sons."

"The woman you knew in Rome?" asked Grant.

"Is a very rich widow again, and those two boys are my sons."

"Twelve years ago."

Milos smiled and looked away. "Well, I guess I'm better at remembering the years than I thought. Obviously, she didn't lose track of time or me. Come, Helena and the family she brought with her, have devised a magnificent feast for our reunion. You and Theodosus are welcome to it."

"But the girl? I don't understand."

"That's her sister, Lydia. The girl has always been a handful, and I guess when their father wasn't watching, Lydia and the boys asked a slave to teach them how to fight. When he left for Rome, she and the boys trained together."

"But they know nothing except how to put on the clothes."

"I know," Milos said with a grin. "Isn't that lucky for me."

"Then you *are* leaving?" asked a worried Grant.

"To be paid to teach students who will never fight in the arena? Why not if it means being with her and them. I'm a free man now. I go where I wish. And where I wish to be is by her side."

"She never forgot you," Grant said half in Latin and half in English.

"So, hurry. They won't wait for slaves. It's quite an honor to be invited."

Grant motioned to Theodosus, and they hurried to get out of their fighter's uniforms and then headed to the bath for a quick dip in the "pool" to wash off some of the dirt and grime that covered their bodies.

"You like fighting woman?" Theodosus was able to say in Latin.

"That was good Latin, Theodosus." Grant tried full sentences with his friend to see how much he had retained as Diana soothed their bodies with oil.

"She points to you. Fight me, ha!" said Theodosus as Diana massaged her lover's back.

"What do you mean by that?"

"She does no want *me* to fight her. I have no workout today with those boys. A woman! Ha! Sword go in the legs."

Grant smiled remembering that he had placed his wooden sword between the thighs of a woman not a Thracian fighter, and that she had done the same to him with her first thrust.

"You're saying that she singled me out because..."

"Sheis haute for you, yes."

"Oh, come on, that's a stretch." He shook his head that it was a crazy notion.

"No...yes, she like you, Grantus. She want only fight Grantus. No want Theodosus though I am better fighter."

Grant raised his right eyebrow. "Really? Seems to me that I've been the victor in our last three matches."

Theodosus just smiled and put on the clean togas Diana had been ordered to give them. The Greek had just learned how to control their conversation. He would speak Latin and New York when he chose and play stupid when the mood struck him.

"Grantus only fight women."

Grant smiled at his friend's teasing. "Just you wait until tomorrow. But, we have more serious things to worry about."

Theodosus looked perplexed.

"We're losing our coach."

There was a big room on the other side of the kitchen that was used for large groupings. It made a perfect banquet hall. There were soft couches filled with pillows upon which to sit and tables filled with fruit and pitchers of wine.

The twin boys raced to the men as if they were the N.B.A. players of the month. Their Latin was fluent, fast, and grammatically perfect. Grant worked hard to keep up with their conversation. They were attractive young boys who seemed older than twelve to him, strong, and well-built with dark brown hair and bright blue eyes. They were about the same size as Theodosus except for muscle mass.

"Did you always want to be a fighter?" said Lucius to both men.

Grant answered for them, "I'm a slave. I was recruited you might say. And my friend here is Greek so talk to me. His Latin isn't the best."

"Did you learn all this from Milos?" asked Marcus.

"Yes. I've learned much from him."

Then the gracious and beautiful Helena welcomed them to a place by the tables. Theodosus sat next to Milos and the boys sat next to him, but Grant saw another spot on the other side of the room that provided a much better view of the lady he'd fought that day.

Helena smiled and said to Grant, "I've always loved to watch true combat, and you gave us quite a show today."

"I'm afraid..."

"Yes, yes, I know. But, my father only taught them basic footwork and very little else. And my sister is...well...not normal," she said, pointing to Lydia who was draped in an ivory chiton embossed with gold stitching on the hem, and a matching palla. Her hair was pulled up to the nape of her neck in a chignon and gold bands were tied threw it. Dangling from her earlobes were gold earrings shaped like fish, encircling her neck was an inch wide gold necklace, around her wrists were gold bands, and she had one ring on her index finger. Her sandals lay at the foot of the couch, and she wiggled her toes slowly back and forth as if they hurt her. Her servants must have placed some rouge on her cheeks and lips, but other than that, Lydia wore no makeup. She didn't have to. Her skin tone was a healthy, tanned beige, and her eyes matched the sable brown of her hair. Her eyebrows were long and thick enough to give drama to every shift of focus. They were intelligent eyes, and their focus shifted and darted here and there inspecting everyone and everything. They changed from bright to dull, soft to tough. He guessed that she'd picked this side of the room so that she'd be able to examine everyone's slightest movement. Now that the mask was gone, Grant marveled that he hadn't seen those penetrating eyes under the visor.

Her smile was teasing and feminine. Soft shoulders held the chiton to her body. A golden fibulae—broach—tied the gown in place on her left side. Her breasts were free under the cloth, and Grant's mouth went dry and his tongue thickened in his mouth. "One snap of that broach, he thought, and I could see that beautiful body of yours."

Though she reclined on a couch, Grant could see that the chiton did not hide her lovely figure. In fact, when he gazed at her, she moved slightly, arching her back, so that he could get a better view, and then dropped eye contact with him as if she knew she had been flirting with him, and that staring at a muscle bound gladiator wasn't something a well-brought up girl did. But, then she might have been stretching a sore back muscle too. It didn't seem that way, however, to a man experienced with wooing women. It looked like a come on. He had a feeling that she was a puzzle, and that made her all the more appealing.

He walked towards her.

"I'm sorry if I hurt you today," he said.

"Did I say you could speak with me, uilicus?" She looked to the left side of the room in apparent disinterest, but there was nothing there that could have drawn her focus.

He drooped his head slightly in a form of bowing to her superiority. "You called me by my first name on the field today, mistress."

She tossed a red grape between her teeth and bit down. "So I did."

"My friend and I thank you for inviting us to this feast. It isn't customary for ladies to dine with men, is it?"

Her pretty brows pulled together in a frown. "Helena has been married twice, you know. Father isn't here. And why shouldn't we all eat together. We fought each other today, uilicus."

Grant wanted her to stop referring to him as "slave" and call him by his real name, but he knew he could not argue with a rich woman.

"Here. Sit down next to me," she said, pointing to a couch near hers. She then motioned for her slaves to bring food and wine for the gladiator. A full chicken, three fried fish, a goblet—that looked like a dish with a handle—of wine, a bowl of red and green grapes, and three oranges were placed before him. Lydia was fascinating, but this was the most food he'd seen since they'd eaten at Tunniclifs, and he had no intention of being polite. He tried not to eat too quickly, but he was so very hungry.

Theodosus received the same treatment, and was surrounded by the two boys who had made a deal with the Greek to teach him Latin if he taught them a move or two. After learning everyone's name, Theodosus was now on to pronouns and verbs and eating plate after plate of food. Apparently, Diana was not permitted in the room.

Milos was sitting next to Helena and discussing something that seemed very important, but Grant couldn't tell what it was from across the room.

"Why did you single me out today?" said Grant, tasting the wine and staring straight ahead. This vintage was superb and making him very drunk. His stomach was full, and his mind was beginning to think of the next level of "human needs" that might be accomplished that evening.

Lydia smiled and drank from her golden goblet. "If we were alone," he thought to himself but did not speak aloud, "I'd minister to those bruises of yours, mistress."

"I was told that you'd be a challenge," said Lydia, looking away from him.

He grinned at how her words had a different meaning when contrasted with his thoughts, and his ego rose similarly. "Oh, who told you that?"

"This new tutor from Greece we just bought from one of my father's friends."

"How would he know that I was any good?"

Lydia motioned to one of her slaves to get the tutor. "It's difficult to find good instructors these days, and he comes highly recommended. He's quite a scholar, good with maps, math, writing, and can speak Latin, Greek, and a new language called New York. It's quaint. I decided to go with his hunch that you'd be the better fighter. He was correct."

Standing in front of him, draped in a scarlet toga with a white palla, and leather sandals, was Bruce Wainwright. "His name is Socrates, and, according to him, he was educated by one of the finest philosophers in all of Greece. Quite a find, don't you think?"

The New York businessman turned gladiator was too excited for words, and by the look on Wainwright's face, Grant would have to say that the time traveler was more than a little bit relieved to find him too.

Grant smiled and said, "A find, indeed." There'd be no way to speak with Wainwright now, but he hoped they'd get together soon.

"I need you to share a toast with Milos and me," said Helena. "My sons have a new instructor."

The boys were delighted, but it seemed as if they had not been informed that he was also their father. Milos beamed with pride every time he looked at them. He didn't appear concerned that they believed their father had been a Roman businessman. That was news for another day.

"I also have two sparing partners for my would-be warriors: Theodosus of Greece and Grantus Tyrellius from...oh dear, you never told me where he was from."

"Ah...I'm from a small city just outside...Pompeii. I was a businessman there until a thief took off with my money," acknowledged Grant.

"A businessman?" Helena said with a twinkle of interest in her eyes. "How wonderful! And you lost all and were thrown into slavery?"

"Yes, that's my story," said Grant whose courage to speak forthright to the Roman aristocrat came from the sight of Wainwright, the headiness of the wine, and the fact that she was struggling with her own business which gave them something in common.

"Then you can give me some helpful clues as to how to run my ex-husband's. Father is too busy with his own affairs to worry about it."

"I would be happy to help in any way."

Lydia squirmed next to him. Was it just his own vanity or did that movement show a slight tinge of jealousy that he and Helena were speaking as equals? He remembered who he was and went silent.

"What about Diana?" said Milos. "She is my slave. May she come to Rome?"

Theodosus's face went ashen and expressed his thoughts. Could it be that he would be taken from her? He placed the goblet of wine on the small table in front of him, looked towards the floor, and said nothing.

Lydia saved the moment. "I think I could use her, sister. That is if Milos is willing."

"You *are* quick," thought Grant. She had seen the expression on the Greek's face and summed up the situation rapidly. Theodosus stared at Milos.

"She knows medicine, tonics, salves, and is useful when it comes to sore and aching muscles. I can't leave her here," he looked at Theodosus. "Of course, she can be your lady, Lydia, if it pleases you."

Lydia looked at Theodosus who returned the glance. A bit of sentiment from a Roman woman? To help two slaves stay together? "What century did you just skip through, Lydia, because you sure are ahead of yourself here?" thought Grant.

No one asked the gladiators if they wished to leave the ludus. Milos could go and stay as he pleased; he was a free man. Grant and Theodosus had no say in the matter; they had just been purchased by the household of Marcus Flavius Antonious.

Chapter Thirteen

Grant tried not to stare at the beauty known as Lydia during the feast, attempted to enter Theodosus's conversation with the two young men, and endeavored to express himself to Wainwright who looked like a wise, mature, Greek philosopher instead of the research detective he'd brought with him from 2000 A.D. Wainwright played it cool; but Grant felt confident that at some point in time they'd get a chance to talk with one another.

Being returned to his cell after the feast reminded him of his distinctively classless state. Good enough to learn from and chat with over dinner, flirt with, tease and play with, but still a prisoner in every way. Use us and discard us.

The sky was clear, and the stars were burning in the heavens when a familiar face peered through the grill above Grant's cell.

"Hey, Grant?" said Wainwright.

"How ya been, Wainwright? Guess what funny thing happened to me on the way to the Roman Colosseum?"

"I guess you took a wrong turn. I am *so* sorry."

"Wasn't your fault."

Wainwright cocked his head to the side and paused to digest Grant's words. "You mean you're not angry with Time Travelers?"

"It wasn't your fault. You asked me to recheck what that professor told me. I believed every word the man said and didn't listen to you. The portal opened just as you said it would, and we traveled to 200 A.D. just as you said we would. I know one Harvard professor who's going to have a lot of explaining to do and a refund for me when I return. But, I don't understand why you were sent to Rome while I'm here in Capua. That has perplexed me."

"Apparently, and I swear I never knew this; I must be on a genealogical or reincarnation transfer. I'll have to check this out when I get home. I thought I knew my family tree from the roots up; this may be a past life for me. I'll need another past life regression session when I get home to see whether I've left something out of my time chart. All of us at Time Travelers have that done so that we know what we're getting into in each time period and can avoid it if we wish. See, you don't *have* to go on a G or R if you don't want to. You can create another persona by choosing to think of the time period rather than the person. I gather that you're on a general transfer, and that the time tunnel sent you to this low-scale lifestyle. If you have no spot in time to fill, it usually places you in an average persona so you don't mess things up."

"You are going through that Gemini thing then?"

Wainwright confessed, "Yes. I can't tell who is in there, and he isn't talking either; but I can see the difference when I look into Lydia's hand mirror; and well...this is sort of embarrassing to admit, but this guy is way smarter than I am. My mind is clicking a mile a minute. I have always been good at researching and retaining information, but this man is a true *thinker*. He is so curious about everything. I awakened from the time travel in the middle of what seemed to be a graduation party for my former student. I was told that this Marcus guy wanted a tutor and that I was moving to a new household. Next thing I know; I'm in Lydia's house with Luke and Mark. Trust me, as far as I know, this separation inside the tunnel doesn't usually happen, but then there have been many things about the time tunnel that have been surprising me lately. I'd say this Socrates fellow and I are fairly equal in strength because I am running the day-to-day life tasks, while he is running my head when I sleep at night. And the truly intriguing part of this for me is that his thoughts and words come to me in these amazing dreams. I'm quiet and still, and then I hear him buzzing in my head about my time travel theories. I think he wants to know about the whole business. He is so *damn* curious!"

"You think you were meant to come back as Socrates, then?"

"I think *he* can help me solve some of the glitches in the mechanism so that we can write the definitive book on this stuff. I thought I knew everything about time travel; but, with more people traveling because of the business these days, we need to know a lot more about well...situations like this. I needed to know that...I needed to know..."

"What, Wainwright?"

"There seems to be someone else running the show." He had a worried expression on his face. "For the security of future transfers, I need to be able to make sure the traveler gets to his destination and returns safely."

"I'm not upset. I should have let you do the research, and, well, I've rather enjoyed the workout in a weird way. I like Theodosus, Diana, and Milos, and I'm learning a lot about myself." He grinned hoping that Wainwright could see his face in the dim light.

Wainwright gave a wry smile. "I like Mark and Luke too."

"Mark and Luke?"

"That's what I call them. They think it's funny. I guess the last tutor got fed up with them."

"Discipline problems?"

"No, they're very curious and quite intelligent. Good boys. But, Granddad has no clue how to teach them fighting and neither does that slave. They also want to try chariot racing! Helena suggested this trip to Capua to find a trainer because they were driving her up the wall. Her second husband just died last month, and I guess he wasn't much of a father figure to them."

"She didn't waste much time," said Grant.

Wainwright lifted and eyebrow. "What are you talking about? You know her?"

"I know Milos. Have to keep mum about some of it, but Milos has been instructing Theo and I in the fine Thracian art of combat. He was a gladiator who won his freedom. He had to leave Rome and come here because of a woman...hint...hint."

"Helena?"

Grant shook his head in the darkness. "Yes, there's more, but it's not my story to tell."

"Well, I'm glad I found you and am thankful that Time Travelers made that new rule about clients not going back alone." He changed the subject. "You'll like the house. It's a work of art. My master designed it for his lovely wife who died two years ago. I guess he's all right, though he hasn't been home long enough for me to tell much about him, and a big deal in Roman society. He doesn't approve of Lydia learning to fight, her behavior, etceteras, but he seems to be light-handed when it comes to telling her what to do. I don't know why, but I'll find out."

"She and the boys actually spar?"

"They *are* pretty pathetic, aren't they?"

"I'm not sure why we're even allowed to fight them. We could have killed them with little effort. But, Theodosus and I aren't the type to take advantage of the weak."

"Is there something going on between Theodosus and Diana?"

"If by 'something' you mean lust and love, yeah."

"I've been given a...slave to assist me."

Grant smiled in the darkness of his chamber. "And your point?"

"It's a young lady, Thea. And they want me to..."

"Oh, yes, the procreation of the slave race. They think that it will give them more slaves. Hello! Does the name *Spartacus* ring a bell? The larger the numbers, the greater the army of angry slaves. Make my day! Get me angry and see what happens when we outnumber you."

"The fall of Rome," Wainwright said in a hushed voice.

"I don't plan on conquering an entire country." He paused for a moment and sighed. "One Roman will do splendidly."

Wainwright smirked, but Grant couldn't see it. "You mean Lydia? I saw you staring at her...or rather trying not to stare at you. Don't waste your time."

Grant tried to see Wainwright's expression. "What do you

mean?"

"There's something wrong there but I haven't uncovered it yet. I'm picking up quiet rebellion, bitterness, chip on her shoulder, 'I don't give a damn'—all sorts of weird vibes from her."

"Well, maybe she just hasn't met the right guy."

"I have to go or I'll be missed. Tomorrow we head by caravan to Rome."

"More marching. Oh, my feet."

"Not anymore. We travel by caravan, and Milos has told Helena that he wants you two to have horses of your own. He promised that you wouldn't try to run away. Since Diana will be with Lydia in her litter, Theodosus won't try to run off without her. And I told them that you looked like the sort who would rather be a slave in a rich man's house than a beggar in the streets."

"Oh, I'm not going anywhere."

"Lydia got that tight a hold on you?"

"She doesn't know what she wants. You can tell by the way she moves. One minute she's as cold as ice, and the next she's flirting with me. She's a mystery, and I plan to solve it. I have lots of time to figure it out."

"A month has passed."

"I know, but it won't take long to break her down."

"Grant, must I remind you that you are a...slave. You're not even allowed to speak with her without her permission. Plus, you'll be sleeping in the stables, no doubt. I have little to say in your future here; I'm a glorified slave myself."

"I have a friend on the inside, Wainwright. One that owes me big time."

"Diana?"

"That lovely lady will be mine. Just you wait and watch."

"I better go. I'll see you tomorrow. Sleep well...ah...can you sleep in that thing?"

"You'd be surprised. I'll dream about a certain Roman lady who *thinks* she has the courage to oppose me."

"Pleasant dreams, Grant."

"Same to you, Wainwright."

Chapter Fourteen

The next morning began as usual with sleepy fighters going to breakfast, the women offering pitchers of water, and the doctores ordering the men to form lines. After breakfast, Grant and Theodosus went to the bath to wait for Milos and Diana.

Wainwright's idea of a horse was erased when Grant saw that they were to ride mules to Rome—or rather a coastline villa just outside Rome. This would be a one hundred to one hundred and fifty-mile trip which, by today's standards, might not have seemed long to Grant, but would take some time by slow caravan. Two teams of four horses pulled two large four-wheeled wagons; the twins, four servants, and Milos rode fine white stallions. Diana and the women were in the two wagons as were the supplies they needed for the trip. Normally, the mules would have been too slow for a trip like this, but, considering the two wagons constantly needed to have a wheel fixed or needed to be rescued from ditches or cracks in the road along the way, the caravan moved at a snail's pace and Theodosus and Grant's humble pack animals didn't seem so slow in comparison.

They traveled along the tree-lined Via Appia that was close enough to the coastline to offer an incredibly scenic view and a cool breeze. Their travel was slow but steady with relatively few stops for mule stubbornness. The skies were clear blue with one puffy white cloud floating along the horizon; the weather was a reasonable eighty-six degrees by Grant's estimation. Milos kept track of the mileage—by reading the frequent roadside markers—to determine when it would be time to 'pull over' and find a 'motel'.

200 A.D. Latin interpretation: Stop for the night and see who lived close enough to the coastline, and who might not mind a few guests for the evening. Hopefully someone we already know.

Since the two sisters had many friends in the area, finding a countryside villa was a breeze. They were graciously welcomed into several spacious villas and given food and wine. They weren't allowed the freedom of dining with Lydia, Helena, Milos, and Wainwright. They spent most of the time in the kitchen area where Diana saw to it that they had the choicest meats discarded from the head table.

Despite the obvious class distinction of being lowly slaves, life on the road to Rome was superior to life in the ludus. The three fighters were placed in the horses' stable for the night; Milos, however, stole away to be with Helena. Grant noticed that the twins seemed to be oblivious to any sexual bonding between their mother and the doctores. They seemed wholly interested in the 'athletes'. "Give them another year or two," thought Grant.

"I wonder how long this will last?" said Grant to his Greek pal.

"Boys teach good. Theodosus un Grant go to arena?"

"That's what I'm thinking too," said Grant.

"Maybe be good house slave with Diana. Find pretty woman slave for you, and we stay?"

"Oh, I have no intention of sleeping with some slave girl pretty or not," said Grant with a smile as he made himself comfortable in the soft, sweet-smelling hay.

"Mistress Lydia?" grinned Theodosus who pointed to Grant and then touched his own chest. "Grantus luv ees haute?"

"Love or lust? I don't know."

Theodosus had a wonderful smirk. His eyes would light up like embers in a campfire, his cheekbones would rise highlighting his handsome profile, and his skin tone flushed beautifully. "She no take

Grantus to bed," he teased.

Grant had an incredibly sexy smirk as well. "You don't think so? You have no idea how charming I can be when I see something I want."

Theodosus saw the look on Grant's face and interpreted his words by his facial expressions and body language, and then laughed. "Grantus sleep with horse in stable."

"I don't think so."

"Breed with she-cow," Theodosus said, turning over in the hay and making himself comfortable.

"Cut that out."

"She-cow think Grantus *very* pretty." He imitated a high-pitched female voice. "Oh, Oh, Grantus, more more."

Grant turned away from his friend so that he wouldn't see the grin on his tanned face.

"We'll see."

The next morning they were treated to a hearty breakfast because they would not eat again until dinner, the midday meal, and that would only be some fruit and bread—hardly enough to sustain one on such a long journey. Wainwright, who could get away from the family long enough for a quick chat, assured Grant that they would be at the villa soon. Grant and Wainwright were in a situation where they could not appear to know each other without arousing suspicion, so Wainwright only spoke with him when the others were heavily involved with luggage.

"We should be home by dusk. You two have definitely inspired the twins. The sisters have caught onto Theo and Diana's little affair and approve of it completely. Lydia needs a private servant as she's had to share one with her sister for the last month. Some of their former slaves were freed a year ago. Manumission is a big deal in this Roman house. It's the way Marcus controls the huge estate. If the slaves can earn their way out, it keeps them in line. Of course, when they get to that point, Marcus has to free the old ones and search for new ones to replace them and that can take a while. I'd say we came along just at the right time. They needed a tutor who could take the boys to a higher level of education. So, basically, they got rid of the elementary schoolteacher. My two students are smart too. They keep me on my toes."

Wainwright smiled and patted the head of Grant's little mule. "I don't mind it really. It could be the other personality pushing this on me, but, I rather like them asking questions and being so curious. It forces me to think of ways to explain things without showing I'm from the future and know where history will take them, as well as the future's take on the lives their leading in this time period. Tricky but a challenge I need right now. It wouldn't surprise me if they ask me whether I think that it's possible for a person to travel through time." He shook his head. "They're really something." It was obvious from the expression on Wainwright's face that he was inordinately fond of the two soon-to-be-teenagers.

"You're in heaven, Wainwright," Grant said when Theodosus was well out of earshot.

"You'll like the house. For one thing, it's cooler than being outside in the ludus's heat. They have mini-Roman baths everywhere almost to the point of looking neurotic about cleanliness. They have ponds and fountains and an open court. Hills. Coastline. Sea. Sunny days. Plenty of sunlight in the atrium surrounded by stone, cement, and tiled marble. This guy has money. They have a kitchen with a grill stove, and a place for baking that looks like those burners people put on their decks and patios back home, and enough livestock to make for fine feasts. They make their own wine, harvest their own grain, and have a place to mill it; they grow their fruit, olives, and create their own oil and candles, and are close enough to the sea to have seafood available once or twice a week. We are far enough away from Rome to be out of the crowds and close enough to ride there for entertainment."

"Have you been to the games?"

"The boys are big on chariot races, but so far we've yet to go to the games in the arena, thank God! I don't know how I'll handle that. I think it must be the most revolting thing in history next to the French Revolution or the Nazi concentration camps."

"Well, Helena just saved Theodosus and my asses by taking us out of the ludus."

"Probably the time tunnel's plan. Nice to know that 'it' brought us back together. The whole time mechanism has been spinning in my head, and I find myself thinking about it when the scenery gets boring."

"Probably why you're the tutor; you have time to think about what it all means."

"I'll talk with you again," Wainwright said when Theodosus turned the corner and saw them.

It was cloudy, and there was a threat of rain as they began their travels back to Lydia's home. Grant had no communication with Lydia but watched for her every chance he got. Diana and Milos were obviously happy with the turn of events, and Theodosus's mood lightened with each mile. The mules showed a bit of stubbornness but sensed bad weather coming and kept up with the horses. Grant was concerned that he would have another headache if it stormed and let his mind wander as his mule plodded along after the others. By high noon, they were at the palatial home of Marcus Flavius Antonious.

Wainwright was correct about the house. On the far side, close to the coastline, was a vast farm of trees and vines. One major house stood in the middle of smaller stone buildings. Horses, pigs, chickens, and one or two cows wandered amid the tufts of grass surrounding the villa. A building attached to the main house appeared to be the kitchen as smoke and delicious aromas drifted around its exterior.

Helena spoke with everyone, "Allow me to show you my father's house. Father is in Rome leaving me to play hostess," she darted a quick look at Lydia, "in his absence." Grant saw the odd glance that was passed between the two women, and it sent his mind swirling with the mystery of it.

Helena took them into the atrium of the home and stopped. She spoke like a tour guide displaying sections of a museum to a paying crowd of tourists. Her sons, not interested in the house tour, exited at this point to parts unknown. Lydia disappeared shortly after the tour began.

"My father loved our mother very much. She adored flowers as you will soon notice when you see the adjoining garden at the back of the atrium and how the individual patios are covered with bushes, vines, and urns filled with flowers. The atrium and garden of the house resemble a flower's stem, and the rooms to the side of this stem are rounded with smooth cement to make it look like the pedals of a blooming rose."

She held her chin up at this point. "There is none other like it in all the Roman world. Senators and even the emperor himself have visited here to see its unique design, murals, and its marble and mosaic tiled floors."

The foyer's floor was formed in a rectangular shape that surrounded a rectangular pool of water at its heart. The floor's pattern was a complicated design of a light rose, solid, block marble border that outlined smaller squares of deep rose tile matched with a light ivory tile. Surrounding the pool was another darker colored tile that was larger and had one heart per block at the center of its ebony surface. The heart seemed to contrast all that Grant had learned thus far about the brutality of the Roman Empire.

Carefully cut stone was used to encase the cement pond; the cement beneath the three feet of water had been painted a pale blue color. At the head of the pool was a statue of Venus clad only from the waist down, who held a double-handled pitcher in her arms. Trickling water poured from the pitcher into the pool. This was not a pool for bathing. however, but one could place a hand or foot in it to relieve one's body of the tremendous summer heat.

Four half-circle wooden chairs rested against the walls of the atrium. Four open arches hinted at attached rooms, and there were heavy drapes tied above it just in case someone in the room wanted privacy. The ceiling, which had been painted with expensive murals of gods and nymphs, was supported by four stone pillars. Above the pool was an open space so that you could look at the sky. Grant noted that it was like the skylight in his apartment and thought, "This would be hell when it rains. Of course," he mused, "the drops *would* land right in the pool."

The walls of this atrium were bordered with pink marble and painted cement covered the spaces between the arches. The paintings that decorated this area were scenes of the valley and land surrounding the estate. There were landscapes of green fields, fruit trees, vines heavily laden with plump red and green grapes, a horse, cow, a few pigs, and blue skies above it all dotted with puffy white clouds. The atrium was relatively void of furniture, but there were two huge wooden chests and an occasional pedestal where an oil lamp waited to brighten a dark room.

"The marble tile you see here had to be imported, and no other house in Rome has this intricate combination. We even have marble and mosaic tile in the stable that matches this atrium's floor exactly."

She moved them into the first room to the left of the atrium. Clearly the dining area, it had one enormous table, a few smaller ones, five couches laden with overstuffed cushions, five half-circle shaped wooden chairs, two chests, and a tall, freestanding cupboard apparently meant to hold tableware and dishes. This room was closed off from the outside save for one window with iron grillwork on it. The half-circle walls were painted cement surrounded by pink marble, and the floor was a mosaic tile. The ceiling was painted in a masculine manner with bare-breasted maidens and muscular men who displayed their genitals to the virgins. One was trying to seduce an innocent maiden by kissing the girl's shoulder and lecherously grabbing a breast with his free hand. Father and grandsons, guests, Helena and Lydia upon various occasions, would eat in this room surrounded by the lustful panorama.

On one side wall, however, was a portrait of a lady having her hair done by a slave while a small boy held her mirror up so that she could see the combs being fitted into her long sable-brown hair. The woman was dressed in a soft, loosely fitting, white chiton, her hair—a strand of which she held up to the slave with one hand—was long and wavy like Lydia's; and, upon closer inspection, displayed a perfectly lovely oval face that could have been an exact twin of Lydia's.

Helena pointed to the wall and the sensuous, young girl in the intimate pose. "That is my mother, Livia. Father had it done while she was pregnant with me. You can see the small round belly under the chiton if you look closely."

This room had another archway that led to a small room that Helena indicated was Diana's bed chamber. There was one small bed—period. They passed quickly through that 'room' and came to an attractive bedroom with an outside patio. The room had a Roman bath at its center with no statue but a few steps at all four corners so that one could enter the water from any side. This really was a bathing pool; the depth of the cool, blue pool must have been five feet. The floor around it was a pink marble border, and creamy ivory tile with flecks of pink swirled inside it.

There were a few wooden chests with gold locks, two freestanding upright cupboards with golden knobs, a wide but shockingly short bed laden with pink and rose covers and tapestry pillows. A soft fur rug covered the cool tiles right at the foot of the bed. Someone had decided to place small pillars around the bed with rods between them so that a thin curtain encircled the bed so that the sleeper could pull it to attain some privacy or throw it back to get the afternoon breeze as they napped. There was a long table by the pool and a small table with toiletries, combs, mirrors, and, what appeared to be a jewelry box on it, and a small backless chair with a soft cushion on it beside that. The room opened into a private patio that had a table and two chairs and was more a garden with green leaves and pretty pink and yellow flowers overflowing the urns beside it. Another curtained arch led back to the atrium.

"This is my sister's room. Diana, you will sleep in the room we just passed so that you will be close to her. Lydia takes her meals on the patio. Remember to serve her there. You will find oils in the chest by the pool."

They walked back to the atrium and then went through a large archway that led to what, at first glance, seemed to be a garden surrounded by a circular cement wall. A rectangular pool rested at the garden's center. At the far end of this pool was the statue of a naked woman holding a jar in one hand and a dish in the other. An open roof similar to the atrium's wider skylight was high above the pool. Grass and a variety of bright flowers enclosed the pool instead of pink and white tile. Four small pillars supported the rim of the skylight's frame, white marble benches sat on either side of the pool; small, smooth, stone steps led into five feet of water which rested calmly in the blue painted cement. The bedroom's decor was very inviting, and Grant's mind presented a myriad of possible lovemaking scenarios he could initiate if this room were his.

"Must be the master bedroom," thought Grant.

The room held chests, long tables for dining, a vanity table and stool, freestanding cupboards, and wooden chests. A melancholy feeling came over Grant as he investigated the living quarters. The woman was gone, but her toiletries remained untouched on the table as if awaiting her return. The bed was made for a couple in love—warm and comfortable with many curtains, covers, and cushions. It was too perfect. A place for everything and everything in its place. Smooth unwrinkled bed cover. Impeccably folded curtains. No crease in either pillow. Deep royal burgundy colors. Tassels on the cushions. Table by the pool with a rolled cloth towel resting on it. No scent of oil or fragrance, which, even after the long trip to Capua and back, still resided in Lydia's room. No need for a patio here. The rounded room had two side windows with grillwork on them, and there were two arches on the right and left of the room for the slaves' quarters. Grant noticed that these slaves' rooms couldn't be accessed by any other room but this one. Whereas Diana's room could be entered by the dining room or Lydia's bedroom, the husband and wife had their own slaves with their own private rooms with curtained archways for maximum privacy.

"This is sad," thought Grant. "These two people must have loved each other very much to want so much privacy. And now that lovely lady is gone, and Marcus Antonious sleeps alone—if he sleeps here at all."

As if reading Grant's thoughts, Helena continued, "The statue is the likeness of our mother offering a sacrifice to Venus which, as you can see, she can see from this pool. Her nudity in such close proximity to the goddess of love tells the story of two people who married for love. Follow me."

Helena led them to the next bed chamber that looked very much like Lydia's except there were three beds. "We are building another small house for the boys behind this one, but we just moved back to my father's home, and they sleep here in their mother's room for now."

"Milos will be anxious to get rid of that tradition, I'll bet," thought Grant.

"The small room to the right and towards the front of the house is for the tutor and his slave. It is larger than the other slaves' quarters because of his need for supplies. The boys take their lessons in the atrium and outside in the gardens."

As if on cue, the most delicate blonde with the palest blue eyes Grant had ever seen, with skin the color of milk, walked into the room and dipped her head to her mistress.

"This is Thea our tutor's slave. If you have need of the tutor, send for her. I do not allow him to be disturbed during the twins' school time which is midmorning and midafternoon. They will have combat lessons first thing in the morning, before school, and just before our main meal of the day. They will have their riding lessons with Crecius before the sun sets. For the present, all gladiators will sleep in the stables. Allow me to show you."

Helena took them outside and into the most glorious garden

Grant had ever seen. He noted the half-built villa behind the house. They crossed through the fabulous garden to go to another building that seemed to be a small version of the grand house. They found six horses in various stages of slumber here. The building was cement and painted with some teal colored vine designs painted around the ceiling that looked like a wallpaper border from Grant's time period. The horses' water and food rested in clean marble basins, there was no aroma of hay or manure anywhere, and the marble tiled floors were spotless. Off to the back of the stable was a livery room. Three cots had been set in this stable.

"This is temporary, I assure you," said Helena apologetically, though why she should care about the slaves' feelings was beyond him—unless she was speaking strictly to Milos.

"As I have stated before, we have just recently moved back to my father's house from our townhouse in the city. My boys were babes when I visited last. I stayed for such a short time, that the need to add on to this house was unnecessary. But, recent developments have necessitated my taking over the handling of my father's house. We are still working on the bath there," she pointed to the boys' cottage, "and I think Lucius and Marcus will be able to move by the end of this week. They will soon celebrate their thirteenth birthdays, and boys that age need some freedom; I want them close to their doctores and their horses. Their slaves have not been purchased yet."

She looked at her sons and smiled. "Next trip to Rome, my loves. Until then, the three of us sleep in the same room, and my body slave, Ariadne, and the tutor, Socrates, stay on either side of us in those rooms you saw by my bed chamber. Of course, with father away, we do have the freedom to use his room if needs permit...but...there is a certain sanctity about that room, and I'd prefer to leave it as it is."

Lydia interjected both physically and verbally. "The food is ready. A light supper I am sorry to say, sister, bread and fruit; but I have ordered a splendid feast for dinner if that's to your liking—or would you rather have it tomorrow."

Those words underlined the domestic demographics entirely. Helena ruled. No one did anything without her approval, not even Lydia.

"Well, it will have to be so today for we are rushed, and the slaves would have had no way of knowing when we would home. I'm sure we are all famished, so let us eat now and rest from our travels. What you have done is good, Lydia, carry on."

The twins were ready to eat, and Grant had to admit that his belly was growling about its emptiness.

Helena pointed to a small fountain with a lion's head that spewed cool water from its mouth into a square basin. "Wash up, boys," she stated and then looked at the doctores, "Milos will join us?"

"If it pleases you," said Milos.

"Socrates, show the gladiators to the kitchen and see to it that they have all they wish to eat, then join us."

"So, we don't get to eat with the family anymore," thought Grant. "How will I see Lydia if I'm stuck in the stables?"

"Mother?" cried Lucius.

Helena turned her head to regard her son's plea.

"I wish to speak with Theodosus and Grant, and I can't do that if they eat in the kitchen."

"You know better, Lucius," said Helena.

"But grandfather isn't here to say one way or the other about it," added Marcus.

"What will people think?" Helena cautioned.

Lydia smirked. "Since when has that stopped you from doing as you please, sister. Or both of us for that matter," she said to Helena and then turned to the twins. "Father would be furious with us, and you would be setting a bad example to the slaves," Aunt Lydia warned her nephews.

Lydia stared at Grant for a brief moment and said, "There will be time to speak with the gladiators later this evening after we have napped."

Grant thought to himself, "You want me to sleep with a horse? Ah, I don't think so." He smiled at her, and she turned away. "For now maybe, lady, but I've got plans for you that would shock both your mother *and* Venus."

Chapter Fifteen

"I was hired to instruct Lucius and Marcus in the fine art of being a gladiator, but that does not include you, Lydia," shouted Milos the next morning after breakfast. She had been pestering him as consistently as a gnat at a picnic.

Lucius and Marcus came to practice with short white skirts over clean white loin cloths that were visible when they sprang into animated play.

"But I thought..." she said.

"I am not a slave, Lydia, and I mean no disrespect to you or your house, but I don't teach *women* to fight. The boys and my Thracian students will be fighting together, and it is man's play. A woman doesn't belong here."

"But there are women who fight in Rome," protested Lydia.

"You plan to fight in the arena, lady?" Milos asked nonchalantly.

She dipped her chin to her chest. "Well, no, but I thought it would be fun to learn *how* to fight."

Her trembling lip and the soft voice had its effect on Milos. "I get so bored here," she said.

"How can this place be boring? There are horses to ride, and you are not that far from the coastline. You have boats and slaves. Go for a ride in the sunshine, or a nice boat ride along the coast. Explore the water's edge for treasure."

"All of which I have *done* since I could toddle by my mother's side."

"Art and music?"

"Accomplished by the age of sixteen. My art is disgracefully bad, and my music is for the cool of the evening."

"Poetry?"

"One can only write *so* many songs, and you need to be in the mood."

"Domestic..."

"Not even in your wildest dreams would my mother's spirit allow me to weave."

"I see." Milos was stumped for any more suggestions.

"Might I suggest something?" said Grant.

They both looked to him for help.

"My lady should not be trained with the boys, I agree with you there, Milos, but she should be trained."

Lydia's eyes glowed with validation.

"Privately."

Theodosus grinned, turned his head so that no one would see him, and gave a soft whistle. Milos placed his hand to his chin as if he needed to inspect something on the ground. The two boys fought over which sword they'd use today.

"If my mistress wishes," Grant said, making a courtly bow, "I would be honored to instruct her in some rudimentary skills with the hope that she would learn how to protect herself."

Lydia smiled.

"Well, Lydia, it's up to you," Milos said.

"When?"

"When the boys go to school, I will train you."

The move was too swift for a country girl like Lydia.

"I agree," she said and then walked into the house and left the boys to start their lessons.

Milos noticed them for the first time. "You put those down right now. You have no need of them today. Do you see the coastline? I'd say it is a good walk from here, wouldn't you?"

The boys shook their head in complete agreement. Grant decided right then and there that he liked the twins. Others would have gone pale at the thought of running or even walking to that coastline and back, but they were more than ready to do as Milos instructed.

"We need to get those legs into shape."

"Do we have to go too?" asked Grant. One could see the coastline from the house, and it didn't look more than a mile and a half across semi-rocky terrain.

"Do you mean to allow yourself the luxury of getting soft?"

Grant and Theodosus looked at each other and then whistled to the boys and began the chase. Grant enjoyed his sleek, muscular body, and he wanted to keep it trim and taut for Lydia. Some instinct bred by sheer vanity told him that she had noticed how good he looked. He planned to teach her many things, and he needed to be one step ahead of her. After all, what was the point in getting into fighting condition if he gave it all up after one month?

The boys were like young colts and dashed ahead of the 'old men' as they referred to Theodosus and Grant, but halfway to the coastline they tired. Young muscles were no match for raw, chiseled physiques. The two gladiators' cardiovascular systems were in tiptop form, and this 'short' run couldn't compare to the long marches up that infernal hill.

Theodosus and Grant reached the shoreline and rested on some rocks to wait for their young companions. Grant scanned the view. The blue-green water of the Mediterranean swallowed the pebble-covered sand. This beach was no place to throw your blanket and take out your suntan oil. The sun rose to the east of them and shed its golden-orange rays upon the water in long silver-white slits. A cool breeze rose from the rocks, and he detected a small cave hidden in the darkness of a shaded cove. Tied to a rock and bobbing up and down with the waves was a pretty sailing vessel. It was probably considered good-sized by Roman time period standards, but from the New Yorker's point of view, it was fit for no more than four passengers. The water looked warm and inviting, but the rocky beach looked painful for the feet. Grant's gaze returned to the cave. "Shades of California living," he thought.

The twins fell at the two gladiator's feet gasping from their pain and exhaustion. They could say nothing for several minutes.

"Can't we walk back?" asked Lucius.

"No," said Grant in Latin. "But, we *can* take a quick swim if you wish."

The boys were on their feet faster than a fallen race horse, stripped off their clothes, and ran down the cliff to the water as if they hadn't run a race beforehand.

"Grantus haute?" asked Theodosus, pointing to the water and then to both of them.

"Why not," Grant answered. They took off their clothes and joined the boys who were now playing a dunking and splashing game.

"Far cry from the ludus," thought Grant. "Wonder what Milos will think when we don't come back right away?"

Grant floated on his back, let the sea water caress his body, washed off the dirt and grime of the long ride on the dirty donkey, and let the sun bathe his face. "Now this part of the time travel mix up ain't bad."

Theodosus followed suit. "Good, yes?"

"Very good. Diana?" Which was Grant's way of asking if Theodosus had seen his girl lately.

"Oh, she fine and good. Happy, yes. In new house. Good clothes. Good food. Yes? Love Theodosus. Soon, yes?"

2000 A.D English interpretation: "She's digging her new location. She's a damn site better off here than at the ludus. Livin' la vida loca with a solid roof over her head, better clothes, better food. What can I say? She's crazy about me. Okay, so we haven't exactly had a chance to be together yet, but make no mistake, she'll find some way to sneak out of that house and meet me for some loving. What a woman!"

Grant let his mind wander to thoughts of Lydia. He'd gained an important foothold. She had agreed to train and fight with him alone giving him access to her time...and her body. As a trainer and a fighter, he would have to be with her as she moved through her routine. And the first place he would bring her was this lovely little cove. "You ain't gonna be bored for long, lady," he thought to himself.

"By all the gods, what do you think you are doing?" shouted Milos from the cliff.

All four swimmers stopped what they were doing and stared.

"Get your butts back to the house right now." He looked at the boys and said, "You two will be late for Socrates, and I don't want your mother angry with all of us."

The men, tanned and wet, wiping the water from their faces and lips, shoulders and hands, moved slowly from the sea. They dressed quickly and began a slow jog and then a faster race back to the house. Again, Theodosus and Grant were home at least five minutes before the weary boys.

Milos pulled Grant aside. "I want to talk with you."

"I'm sorry about the lack of discipline today."

"I don't care about that. Boys will be boys. It's Lydia. You may be fooling her, but you aren't fooling me. Are you crazy? Do you have any idea what you're doing?"

"Yeah. What you did for yourself back in Rome with Helena."

Milos shut his mouth. There was nothing more to be said.

Chapter Sixteen

Lydia returned after the midday supper. She was wearing what would be termed in this time period as a dancer's costume. It was a dress, so to speak, the skirt of which barely covered the thighs; for modesty's sake, the bodice was tied at both shoulders with no broach. From Grant's point of view, it was most disconcerting. He assumed that she was wearing some sort of linen underneath, but he could not tell, and it was blatantly conspicuous that nothing was prohibiting the swaying movements of her beautiful breasts. His manhood responded which was not exactly what he wanted now. If Lydia only knew that she had disarmed her opponent with only a smile and a jog across the courtyard. But she didn't. She was naive about many things not the least of which was how men reacted to half-naked women.

"I'm ready for my first lesson. Are we going to run?"

"Lord in heaven no!" thought Grant to himself trying to think of non-sexual activities such as cold showers and playful puppies. His body was fit, healthy, and happy in its new setting of good food and morning swimming sessions in the sea. His libido was working overtime. He wasn't used to the Roman way of targeting all decor, paintings, statues, food, clothing, drink, architecture, entertainment, and recreation to sex. The fact that Theodosus and Milos were having gloriously satisfying sex lives didn't help the problem, either. And he wanted Lydia so much. Lord, how he wanted to take her in his arms and smother her full lips with his. To press his tanned muscular body right up against those full breasts of hers and tell her any lie he could invent to get her to comply with his sexual advances. Then he'd look at her and see her eyes twinkling with happiness, her hair fly around her perfect face like an angelic halo, and her hands moving every which way with excitement and feel his heart burn in his chest. He wanted more than just sexual gratification from Lydia.

"Can we start now or do I have to wait longer?"

Grant closed his eyes and smiled. "No, mistress, we can start right away. But, you will have to change into better shoes. Those sandals will not protect your feet. Also...do you have some sort of..." he said, moving his hand sideways across his chest. "I wouldn't want you to get...hurt."

"Oh," she looked at her breasts, "a brace? Of course, I'll change and be back immediately." And she was gone.

Grant bit his lips and closed his eyes forcing his body to remain under his control. When she returned, she was wearing a soft, white, goat skin brace across her chest and Marcus's boots.

"I'll have to get some of my own, but these fit, so I stole them. I'm ready."

"So am I," said Grant. "The first thing we need to do is condition your body," he said in Latin terminology. "Make you strong and graceful so that you can count on your muscles to help you parry and attack. It means a great deal in warfare."

"I see. So, you want me to run?"

"Well, we can begin more slowly by *walking* to the coastline."

"But I thought the twins ran the whole way?"

"Well, they didn't have a very good start. Didn't pace themselves very well and finished exhausted. Since the sun is directly above us, I think you would be at more of a disadvantage."

Lydia removed the leather ties that held her hair in place and pulled her sable strands back into a ponytail and then retied the style with the leather bands. "Really?" she said and then began the race of her life. "Try to keep up," she called back to him.

Something about the surprise challenge calmed his desire for her, and he could sprint fast enough to catch up with her. To win or lose was the question in his mind. He certainly could beat her even if she did look as if she could run a marathon in twenty minutes. She would certainly tire...eventually...and he could catch her. But did he want to win was the thought flying through his mind? If he lost, she might think she was superior to her teacher and that wasn't a good thing. The teacher must never appear inferior, at least not on the first day. She plainly wanted to show off for him. To show her worth as an athlete. So? He decided to let her stay ahead of him by a foot or so, and then dart passed her when they got to the shoreline.

Easier said than done. Grant soon became aware of how strong her leg muscles were, and how they had more power than the boys'. She was older, and her body frame was mature compared to the boys' who must have spent more time on horseback than she had. How she managed to build that leg strength was beyond him. Walking to the gardens once or twice a day wouldn't have given her this incredible stride, and Grant found it increasingly difficult to keep up with her. She never turned around to see how close he was to her. Her arms were above her waist, and she used them to help her pace herself. The boots were protecting her feet nicely; the brace kept her breasts in place as she moved. As he managed to close in on her, he noticed that her mouth was open, and she was controlling her breathing. It occurred to him, that she was a better athlete than the twins, but after the grueling sessions back at the ludus, he would win. If he died after this race, he would beat her.

His heart was pounding against his chest, and his lungs ached; but, if he didn't pass Lydia, they would have no future together. He pushed his legs and lungs to the limit and finally came up behind her. He heard her laugh and surge forward. She had energy in reserve. Grant hadn't counted on that. His body was so much stronger than hers, but her litheness was working to her advantage. He was a giant next to her. She had lived in this heat all of her life, and the noonday sun was no hurdle for her to overcome.

The tie flew from her hair, and her long, dark curls became a playground for the breeze: hurling them, tossing them, finger combing them around her shoulders and face. She laughed and shook her head. The sweat on her skin shimmered in the sunlight. She let her hands dangle at the wrists. Her dancer's dress was soaked and clinging to her body. The outline of a loin cloth was now visible under the skirt.

"How did she learn to do this?" thought Grant whose body was now relaxed and working to his advantage in its own mode of pacing and momentum.

Grant accelerated just as they came to the coastline. He stopped there and gasped for oxygen as he kept walking in circles to cool down his body temperature. She came up behind him and stopped abruptly.

"Don't stop like that," he gasped. "Keep moving. Your muscles will tighten on you."

"You won," she said smiling.

"Pure strategy, mistress. Let the other runner take the wind in his face, opening a tunnel of easy flying for you, and then pass them just before the finish."

"I'll remember that." She looked at the waves that were calmer than they'd been in the early morning hours. "Marcus told me that you four swam today."

Grant pressed his hands to his knees and bent over to catch his breath before speaking. A swim with Lydia was everything he wanted and exactly what he should not do at this point in his relationship with the headstrong daughter of a rich man. "Not a good idea," he said.

"Why not?" she said, starting to strip.

"Ah..." he said, thinking fast. "Cramping."

"Cramping?" she said, tilting her head flirtatiously and throwing her hair away from her face with one hand so that she could see him.

"Yes, until you get those stomach muscles in shape, that fast race you just had will...cause...major cramping...and...you'll...probably die."

"Really?"

Grant was able to relax his speech and move calmly towards her. "Absolutely. Where did you learn to run like that?"

"Oh, I've done it all my life. Ever since I was a girl. Helena and I used to race to the coast all the time and swim."

"Your father allowed you to go near dangerous cliffs and swim without adult supervision?"

Lydia closed her eyes and smiled into the bright sun. "My father is rarely home, and my mother couldn't control Helena and me, anyway."

"I see," he said.

"When Helena married and moved away, I continued my frequent swims. Sometimes I would take Thea or Ariadne with me, and we would swim and imagine tales about handsome, dangerous, renegades who would come in a ship and carry us away."

"Pirates," he said.

She stood erect and moved towards him so that they could hear each other. "Yes." She looked away for a second. "We saw a pirate ship once."

Grant showed his disbelief by closing his lips and raising one eyebrow. "Really?"

"You don't believe me?" She placed her hands on her hips and spread her legs to balance herself on the rocks.

"I think you're a bit of a storyteller, mistress."

Lydia scowled at him, looked at a small rock, bent over and grasped it, and then hurled it into the waves. A long distance, high-flying, solid toss.

"One afternoon, when I was about fifteen, Ariadne, Thea and I were sunning ourselves on the deck of the Athena. A pirate ship came close to shore, so we hid in the belly of the boat but peeked out occasionally to see what they were going to do."

"How did you know it was a pirate ship?"

"The evil eye on the bow of the boat."

"I see."

"They were looking to plunder and saw our little sailboat. I was *so* frightened."

"Did they stop?"

She looked at the sky as if the clouds would tell her the next chapter. "Not that time. But later. On another day. Thea and I were hiding in the cave because a bad storm spoiled our swim. And we found some gold coins."

"Really?"

"Yes, I took them home with me. I still have them at the bottom of my chest."

"I'd like to see them."

"I also found some gemstones, but I gave them to Thea since she's the one who found them."

"Valuable gemstones, mistress?"

"I really don't remember. Probably. Pirates horde their treasure on small coves like this one."

"I've heard that."

"Shall we swim now that we have calmed a bit?" She started to strip again.

"Well, I thought you wanted to learn some moves today."

"You said conditioning came first."

"I did, indeed, but I think you've shown me that you are very much in shape, and we can proceed."

"Are we going to run back home?"

"Actually, I was hoping you would tell me more of those pirate stories."

"There isn't much to tell," she confessed. "But," she looked at him directly, "I would like to hear about your life as a businessman, and how those men were able to steal all your money, and what it was like to be a slave at the ludus and all."

Grant Tyrell wasn't much of a storyteller, and he had only a rudimentary, calculating sort of imagination at best, but he would have to come up with something good because Lydia expected a good story, and it was a long walk back home.

"Well, I was...living in Pompeii..."

He moved to her side and motioned that she should lead the way. She grinned coquettishly and moved away from the rocks. It would be a long walk home, but, Grant thought, he couldn't think of a better way to spend his afternoon.

Chapter Seventeen

The twins progressed nicely during the next week's workout

though they were hampered by the usual aches and pains of a new regime. They moved awkwardly at first, stretching their thighs and pressing down on their toes while raising their heels from the ground repeatedly to alleviate the pain in their calves. Milos noticed every movement and smiled. He was helping his sons learn how to fight. Nothing could be more satisfying for him except, perhaps, some privacy with Helena.

Theodosus and Grant gave them a slower run to the coastline for a few days, and subtracted the swim from their daily task until they proved worthy of such a break from their lessons. They took their wooden swords and hacked away at the two stakes Milos ordered to be placed in the courtyard. They grumbled about not being able to wear the uniform of a Thracian, and why they could not use their real swords; but because they wanted to learn, they quieted with a glowering look from Milos. They exercised for five days and were given two days off from both scholarly and physical pursuits.

Helena was still very much in charge of the house, and Grant wondered if they really had a father who would be returning any day. Wainwright found brief moments in the evening to speak with Grant.

"You are sure giving Lydia a workout," he said.

"Oh?" Grant smiled and let his focus fall. "Why do you say that?"

"She won't let on to you, but Diana has been talking to Thea about how her mistress can't move in the morning, that she has to blend special oils to soothe Lydia's stiff muscles, and how Lydia's been taking her meals in her room because she doesn't want her sister or the twins to see how bruised and hurting she is. She's very afraid that Helena will give her trouble about learning the art of being a gladiator. I guess her sister has doubts but is giving in because of what happened two years ago."

Grant was instantly alert. "What happened two years ago?"

"I guess Lydia was supposed to marry this army guy. One of those matches made of love—one of a kind things. They planned on marrying when he came back from this campaign with Emperor Severus. Only trouble was he came home wrapped in funeral cloth."

Grant flinched. "I felt there was something going on with her, but she's not about to open up to her slave/coach."

"I guess Daddy is pushing her into marrying again, but Lydia just drops the subject as soon as it's brought up."

Grant was touched by the story. He'd grown fond of this feisty, independent, ahead-of-her-times woman. He knew she was hurting when she showed for her lessons, but she never complained or held back. Always gave him one-hundred percent every day. She'd been struck several times with the wooden sword, tripped, stretched, fallen, her feet lanced by stones; and yet she kept her lips sealed. She had also kept them closed whenever Grant had tried to get her to talk about herself.

At first, Grant just wanted the woman. Challenge. Conquer. That sort of thing. But gradually over the course of the first week, he'd detected a certain sadness in Lydia.

He'd lie on his cot at night and think about her. Such a puzzle. She was the exact opposite of Helena in so many ways. Helena was more domestic, maternal, protective, and very strict with the slaves. Lydia was the silent shadow who rested in the wings allowing everyone else to do, say, behave in any fashion they wished. Her voice was soft when she spoke with Diana who lauded praise on her mistress when she had spoken with Theodosus and Grant during the day. Diana never felt like a slave to Lydia. She spoke of Lydia's melancholy, distance, and need. Quiet and hurting. She'd even mentioned that she thought she had heard Lydia crying during the night.

Now some of the pieces of this puzzle known as Lydia could be placed onto the picture. The portrait was in no ways complete, but she was coming into focus.

Grant tried every way he could to touch her during practice. Theodosus had teasingly commented on Grant's 'new' way of fighting. Lydia would never have guessed that she wasn't supposed to get quite that close in battle. And Grant had found her handling of the sword so inferior that he had had to stand behind her, wrap his arms around her, place his face and lips against her neck, his stomach against her back and show her repeatedly how to hold her weapon.

Of course, her leg placement was forever sloppy, and he had had to move her long limbs to the correct placement thereby touching her calves. If she flinched, he immediately stopped all work to inspect her graceful arms or taut thighs. And if her feet looked bruised, he made her sit down, undid her boots, and gently massaged her toes. He had a line for all this interest. It was completely wrong to continue any movement until the pain was deadened. He had told her that serious injury could be avoided if he acted quickly to mold the soreness from her aching body.

Lydia was an excellent student, did everything he asked, never argued or complained, and appeared to be naive about her coach's solicitous behavior. Theodosus was wise to Grant's plans, but Lydia either didn't know, or didn't mind, for her face never reflected any emotion but relief when he touched her.

She talked about pirates, ships, and childhood memories when they rested from their morning run to the coastline, but had never told him about the handsome warrior who had stolen her heart and died honorably on the battlefield.

Wainwright's words struck some cord of compassion in Grant's heart. A stirring he hadn't felt since he was told that his father was never going to live with them again. He was silent for a few moments before saying, "Keep me informed."

Wainwright shook his head. "And how are *you* doing?" he asked with obvious concern.

"Me? Oh, I'm fine if you consider sleeping in a tack room great accommodations."

"I think they're moving the boys to their own house today. That's why I am free to do as I please."

"Want to take a walk to the coast?"

"Is it pretty there?"

"It's awesome."

"Well, I could use the exercise. Sure. Lead the way."

When they were far away from earshot, Grant said, "This whole villa is extraordinary. Do you think Milos will be in Helena's room tonight now that the twin's are moving?"

"Oh, yeah. In fact, they might allow you two into some of the empty rooms. Thea told me about Diana's love for Theodosus, and I guess Helena has given her approval for them staying together so that they can make children. That leaves you all alone, and since Daddy isn't home yet, and there is this small room by the master bedroom; they may let you stay there for security's sake. That would leave Theodosus on the western line of the house, Milos on the eastern side, and you close to Lydia's room. The boys and one male slave will stay in that new addition. Oh, yeah, the boys are getting a chariot and two dogs as a birthday present. Their birthday is in three weeks. But, the chariot hasn't arrived yet, nor the dogs, and I guess this is a real irritation to Mom. I think new horses are coming with the chariot. These kids are spoiled rotten," he said and then smiled, "but I like them, anyway."

"I'm Lydia's protector?"

"That's the way it looks. And that room by Daddy's is much bigger than any of the other slaves' quarters."

"That'll work," Grant said smiling.

Wainwright paused for a full five minutes and then said, "I must applaud your attitude. I mean none of this has worked out the way you wanted it to."

Grant stared at the rocks ahead of them. "On the contrary, this trip has been more than I bargained for in all ways."

"How so?"

"I'm not sure I can talk about it right now. It's still swirling in my head. Let's see. I never realized that I have no real friends back home. Come to think about it, I never had friends before. For a while I had some pals in high school, but once I made up my mind to climb the ladder to success, I thought only about that goal and ignored them unless they could help me. No one and nothing was going to get in my way. Now that I'm on top, I live a secluded life. Until I traveled back through time, I never acknowledged that I'm not really very happy. I'm not quite sure what it is that *will* make me happy, but I have learned that being at the top doesn't mean you can see everything. What's really scary, Bruce, is that I had no clue I was miserable. None. I thought having manicures, gourmet food, and unending digits in my bank account made one secure. Financially, it does. I won't lie to you there. Money does buy you security and a certain amount of pleasure, and I would never go home and suddenly throw it all out the window. I've worked too hard for that. But there's something else I'm missing. Until I fell back in time, I never would have figured it out. I was on autopilot. Just cruising along in my own space. Very in-control, and, to some degree, quite satisfied."

"But now you realize that you're miserable? Forgive me if I've missed something but I'm not sure how we've helped you."

Grant stopped and looked at Wainwright who paused beside him. They were on the coastline now; they could smell the sea and feel the cool breezes.

"I could have lived the rest of my life numb. I could have gone to work for years before some young fellow takes me down like I did my old boss. And then, when I had nothing else to think about, it would have hit me. I have everything and nothing. No human contacts who would care if I lived or died. In fact, some who might just be hoping I hit the bricks. Like..." he stared at the sun, "like a certain secretary who asked me for one small favor I should have granted but didn't. She's always been there for me, and she needed help. I responded like an oaf. Nice way to treat loyalty, huh. Give her ten years more in my employ, and she'll be going back to her apartment every night and stabbing little voodoo dolls made with my face on them."

"It isn't just about Lydia then?"

"Oh, no, not at all. It's everything, Bruce. All of it. Theodosus.

Diana. Milos. The two boys."

"I'm glad you feel that way. Real glad."

"You still worried I'm mad at Time Travelers. Don't be. In fact, when we get home, if you like, I'll go over your books for you and give you some ideas of how to increase your profits."

"Well that would work." Wainwright scuffed at a rock with his sandaled toe.

"Something going on with you?"

"Well, yeah."

"Spill it," Grant said, sitting down on one of the smoother looking rocks.

Wainwright did likewise. "I'm learning some things about myself too. Thea..."

"The slave girl?"

"She thinks I'm the greatest thing since computers."

Grant smiled. "Way to go, Wainwright."

"She does everything I ask her to do in triplicate. I thought it would be weird having a...servant, but she isn't what I expected at all. I thought she would be unhappy, growling, lazy, and spit in my wine or something, and it's not like that. She wants to please me. And...I get the impression that if I showed some real interest in....you know...she'd oblige me."

"Like in...what way exactly."

"Like in 'may I bathe your body with these sweet smelling oils, Socrates?', and 'could I fill your goblet, master?'stuff. Sweet. Flirtatious."

"So what's your problem?"

"I've never had this happen to me before. I'm used to challenges. Ones I usually lose."

"What are you going to do?"

Wainwright paused and then smiled. "I'm not sure, yet. I might take her up on an evening's entertainment, if she'll have me."

"That'll work."

"Well, yeah, except one little item is missing. I mean, she's almost *too* submissive. If I tell her something, she gives me this 'oh that's cool' look and goes right back to what she was doing. She isn't interested in what the boys are studying, and she's right there. She sews or weaves something and smiles."

"Cute but dumb?"

"I don't know. She wears a silver fish pendant on a thin rope chain around her neck. What's that all about? Now Diana has this curious spark in her eyes. She watches everything I do, and listens to what I say to the boys. Something's clicking behind those pretty eyes. She's learned Latin faster than Theodosus, and it's because she's always paying attention to what everyone is talking about."

"Ready to go back?"

"Can we go down to the water? I love the Mediterranean, and it might be rather intriguing to see it from this century."

"I'm game."

They walked to the water's edge where Wainwright took off his sandals and walked around in the water for a while. Grant chose pebbles from the beach and made a game of seeing how far they could skim across the water's surface without disappearing.

"So your learning something too," said Grant.

"I guess. See, I had this girl once whom I just adored, but she was a slot transfer so I lost her. I thought we had so much in common, and I guess I just haven't ever said goodbye to her in my head."

"Need to move on, pal."

"I know."

"Do you mind my asking something that's been on my mind since we met?"

"Sure go ahead."

"When did you first time travel?"

"Oh, that. Well, I was fifteen and studying with my father who was a UCLA college professor recently transferred to a private academy in England. My mother divorced my father when I was twelve. Ran off with another man who was more available than my dad. So, Dad and I became glued at the hip. I was an only child. He was a historian with an interest in scientific theories. Actually, he'd written several books on English history and on the subject of time travel that are still in print today, by the way. He wanted to test his theories of portal/solstice time travel. He'd manage to read some ancient books on the subject. Books that went as far back as the Middle Ages. They were written in Latin, and that's how I learned to read a little bit of the language because I helped him do his re- search. He always made a big deal about whatever I found so my ego blossomed, and I became proficient in the fine art of finding lost scraps of history."

"And you became a research analyst because of that."

"Correct. We traveled to this ancient church in England that my father had learned was a major portal. There is a circle design on the center tiling of this church. It rests halfway from the back and halfway to the altar. Since my father was ill, I volunteered to test our theories by being the time-traveling guinea pig. I had always loved the Arthurian legends and chose that time period in English history so that I could uncover the truth about the existence of King Arthur?"

"Did he exist?"

"Yes. I bid goodbye to Dad and flew back to Arthur and the Knights of the Round Table. I met an alchemist named Merlin."

"Arthur's wizard and tutor?"

"Well," Wainwright chuckled, "he really wasn't a wizard but loved letting the people think he was mystical. He'd perform some tricks for the people, acted eccentric, and healed the sick, so that they'd leave him alone. Once Guenevere showed up, Arthur refused to listen to anything Merlin said which suited Merlin fine. He now had plenty of time to do research on time travel and medicine. He was a man ahead of his time, a wise scientist, and a creative thinker."

"The first time traveler?"

Wainwright shook his head. "Not by a long shot. He told me that people had been time-traveling since the Egyptian time period, and that the Etruscans had actually dictated entire trips, as well as documented the five ways to travel and a few portals that they'd used long before he ever heard of such a thing as time travel. He'd found some of those ancient journals and started intense exploration of the portals in England. He told the people he was 'under enchantment', but he was actually locked in his 'white tower' with a big 'Do Not Disturb' sign on it."

"What did he tell you?"

Wainwright was pleased to have such a willing ear. "That the portals are all over the earth's surface, and that he would look for a slot transfer for himself by standing in the middle of Stonehenge on the next solstice. Wanted to know whether I wanted to come back and try a twin travel with him. He wanted to go to Egypt and told me that if I went to Stonehenge and thought about Egypt, we would probably go together though we were from different time periods. I agreed to try it. Went home and told my dad who wrote all that I said in his books. Then, on the following solstice—June—I went to the Stonehenge of my world to meet Merlin in Egypt."

"Did it work?"

"Yes, and oh, what a time we had. Merlin had just finished his Book of Arthur which he had hidden under that circle of tile in the church. Locked it with a special key and placed the key behind the altar."

"Mallory?"

"Must have stumbled upon it, then plagiarized it, I guess. See, Merlin didn't want anyone to know about Arthur who blew it in his mind because he used his emotions instead of his head to work things out. Plus, Arthur never listened to anything Merlin told him after he became king, so he figured history could live without the legend of Arthur. Apparently, time refused to keep the legendary king under wraps."

"What happened to Merlin?"

"He met Imhotep."

"The Egyptian mystic?"

"Correct."

"They left me out of some of their discussions. I know he wanted to return to Egypt and was hoping he was a slot transfer. I've always wondered about that. Merlin was really evasive about the whole thing. Just told me to go back to Arthur on the December solstice and tell him that a nymph by the name of Nimue had seduced him—actually there was this slave girl who worked for Imhotep who had stolen Merlin's heart— and tell him that she had trapped him this cave, and he could never return to Camelot."

"Sweet."

"Yeah, I know. I did as he asked."

"You ever see him again?"

"No, actually I never had a reason to go to Egypt again. Too hot for me."

"And your dad was thrilled I bet."

"It was the find of a lifetime, and that was good because he died two years later."

"I'm sorry."

"Yeah, well, I continued his research until I met Trudy."

"The one who got away?"

"Yeah. She just knocked me off my feet; I was a bit too controlling, I think. But, anyway, I had always planned to take her with me on one of my trips, and then she sort of wondered right into a portal at Sam and Jim's and the rest, as they say, is history."

"You actually met Merlin, Arthur, and Imhotep!"

"Yeah, I know why they can't find Imhotep's tomb too."

"Can you tell me?" Grant was so fascinated at Wainwright's words that five hundred soldiers could have marched right up to him at that point, and he would never have noticed.

"If you really want to know."

"Sure."

"I don't think he's dead."

"Come on! Where is he, then?"

"The two became involved with the whole time travel thing and told me that they had uncovered the truth about reincarnation."

"Reincarnation," mumbled Grant. "Go on."

"Reincarnation is time travel."

Grant shook his head. "I don't get it."

"We follow the circle—the cycle of life that is dictated by time."

"Live now—die later."

"Lived then, live now, will live. And we can go back and see how we lived before. The slot transfers are the only ones who can stay. They are chosen to help evolve the earth through its tough times."

"Could we be..."

"Just spinning our wheels in recorded time? In what we think is our time but isn't?"

"Yes."

"I don't know the answer to that one. I'm still working on it. It's all about learning from our mistakes so that we can evolve into wise and wonderful souls. I know they stumbled on something very cool and refused to share it with me."

"At that time."

"Yeah, at that time. Maybe I can go back and uncover it. I just know that Imhotep lives...and so does Merlin. In time. They were recruited to transcend time. There may be others, but I have no knowledge of them."

"Are you saying they can go forward and backwards?"

"Remember what Merlin said in the book, 'I don't age; I youthen'?"

"Yes. I always thought that line was sort of cool and mystical."

"Well, I haven't uncovered all the parameters, but there are some Chosen Ones, ancient priests, who can do that. Not you or I or Trudy or Sam or Jim. Only the Scholars of Time."

"Who called them that?"

"Me," he said with a boyish grin.

"You are something, Wainwright," he said.

"Yeah, I know. But I'm still a flop with chicks."

They both laughed, and Wainwright lost his balance and almost fell into the sea.

Grant stood up quickly, grabbed him, and then motioned towards the villa where a girl named Thea waited for the 'professor'.

"Well, maybe not this time," Grant said, patting Wainwright on the shoulder. "This time you might get lucky."

Chapter Seventeen

The move to the small villa was completed on Sunday—or rather the seventh day of Grant's week which he and Wainwright called Sunday. Milos moved into Helena's room. No comment was made about this maneuver. Theodosus was allowed access to Diana's tiny room, but he and Grant would live with the boys for now. Milos and the other servants and Wainwright would be the men of the household and serve as protection for Lydia and Helena. The two gladiators were to protect the boys. As expected, Grant was disappointed. He'd been envisioning a stay in that beautiful master bedroom that had been dedicated to love.

Lydia had been given two days' rest from practice to heal from her first week of it. He'd given her private instruction, but when it actually came to teaching her how to protect herself, he had held back nothing. He attacked her as an opponent would. Lydia had sore muscles and bruised skin from these encounters. He took no joy in hurting her, in fact, he disliked it immensely; but he knew that he would be gone in a few months, and that whatever danger might come to her, she needed to know how to defend herself. An aggressor wouldn't be gentle; so it was out of a sense of affection for his pupil that Grant Tyrell showed Lydia how to ward off any threat. Because of that practice, Lydia stayed in her room much of the 'weekend'.

She was ready for her workout on Monday though and showed earlier than she had the previous week. "I want double sessions this week."

"Of course, mistress, anything you wish."

He had to hand it to her; she was courageous, determined, a quick learner, and talented. Lydia seemed to be tossing away her grief with every parry and stabbing the dark shadows of her loss with each thrust. She never tired and shook off defeat promptly, hurling herself back at him for more. No ache stopped her from wanting to learn every one of the skills needed for obliterating someone from the face of the earth through hand-to-hand combat. It was as if she were possessed by an exigency to hurt someone or something with the same fierce brutality fate had handed her. Grant took a fair amount of beating from her, as well. His body was scared with some unattractive bluish-purple welts from her smacks and kicks. That was what she did when nothing else worked—kicked at his legs, making him fall and then stabbing him with the tip of her fake sword. If Lydia ever got a chance to fight in the arena, Grant mused, woe to her opponent.

Grant noticed that his attitude with Lydia changed because of what Wainwright had told him. His heart softened towards the spirited Roman lady, and his voice dropped in volume and softened when he spoke with her.

"My lady feels better today?" he asked as he checked her boots for their run.

"I was never weary, warrior," she said.

"Might I ask a favor of my lady?" he said.

"What is it you could possibly want that you don't already have?"

"If it pleases my mistress, I would like to be called by my first name."

"You want me to call you Grantus?"

He winced. "No, Grant will do."

"You want me to call you by your first name?" She was incredulous.

Grant could tell that this idea wasn't sitting well with her, but he had to give it a try. "We work so closely together that it..." he was watching her facial expressions, "might be nice to be called Grant instead of slave or warrior. I am your tutor, and I've noticed you calling Socrates by his first name, and he is a slave such as myself, isn't he?"

She thought it over for a while. "You're correct, Grant." She smiled. "I think it would be nice to call you Grant. I like the way it sounds though it is such an unusual name."

"Thank you, mistress."

"And..." she hesitated and looked at the ground, "when we are alone and not in front of my sister or my nephews and all the servants, you can call me Lydia."

Grant was aware that he had involuntarily blushed. "My humble gratitude, mistress...I mean, Lydia. Are you ready for our run?"

"Completely refreshed," she lied for he had seen her limp to her morning meal.

Grant looked at the sky. "Those dark clouds portend a rainstorm unless I miss my bet, so we had better move."

She started a brisk run, but her pace was not as spirited as it had been on her first day of practice. He stayed with her but did not wish to hurt her pride by passing her. He'd grown stronger since their move to the villa, and it was due in large part to good rest, good food, and stress-free workouts with the twins. So, he was mentally and physically stronger than he had ever been in his whole life.

She fell. Just like that, without warning, she tumbled to the ground and screamed in pain. They were not far from the coastline, and she had tried to speed up her pace for some reason—perhaps to show him that she had recuperated from their last session; but it had been too much for her feet, and they gave out without warning.

Grant was by her side within seconds. She was sitting on the rocky ground and nursing her foot. "Let me see, Lydia."

"It's all right," she winced. "I can go on. Oh, what a thing to happen so far from home!"

"Let me see it. Now, don't pull away from me like that. Let me look." He examined her ankle, foot, and calf for the problem. He gently maneuvered her foot, and she cried out in pain. "No! Stop that! You're hurting me."

"All right, you've sprained your ankle, and you'll need a brace and stay off it for a few days."

She was wearing a bright blue linen headdress that wound around her curls and tied them in place. He took it from her hair and wrapped it around her ankle. She tried not to cry, but Grant could see that she wanted to.

"I can't walk?" she sighed.

He looked at the sky. The fat, dark gray clouds were right over his head, and he was starting to get a headache. He remembered that Wainwright had warned him of the effect of storms on time travelers.

"Put your arms around my shoulders, Lydia."

"You can't carry me all the way home."

"Well, for right now, I'm going to carry you to that cave you told me about."

"Over those rocks?"

"Would you rather me leave you here to get drenched with rain?"

She looked up. "Very well," she said, placing her arms around his shoulders. She was so close to him now, and he could smell the oils on her body, and the perspiration covering her skin from her fast run. It crossed his mind that he would have carried his mistress to the ends of the earth if she'd asked him to, and that was when he realized his true feelings. The story of the lost soldier and the detoured love affair had touched Grant's heart. She had been offered a half-life for there would be no one to take her first love's place, and no matter who she eventually married, she would wonder her whole life what might have been if the soldier hadn't died.

"Lady," he whispered deep in his own private thoughts.

"What? Did you say something?"

"Ah, nothing really. Drop your head onto my chest; it will be easier for me if you stay close to my upper body when I go down those rocks."

She cuddled against him and said, "Can you see the opening to the cave from here?"

"Yes, barely."

It was tricky getting her down the cliff, but Grant could show no sign of fatigue now. She trusted him, and he was in control—for once since he'd arrived in 200 A.D.—of the situation and the lady.

Just as he set foot on the beach at the front of the cave—which was the only spot on the coastline that had soft sand and very little pebbles—a large bolt of lightning streaked from heaven to earth as if Zeus himself wanted to warn them of the approaching storm.

"We just made it," she said, dropping from his arms onto the floor of the cave just as he doubled over in pain.

"What's wrong?" she asked, crawling over to his side.

He remembered how he'd been struck with the migraine back at the ludus and how quick Diana had been in helping him feel better.

"Head...aches...it's the storm. I get ill when we have a bad thunderstorm. I feel lightheaded...sick to my stomach. Don't worry. It will pass with the storm. You just rest that sore ankle."

"Lie down. Don't crunch over like that. Here, rest your head in my lap."

At any other time, the thought of his head in her lap would be a dream on earth, but right now lovemaking was far from his mind. He doubled over and wretched.

"My, you really do get sick, don't you?" she said.

He tumbled into her lap and rested with his eyes closed. The rain poured outside the door of the dark cave. The heavens were so black, that the cave was almost like night, and it was difficult to see whether they were alone.

"We're all right," she said as if reading his thoughts. "It's a big cave. We can ride out the storm. Maybe Marcus will come for us when we don't return."

"Yes, that's a comforting thought. Oh!" he said unable to look at her because of the intense pain in his head. "I'm so sick."

She smoothed back his hair from his forehead and soothed his temples by massaging them with her fingers. "Well, I'm here," she whispered so as not to upset his aching head with loud talk. "I'll take care of you as you took care of me."

Her lips were close to his face as she soothed his forehead with her hands. "There, there, Lydia will take away the pain."

He opened his eyes on those words. "Lady."

"Hush now. Don't talk."

"I'm so sick."

"Just relax and let me watch over you. Actually, the storm is rather interesting to watch from here; and, for some reason, I don't feel the pain in my ankle anymore. Isn't that funny?"

"I'll be all right when the storm passes."

"I don't want to make the matter worse, Grant, but I'd say it looks as if it may be a few hours before that happens."

"Then if it pleases my lady, Lydia, I'll sleep here in your lap until it's done."

"Yes, sleep now, Grantus...I mean Grant. I'll watch over both of us."

He slept for possibly twenty minutes in her warm lap until he felt the rays of the sun trying to illuminate the cave. The sand outside their tiny home was wet, but other than frothing waves, all looked relatively calm on the beach.

"Do you feel better?" she asked, showing no sign that she wished him up and walking her back home.

And he did. He felt like a totally new man, completely refreshed, and ready to tackle a Viking army. "I do. Isn't that strange? I feel completely invigorated." He moved away from her and stood up. His stomach did a flip-flop, and he almost vomited. She smiled and then sat back on her bottom and watched him.

"That was fun?" she said with a smile.

He shook his head at her in disbelief. "What was fun about it?"

"Well, I mean spraining my ankle wasn't fun and watching you get sick wasn't fun, but playing house in the cave and watching the storm made me feel like...oh I don't know Greek sailors stranded on a lost island."

He coughed and almost vomited again. "Pirates?"

"Yes, like pirates coming to the cove for safety. Leaving the ship out there and running for cover into the cave."

The words escaped his lips before he could stop them. "That's a unique perspective."

"What?" She was evidently offended.

"Everything to you is this wonderful, romantic fantasy...this made-up fiction. Why can't this be just a cave? Why can't the cove be..."

"I've had a hard time lately with the real world," she interrupted, staring at the floor of the cave and trying hard to hide her tears.

"I heard about the death of your fiancé."

That did it. Totally wrong thing to say. Lydia started to sob loudly and from her heart.

"Hey, look, I'm sorry. I didn't mean anything...oh hell with it...look, I know what you're going through."

"How could you possibly know what I'm going through, slave?"

There was that word again.

"I know how it feels to hurt inside. My father and mother...that is to say...I lost my father at a young age, so I know what it must feel like to lose someone you love."

"Your father was killed in battle?"

"Well...sort of."

Lydia tried to stand.

"No, don't do that. I'll help you get home, or your nephews will come for us, or Milos. If we don't return, I'm sure they'll look for us."

"Yes," she sniffled, "I suppose you're right about that."

He moved down to her side. "Hey, look, you can't do anything about the past. That's over. But, you can have a bright new future."

"Married to some seasoned senator my father picks for me? I have no choice now. Oh, yes, they always say that women and men of Rome marry for love and family, but that is a lie. Well, except for my father and mother—they really were in love. Helena's first husband was chosen for her. And she really had no choice in the second one either because it was such a fortuitous arrangement. It all comes down to pride, money, social status, politics..."

"I see. And your heart?"

Her eyelids opened wide, and she looked up at him. She was so vulnerable right now. "Doesn't feel anything anymore."

"What was he like?" he thought to ask in order to keep her talking.

She smiled. "Oh, he was brave, strong, handsome. We'd been friends for such a long time, and when he asked for my hand I quickly agreed."

"How old were you?"

"Fifteen."

"That long ago?"

"The emperor has been far from Rome for some time with infrequent trips home. Justus died last year. It was to be his last battle too. He was going to retire from the army and start a life with me, then go into politics like his father. He refused to marry me while he was gone from my side, stating that it would be cruel to leave me so soon after the marriage vows." She shrugged her shoulders. "That seemed so romantic to us then. But now..."

"You could have at least been a veteran's widow?"

"I would have had to remarry anyway, but at least my first love would have been a beautiful memory; instead, here I am twenty-one-years old, and I've never known...physical love."

"You are a wonderful woman, Lydia. You deserve better than you got."

"You think well of me?"

"Of course. All right, you have a bit of an imagination, and normally I think it's nice to hear your stories so I shouldn't have said what I did. I was still reeling from my headache, I guess. But truthfully, I have never known a woman like you."

"You're just saying that," she said obviously fishing for a compliment.

"I speak the truth, lady. You're smart, talented, strong, brave, gutsy, determined, stubborn, clever. You can fight too. Got a real aggressive streak most women don't have. Not to mention the fact that you're beautiful."

"You think I'm pretty."

"Oh, not just pretty. You take my breath away."

"I do?"

He moved closer to you. "I've never known such beauty. Venus herself must envy you."

Lydia placed her fingers on his lips. "You mustn't speak blasphemy. She'll hear you."

He took her fingers in his hand and kissed them, never dropping eye contact with her. "Let her hear me; I don't care. For she placed you inside my heart, and it's her fault if I dream of no one else but you."

"Slave?" she said, moving away from him.

"Oh, yes, indeed, I am. Slave by purchase and slave by love. I wouldn't leave your side if you shackled me to a post in the middle of Rome. I'd find some way to cut through those chains to be with you."

"Grant."

"Let me speak before I lose my nerve. Venus has made me bold I think, or the illness has given me courage."

"You mean what you say?"

"If I didn't..." and suddenly he realized that he *had* fallen in love with the high-spirited Lydia. "I *am* in love with you. I wouldn't hurt you for the world, and I would never have left you behind even for a politically advantageous military post."

She looked at his expression, searching perhaps for a sign of a lie. "I can't..."

"Love me? Oh, I know that. You're still hurting. But, you need to know that I will defend you with my life."

Long, dark lashes wiped away her tears, blinking them away just like the sun had chased the rain clouds from the sky. "You mean what you say?"

"Zeus strike me dead if I speak falsely."

She moved her fingers again to his lips. "You mustn't say that! He'll hear your spoken oath."

"Oh, I don't mind if the gods hear me." He laughed. "In fact, it's fate that I should find you, isn't it? And fate that I should end up in love with a woman I can never have. What a turn of events!"

She hobbled into his arms, keeping the sore foot elevated from the ground, and rested her head on his chest. "My protector?"

"You can take care of yourself, mistress; but, if you wish to think of me as that, I will be your protector until my last breath."

Then she tilted her head up to look into his eyes and parted her lips.

He took her face in his two hands and gently kissed her. A quick kiss filled with emotion and with no trace of lust. He didn't want to frighten her. She didn't move away.

"Aunt Lydia. Grantus!" came a cry from the hills surrounding the sea.

Grant walked to the mouth of the cave. "Down here, Marcus. Your aunt fell during her run and hurt her ankle. She cannot walk home. Bring a cart. Hurry."

The boy was off like a shot.

When Grant turned around to see Lydia's reaction to his embrace, she was crying again.

"No more tears, lady," he said in a soothing tone. "I am your slave. Whatever you want, I will gladly give."

"Pirate!"

"What?" he asked stunned by her words.

"You mean to steal my treasures!"

"Never." He reached out for her.

She moved into his arms again.

"Just think about what I said, Lydia," he said to himself while he held her as she cried. "I take nothing that isn't offered with a full and happy heart. But, you need to heal first before you can love. I'm in no hurry. I've waited a lifetime to find you."

Chapter Eighteen

Grant's life changed when he moved into the small house. He was allowed to walk into the main house whenever he felt like it and investigate the rooms. He noticed how little contact the sisters had with each other, and how no one ever ate in the dining area. Helena gave chores to the servants, created the daily menu, saw to it that the work in the fields was completed and, in general, was the one who kept the household and farm running smoothly. It was a monumental task and consumed Helena's entire day. She stayed in her room with Milos during the evening hours. This appeared to be her only stress-free time, so there was an understood sanctity about not disturbing the mistress for any reason when she was alone with Milos. Once a week, Helena and Milos rode on horseback to the coastline, had a private meal there, and returned several hours later. She spoke with her sons several times a day and showed interest in their schooling with Socrates, education as gladiators, and training in the equestrian arts. That was the extent of her physical activity.

Diana told Grant a great deal about *her* mistress's thoughts and habits, for she was responsible for bathing Lydia with oils, massaging her sore limbs, preparing and cleaning her clothing, bringing Lydia her meals, and keeping her mistress company when she was lonely. Lydia stayed in her room for her meals and occasionally spoke with Socrates when she rested in her mother's garden before retiring for the evening. Diana remarked that her mistress found her workouts grueling but satisfying, and her long discussions with Socrates fascinating.

Grant and Diana forced Lydia to stay put for three whole days to nurse her swollen and sprained ankle, but no one could keep her from coming to her lessons after that. His words must have inspired her because she became a tiger during their pretend battles.

Marcus and Lucius garnered a modicum of praise from Milos and were anxious to show off for Aunt Lydia; but when they saw the way she attacked Grant at practice; they remained silent. The entire household was aware that the three aristocrats were mastering the skills necessary to be true warriors.

"You know, Lydia, Father will put an end to this once he comes home," Helena teased after watching a few practice sessions.

Lydia smiled. "When and if he comes home. Well, he always wanted a warrior son. Now he has three." There was a trace of bitterness in her tone.

Milos spoke with Grant one afternoon when the boys were tardy due do to an extended lesson with Socrates.

"She's changed."

"Who? Lydia?"

"I didn't know her very well when Helena and I were lovers in Rome. She was just a child then. But, Helena spoke lovingly of her. Of how she always wanted to play boy games and pretend she was a soldier or a pirate, making the children of the servants perform with her in her imaginary plays. She's been hurt I gather."

"Yes, she lost her fiancé who was a good man, a noble warrior of Rome."

"Helena told me that her sister's been depressed for the last year and only took interest in this hobby of hers when the boys began to learn combat. Boredom, I guess."

"Or the need to hit something," Grant looked at Milos and grinned. "Sometimes that's good for people. To hit or throw nonliving things to vent their anger at the world. She likes to hit me instead," he said grinning. "It doesn't bother me."

"Helena's aware of your flirtations with her sister."

"What does she thinks?"

"That whatever brings a smile back to Lydia's face is worth gold."

"Then she approves."

"Well, I wouldn't go that far, but she won't prevent Lydia from taking pleasure whenever or however she can. I was worried about you, but it appears that you're the remedy for what ails the girl. You and Socrates. Lydia listens to everything he tells her as if he were some sort of god."

Grant smiled at the remark. "She's a clever girl, and I would never hurt her. Understand that. Socrates is good for her too."

"Oh, that's for sure. Zeus's gift to her. And you must be the reward for her offerings to Venus. But, a word of caution, Grantus. Causing grief to this family could be fatal to your career. You're living the grand life now, even if it is in servitude; but they could sell all three of you to the next passing lanista if you anger them."

"Can't happen. I am drawn to Lydia as a thirsty man is drawn to a full well. Why would Helena, or anyone for that matter, get rid of the balm that's healed Lydia's heart."

Milos grinned. "I'm glad for you...for her...for all of us. Helena is my heart, and I will love her forever. My boys make me proud, and I adore them. This house must be ruled by Venus for love grows here."

"Yes," Grant smirked, "Venus, indeed." Grant thought of how the time tunnel had helped Lydia not Venus, but, of course, said nothing.

"I can't run to the coastline today," interrupted Lydia, "but it is such a beautiful day, that I thought it might be nice to ride my horse and sun myself on the sailboat. I have a horse that you can borrow." She smiled and tilted her head sideways.

Milos patted Grant on the shoulder and whispered, "I'll tell them to ready a horse for you."

"How does your ankle feel?" he asked her.

She let her horse trot around in the courtyard. "Better. Diana suggested that I take a swim in the sea and try to move it in cool water instead of my bath, so I'm going to give it a try. I don't want to go there alone."

"I know. Pirates."

"Precisely. And Diana doesn't really know how to ride. I thought you might."

Grant thought of his summers at camp learning how to ride horseback. "I would like to accompany you."

As soon as he had checked the horse's girth, they began a pleasant gallop to the coastline. She did not race the horse in the heat, but kept the pace relaxed and noncompetitive. She had a bag of food and a jug of wine with her. When they stopped by the rocks, he leaped from his horse and carried her to the smooth, sandy cove so that she would not have to walk on the stones.

"Go back and retrieve the food," she demanded.

He turned his back on her to walk up the hill, and when he swiveled around to return with the picnic lunch, she was already in the water—completely naked. "Now what was expected?" he wondered.

"You have my permission to swim if you wish. Put the food down by the cave. This feels wonderful," she called to him, splashing the water around her.

His masculinity was at full attention and leaving him completely helpless and unable to think of anything but her perfect body under his. If he went in there now, he would ravish her. If he didn't go in, she'd think he was uninterested in her. He would be stranded there sitting next to the cave and suffering from an unsatisfied libido. At least the cool water would help. He undid the skirt that covered his hips. She dove under the waves. He took that as a sign to slip out of his loin cloth and dive into the water. He felt immediate relief until she emerged from the waves. How could he not notice how the waves licked at her breasts?

"Isn't it lovely?" she sighed.

"Oh, lovely can't begin to describe it," he answered.

"Can you swim?"

He surface dove and came up beside her. "At your service, mistress."

"Oh! you surprised me. Put your arms out and let me float against you so that I can move my ankle in the water."

He did as she commanded. Her wet hair stuck to his skin, her breasts appeared above the waterline, and her skin glistened like burning copper in the sun. He averted his focus as she gently moved the foot. "This is a good idea," she said.

Grant thought, "Oh, *sure* it is! If you want to torture me beyond my senses." He tried not to touch anything but her side and back.

"Oh," she sighed as she let her body relax against his chest. "This is heaven. I'm so happy."

"I am glad to hear that, mistress."

She turned in his arms so that her breasts touched his skin. Her eyes were sparkling like the sun on the waves. "Do you like to swim, Grant?"

"Yes, Lydia, it's just fine, but..."

"What's troubling you?"

"You told me that you have never experienced love, so you have no idea what you're doing to me."

"I don't?" She swam away from him. "Race you to the sailboat."

He followed the enigma to her boat. She struggled to get on board managing to shift her weight onto her stomach and then swing her legs over the side and onto the deck. She stood there completely naked, with no apparent problem with the ankle, smiled, waved to him, and then dove back into the water.

"Ancient Rome! Lord have mercy," he said to the sky. He didn't join her but waited until she swam back to the cave. Then she ambled carefully back to their spot and dressed.

Grant joined her at the water's edge. "I'm coming out of the sea to dress now."

"That's fine," she said avoiding his gaze. Then she plopped down by the food and began to make their meal.

"Lydia, we need to talk," was all he could say at the moment, and it was said with a scratchy voice at best.

"What about?" She offered him some bread and a small wooden bowl of wine. He drank the liquid but hesitated eating the bread.

"I told you how I felt about you the other day."

"Yes, I know." She sipped her wine.

"And when you...stood so close to me...well it encourages me to make love to you. Is that what you want? Is that what you're getting at?"

She came close to him. "Do you want to make love to me?"

"More than anything," he said reaching for her. He smothered her lips against his.

"But you did not touch me when you had the chance to out there. Why?"

"Because I love you. It would be so easy to take you now and give you the pleasure you deserve and the satisfaction I need."

"But?"

"That would be all it was."

"You mean because I can't love you in return?"

"Yes. There's more to it than just physical pleasure. Were you trying to get my attention out there?"

"Yes."

"And what did you want me to do?"

"What you did."

"I didn't do anything."

"Exactly. You had a chance to steal what you wanted, Grant, and you waited."

"I waited because you're my mistress...and I didn't want to anger you...and I..."

"Couldn't."

Her words struck a cord inside him. She was right.

"Well, I certainly wanted to, Lydia."

"Oh," she giggled, "I know you did. I was watching when you undressed and was so embarrassed I dove under the water."

"Then why did you tease me?"

"I wanted to give you every opportunity to prove to me that all you wanted was sex."

"To show you that I was a thief—a pirate."

"Yes."

He held her in his arms. "I want more than that."

"I know, and I can't give it to you. I'm still grieving."

"Lydia, I love you. When you want me to show that to you, tell me that you love me too."

She turned away from him. "How can I feel that again for another man?"

"By admitting how happy I make you. How good you feel right now." He turned her face so that she could see his eyes. "And that I'm telling you the truth. I don't want half a love, Lydia. It's all or nothing."

"So you chose nothing when you could have had me at your mercy."

"Nothing *is* something. It means that some day you'll come to realize that what I'm telling you is honest and real. I love you, and I want to make you happier than you have ever been in your entire life."

"So you won't make love to me now?"

"Well, if you order me to, I will. Is that what you want? Do you want me to make love to you, mistress, for I will always do as you wish?"

She looked at her dish of wine. The tears fell swiftly, streaming down her cheeks. "I don't...feel...anything...inside, yet."

"I know."

"I don't know what I want, Grant."

"Of course you don't. But you will." He held her close to his chest and let her cry. "I only hope I'm here when you figure it out," he said to himself. Then he made her look at him again so that she could see the truth in his eyes. "A man can make love to a woman in many ways. But, I want to touch more than your skin, Lydia, I want you to be *with me* when we love. I want your heart; you know you have mine. You don't understand who I am. Where I've come from. What I've been through to get this far. I never do anything halfway, and I've never loved a woman as much as I love you...never."

"Never?"

"Oh, lady, you're a whole new experience for me. I want to savor every minute of it. Do you understand?"

"I think so."

"Then no more teasing games, Lydia. It's not fair."

"I'm sorry."

"And when you want me...you come to me. Not like a girl who is bored with her lessons, but like a woman ready to be loved by her man. I'll be there."

"You do love me, don't you."

"You're not half as surprised as I am. Now let's go home."

They gathered their clothes and supplies and rode quietly back home.

Chapter Nineteen

The twins' birthday came in the middle of the week, and grand scale plans were made to celebrate what Helena called their 'coming of age'. They would be thirteen-years-old and, by Roman standards, they had reached maturity. They lived in a small villa of their own, would be given female slaves if they wished, and could start planning their futures and arranging for their brides.

There would be an outdoor feast at twelve o'clock, and all members of the estate would be allowed to enjoy it. The kitchen was in chaos because the twins had been allowed to choose the menu for the feast; and, since the boys wanted plenty of sweet desserts as well as specific recipes they'd acquired a taste for when they lived in Rome, the cooks were beside themselves trying to follow new recipes and not destroy traditional favorites that they had not prepared for ages.

There would be homemade wine; Lydia was to sing some of the boys favorite songs; Milos promised them that they could spar wearing their new Thracian outfits; and Helena promised them a special gift she had hidden somewhere on the estate. The boys—who had tried for two weeks to disclose the whereabouts of the gift—pestered her incessantly until she told them that they could have all their gifts after their morning lessons.

Ariadne's present was a dance she had learned in Rome. Diana had made a gift of two jars of scented oils she had been allowed to hand make from the flowers in the garden, and the families personally cultivated olive oil. Grant and Theodosus promised a 'real gladiator battle' for their birthday. Socrates promised to tell them a special time travel story he'd learned from his Greek teacher.

The only thing missing was their grandfather who hadn't made it home from Rome as he had promised. According to Wainwright, Helena was enjoying his absence as she liked to be in control of this household. She feared that he might send them back to Rome to live in their other house. He told Grant that Helena loved the country and wanted to remain there for as long as she could. She was thinking about selling her house in town as well as her ex-husband's business. Wainwright further intimated that Milos might not be met with proper respect in the social circles Helena would have to move in to keep her business afloat. She received mail from a carrier once a week and knew in her heart that the man she had left in charge of the business was stealing from her. She didn't seem to care that much. She had found happiness with her new family whose happiness rested in this house of

Venus. She loved her sons, Milos, and her sister too much to force them to follow the dictates of Roman high-society. She had even told Wainwright that she wanted her sons to be free thinkers, unvarnished by the ways of the Roman world she'd been forced to live in for twelve years. She loved Milos and saw no reason why she should live without him for even a moment, or why she should alter everyone's happy life by moving back to Rome. Lydia was smiling for the first time in a year, and her smile brightened the whole estate. It, and the joyful noise generated from playful, maturing, young men, made a house no Roman businessman, senator, or emperor could purchase. Helena was lucky, and she knew it, even if her stern running of the household seemed restrictive and contrary to that fact.

Grant told Lydia that she too could wear her uniform for sparing practice today. She had lost some of her usual aggressive nature in practice while her ankle mended, but in the last two days, she'd countered with renewed ferocity. She puzzled Grant, and he had the feeling that she would always be a mystery to everyone who knew her; that no one would be able to decipher her whims.

The twins received their gift in the courtyard. The artisans on the estate had built a beautiful chariot for the boys, and Crecius had attached two new white stallions to it. He rode the present into the courtyard with noticeable pride.

"I've practiced with the horses so that they will receive the chariot's bridle. They're ready for you, but you need to learn how to handle them."

"Well," thought Grant, "that should occupy the boys while I practice with their aunt."

He waited for her to put on her gear before saying, "Lately, I've noticed a tendency on your part to play by your own rules of combat, Lydia; but Thraceans have a code of conduct that, if you wish to learn their art, you must obey."

"I understand," she said, securing her face guard, and pulling her sword up to defend herself.

He knew better than to give her less than a full workout. Gentle combat infuriated her for she knew that he was only doing it because she was a woman. So, he attacked her upper body aggressively, and she cowered, holding her shield up to protect herself. She carefully angled her weapon, and, conserving energy as he had taught her to do, counterattacked with sharp, quick thrusts to his midsection. He protected himself and then thrust at her midsection, almost making contact, but she darted backwards to avoid his sword. He swung at her head; she ducked. She thrust wildly at his legs; he turned around sharply then swung his sword at her shield. She did not drop it and remained balanced with her legs parted. She waited before she moved towards her opponent.

"Good, Lydia, that's the way. Anticipate. Think. Feel. Attack," he said. "Don't come at me with anger, though. Remain cool. I'll beat you if you come at me in a temper, for you will lose your focus. Calculate your strength, my strength, and never feel the pain."

She shook her head, tripped him, and placed her wooden sword at his throat. It was a tiny replay of their first combat session at the ludus. As if she had been dreaming of the moment when she could use it on him. She pulled off her head gear. Grant lay defeated in the dirt and finally laughed. She had her full body weight on top of him, and her lips were only a fraction of an inch above his.

"Good job," he said.

"I didn't play by the rules," she reminded him.

"You thought it through, and that was what I wanted. You knew I wasn't focused on your moves because I was teaching you. I'm supposed to do that, but I *had* just told you to think before you moved. And you did. I was off guard, and you played on that knowledge. You're a clever fighter."

"I am?" she said bewildered and pulled the sword away from his neck.

He pulled off his head gear. "Isn't that what you wanted? I thought that was the point of all this."

"Well, yes, but I..."

He rolled on top of her and placed his sword against her throat. "Yield!"

"What?" she gasped and tried to get up.

He pinned her body flat to the ground. "I never said that we were through fighting; I never yielded to you. Now give up or I slit your throat—metaphorically speaking, of course."

She was in shock. "But..."

"My strength over yours. You can't push me aside." He felt her knee move to his groin and pinned her leg with his thigh. "Now that's not a very nice thought, Lydia, even if it would have given you the upper hand." He pressed harder on her arms and legs and stared into her eyes. "Now yield, mistress, because I'm not budging until you do."

She wouldn't say a word, so Grant pressed his lips passionately against hers until she could no longer breathe. Her whole torso relaxed under his. His manhood stiffened against her thigh. She gasped for air, and he let her breathe. He whispered, "Yield."

"Yes." She returned the kiss. "Yes!" And then, her limbs went limp; she dropped her sword, and placed her arms around his shoulders. "I yield."

She stopped kissing him to look at his face. "What are you doing to me?" She kissed him again and his entire being wanted her. The heightened tension of physical combat and sexual stimulation was a wonderful aphrodisiac.

"I want you, lady."

"I want you too."

"When?" He placed his right hand on her cheek, let it smooth her hair from her forehead, let it rest on her neck—her shoulder, and finally let it settle on her left breast.

"Grant, I don't know how to...to...I'm not feeling anything but...heat. Hot, burning, driving, heat."

His manhood was so erect now his mind lost track of everything but lust. There was only one way to ease that sort of torment. As long as he loved her, did it really matter if she didn't love him when their bodies were so close like this?

"You're so beautiful. I need you, Lydia."

"Is it all right, then? Will you show me how to love?"

"As long as you want me and I want you..."

Just then there was a scream.

The twins had been circling in their new chariot under the ever watchful eyes of their mother, Crecius, and Wainwright, when for no apparent reason the horses whinnied in horror and began a race to the coastline. The two boys held onto the reins but did not have the strength to keep such fiery stallions from galloping to what would assuredly be their death.

No one had a moment to wonder what was lying in the dirt that had caused them to rear and run. Helena screamed, and Crecius ran for his horse, but Grant was there a moment before him, and, with a loud whistle, forced the thoroughbred into a Derby winning pace. He didn't think of his own neck, or the fact that he had no idea how to stop a chariot, only that he had to save those boys if he could.

The horses stampeded directly to the shore, but because of the chariot's weight, and the boys trying to stop them, Grant was able to get close enough to catch the back of the chariot.

"Okay," he said aloud to the wind that was pressing against his face, and the dirt that was flying into his hair, "what did they do in those Western movies when they wanted to stop the stampeding wagon train?"

He was afraid his horse would not overtake the spinning wheels of the chariot; that the animal would be frightened by the snorting, terrified stallions; but he obeyed Grant and moved fearlessly to the side of the chariot at the very moment it hit a rock. Both boys lost their footing and were tossed into the air, they dropped back onto the carriage only to lose their balance for a second time as well as the reins.

"Grantus!" screamed Lucius, "stop them!"

Without really thinking about what he was doing, he grabbed

one of the loose reins as it flew into the air. That only made the chariot teeter further out of control. He jumped onto the chariot, leaned over its gilded edge, snatched the other section of the reins, closed his eyes, pulled hard, and screamed at the top of his lungs, "Whoa! Stop! Now!"

And they did.

Both boys fells from the carriage. Grant refused to open his eyes, holding steady on the reins to make sure he had control of the fiery steeds.

"Grant!" called Marcus from somewhere behind him.

He opened his eyes and saw that they were on the very tip of the rocky cliff, that the horses were pawing hysterically at the dirt and rocks with their hooves. But they did not fall. Just barely. Lucius ran after Grant, pulled the horses around so that they pointed towards home, and tried to calm the frightened beasts.

"You take them back, Grant. We'll get your horse."

Carefully easing the bewildered creatures into a slow walk utilized every muscle Grant had in his shoulders and back, but the stallions obeyed him. "Indiana Jones couldn't have done any better," he thought. His heart had been racing as fast as the horses, so he tried to breathe deeply and relax.

He was soaked with his own perspiration. The horses, drenched in sweat, were spewing white foam from their mouths by the time they returned to the courtyard.

"Grantus! Praise Zeus, you were so quick witted," called Milos.

He gave the reins to Crecius and dropped from the chariot onto the ground. "What spooked them?"

"Not sure. Are you all right?"

"It looks like I am. I'm still in shock, though."

"I imagine so," said Wainwright. "Boy, that was lucky. I thought we'd lost the boys. The way they were tossed from the chariot. It looked bad. You stopped right at the edge of the sea! It was like some wild west mo..." he saw Helena coming near enough to hear him, "ah...moves I've ever seen. Took my breath away I can tell you. Splendid work, Grantus."

"Thanks...ah...Socrates. Actually, I didn't even think about what I was doing. I just did what I had to do."

Helena was sobbing. "Spoken like a hero," she hugged him for a good moment and then stared at him. She smiled and said, "I was so frightened. You have been a gift from Venus to this family for so long. The boys. Lydia's lessons. I owe you for the lives of my sons." Her tears streamed down her cheeks. "And my sons owe you, as well."

The boys came running to their mother after giving the horse to Crecius.

Marcus said, "I owe you my life, Grantus."

"Me too. And on our birthday yet. I was so frigh...well...not scared but..."

"I understand. But really, I just acted as if by some silent command."

"Zeus, I knew it the first time I saw him. He has been charmed with good luck from Zeus himself."

Grant thought, "Yeah, okay, whatever." He looked for Lydia. She was standing in the spot where they had practiced. Her hands were clenched, and she had been crying. Oh, yes, she must have been frightened. He smiled at the thought that she might have been worried for him also.

Milos spoke, "A Roman can only thank you in one way. Boys."

"For my honor and my life," said Lucius, "I will fight for yours if need be, Grantus Tyrellius."

"And I too. May Zeus grant us the chance to show you our gratitude."

They grasped his arm in a solemn token of eternal friendship.

"Ask anything," Helena said.

"Well, right now, I'd like some of the food you've been putting on the table for the last half of an hour.

Theodosus laughed and walked with him to the chairs placed in the garden. "Good. Very good, Grantus. I saw the race. You very good. Hero. I am small next to you."

"Come on now, Theodosus, cut that out."

He patted Grant on the back. "Charmed by Zeus," Theodosus mimicked Helena's line.

Grant saw Lydia holding back from the crowd. "Go ahead but save some for me."

He walked over to Lydia and stared at her silently. After a moment, he smiled at her. He was sweaty, hot, dirty, and sore.

Lydia went to the well and poured some water into a jug. Then she found a cloth and returned to him. "Allow me," she said as she washed away the dust from his face, arms, and hands. "You are charmed by Zeus himself."

Suddenly, she was in his arms. "I was *so* frightened, Grant. I thought I'd lost the boys, and then I suddenly realized that I might lose you as well. I felt the pain inside my chest. The same pain that I felt when my fiancé returned from the battlefield dead." She held onto him tightly. "Helena was correct. You are a gift from Zeus." Then she whispered into his ear, "And Venus has given me back my heart."

He pulled away from her so that he could examine her face for that whimsical expression she used so often. "Do you mean that, Lydia?"

"Yes." She smiled into his eyes. "I know it now."

She held on to him tightly. "Never leave me, Grant. Promise me that you won't ever go away. Now that I have found my heart, I give it to you completely. You must keep it safe for me."

Grant closed his eyes and smiled.

Chapter Twenty

The late afternoon's activities seemed subdued in comparison with the earlier excitement. Still reeling from their near fatal adventures, Marcus and Lucius decided to spend the rest of their birthday inside the main villa where they could celebrate with the household. The servants were allowed to finish the leftovers from the midday meal and delighted in the sweet new dishes the cook had prepared in honor of the twins' special day.

Lydia stayed close to her sister but never missed a chance to make eye contact with Grant who bowed his head in a show of submission to her authority, and then smiled wickedly at her. When everyone was very drunk, and the sun had not yet bid good night to the heavens, Lydia stole away to the stables, saddled her horse, and took off for the coast. Grant watched her, found a small, soft fur bed cover he'd found lying at the foot of her bed, took the horse she had given him to ride the day before, and rode after her. She wasn't going very fast, so it didn't take long for him to catch up with her. The grin on her face told him that he had done the right thing in following her.

"Sunset," she said to him while remaining seated on her horse.

"Almost. Shall we ride close to the shore and watch it fall into the horizon?"

"I'd like that."

They said nothing for a while, just rode along the ebbing tide. They commented on the sky's varied colors, the sun's reflection on the waves, the quantity of pebbles and seashells, the horses' hooves' soothing sound as they splashed across the cool water.

Lydia stopped her horse and slid off. The action surprised Grant, and he followed her. When he came from behind his horse, she had already stripped off her clothes and gone into the water. He took off his clothes and walked into the water, then dove into the refreshing waves. He swam to her side.

She wasn't in her usual playful mood. She had no intention of teasing Grant now. She was staying afloat by slowly kicking her legs back and forth and moving her arms like someone making angel wings in the snow, but Grant was touching the bottom.

"I can't help thinking...what would have happened today if you hadn't been so quick to act. You thought nothing of your own safety, only the boys' lives." She shook her head. "Thank the gods you were there."

"I did what I had to do," he repeated the statement with true modesty.

"Humble servant."

"I obey my mistress's command in all ways."

"Do you mean what you say?"

"Do my eyes lie?"

She looked deeply into his blue eyes. "No," she agreed, "they speak the truth."

"Does it amuse my mistress to tease her slave?"

"I would not for all the world," she said and swam into his arms.

He covered her lips with his mouth, consuming them with greedily. Her body was cool, wet, soft, helpless, and so small against his.

"Give me your love," she said.

"My lady?"

"Yes, Grant, do as I command. Touch me."

He took his wet right hand and held her breast, first a gentle touch, then playfully teasing its tip, then tasting the water on it with his tongue, then kissing its swollen bud until she moaned, then pressing it cruelly into his palm until she groaned. "I'm sorry. Did I hurt you?"

"You can't hurt me," she whispered and rested her head against his chest. Her right hand crawled up the strong muscles of his stomach; her fingers found his nipple and played with it between her index finger and thumb until it grew hard. He moaned deep in his throat.

"You can't hurt me, either. Anything you do to me will only increase my appetite for you."

His lips went to her neck, and his teeth bit down hard on her flesh while his hand caressed her shoulder. She tossed her head back and cried out. His fingers moved easily down her spine, and he pressed her legs against his. He carefully moved his knee between her legs and pushed her hips towards his thighs, almost placing his manhood close enough to enter her in a second if she moved correctly. She had to have felt his erection moving up and down, pulsating next to her skin. Even in the cool water, it wasn't wasting any time.

He kissed her until she could no longer breathe. Both of Lydia's hands found the thick flesh of his muscular buttocks and squeezed it. Then her fingers moved like a floating fish through the water until they enclosed his manhood in both her palms. Her eyes shimmered in the final rays of the day's sunlight.

"Give me pleasure," she demanded.

"My lady could not ask me to perform a more delectable task." He picked her body up in his arms and took her across the water to their cave. She watched him, smiling at his every movement.

"I brought you a fur in case you caught cold while you rode. Allow me to fetch it."

"Please."

He walked gingerly back to his horse which was not an easy chore for at least two important reasons. He took the reins of both of the horses and walked them to the side of the cave. They stood there contentedly as if they knew what was going on and had no interest in destroying the magic. The cover was lying over his saddle. He cuddled it against his stomach and took it to Lydia.

He covered the floor of the cave with it. "My lady's bed," he said, patting it for her to sit upon.

She moved to the soft fur and stretched like a cat or an elegant nymph of Venus across it.

"You are so beautiful, mistress. Allow me." He motioned that she should roll over on her back. "Does your foot still bother you?"

He took her foot and softly kissed the inner sole. Then he

massaged her ankle, winding his fingers around her heel until she moaned softly. He rubbed and gently twisted one foot and then the other. He could feel her body relax. He used his hands to kneed the calf muscles of both legs, but when he moved to the back of her thighs, he began a different attack. He massaged her buttocks and hips, gradually moving his hands further down her abdomen until he found a warm, sensitive spot. He had no intention of doing anything more than titillate this area with the tips of his fingers. Her body instantly ignited with passion, but Grant had no intention of rushing this innocent virgin turned vixen. The more her body temperature rose, the more her tanned skin heated with the scent of floral oils, a scent that overpowered him. He wanted to kiss her, taste her luscious skin, and make her cry with delight, but he wanted her desire to grow into an ecstatic ferocity; he wanted her beyond reason, deliriously in love with him, and begging for his touch. He wanted her to cry out to him that all she wanted in life was to make him happy, and then he would show her how. He had to make her libido go beyond the initial novice fear and into base, animal hunger.

His index finger massaged the tender skin between her legs. Rubbing then playing then withdrawing and waiting for it to moisten so that he could try again. It reacted to his touch the way he wanted it to. It moved closer to his hand, moistened, then softened in his hand. He felt her body's heat, its yearning to be entered, its lips opening for his manhood, the oil on her skin warming and inviting him to take her. The signals Lydia's beautiful body was sanding him encouraged Grant to waste little time with this foreplay and go for the goal. But, she was new to the fine art of lovemaking, and he loved her too much to rush anything. He was older and more experienced. He knew how to hold onto his passion and temper his erection to be there when she needed him. Suddenly that was more sexually stimulating than the knowledge that he'd conquered her. He was in control. He didn't care about his satisfaction as much as he cared about hers. Grant smiled. Wasn't that a unique turn of events?

Lydia tried to turn over.

"Not yet, mistress."

He took the tip of his tongue and ran it up her spine, moved her hair with his hand, and bit her shoulder lustfully. Nothing he did displeased her. He sat back and massaged her shoulders and then moved down each arm, ending his therapy with a kiss on the inside of her hand.

She rolled onto her back. Her beauty was too much for his plan, and he had to look away for a second to control himself. His manhood protested violently.

"Lydia," he said as he gazed into her eyes again. She parted her lips.

"Isn't this the perfect place to make love? Here on this fur? In the cave? With the wind and the fragrance of the sea?"

"I can't think of a better place, mistress." But, there was no way he could hide his insatiable desire to taste her full breasts or their hardened tips. And no way he could convince himself to delay taking her any longer. His mouth moved to her breasts hungrily and kissed them one at a time in a gentle, reverent fashion so that she would not be afraid. Then he took them into his mouth allowing his tongue to tease them, took the small buds between his lips and his teeth. Anticipating what her reaction would be, he pulled her into his arms; he bit down.

She murmured a soft shriek, then moaned in a manner that indicated that she wanted more.

"Did that hurt?"

She dug her fingers into his arms, drew up her body, pressed her breasts into his chest, and bit him savagely on the fleshy part of his shoulder.

He was on her in a flash, pushing her frame roughly against the fur and using his right hand to force her legs apart. Would it be over quickly then? His plan to make her beg had been ruined by her eroticism, her subliminal call to fight him unless he took her; her sudden need for him to end the delightful torture. Her hands abruptly moved to stop him.

"Why?"

"I want you, but I'm...afraid."

"No, you're not. Don't ever say that, Lydia. You're not afraid of anything. You're the bravest woman I've ever met."

Apparently, the sudden movement of thrusting her legs apart, of making her helpless, immobile under his strong, muscular torso, was too quick for what he wanted, and his mind deadened his ardor. He'd envisioned this moment so often, that it just had to be more. She must call to him, speak his name, and beg him to take her. Her slave? Never. He was slave and master all in one. He would love her with devotion, but conqueror her as an emperor would. She must be *his* slave, must want him more than air or food. He must make *her* submit to his sexual superiority, his experience, his love. That tenet startled him, and he stopped all movement to let it blossom. Love? It was what he had wanted from her. He had wanted her heart, and he'd earned it, fought for it, suffered for it. And she had his as well. It occurred to him that he wasn't lying to himself anymore. He really did love her.

Grant rested his body on hers, pushed the dark hair from her forehead and temples, stared into her eyes, and smiled. "Oh, Lydia, how I *do* love you."

"Yes, oh yes, and I you."

He put his hand under her buttocks and pulled her up to meet his. It could be now. His erection rested so close to her anxious lips.

He pulled his body from hers and rested beside her. "Close your eyes," he said. She did once, then opened them again, smiled nervously, and then closed them tightly.

"What are you going to do?"

"Do you want to know?"

"Do what you want."

He did. He rested his hand on the heat between her legs while positioning his head on his hand and resting his body's weight sideways on the fur, then he slid his two fingers into the velvet folds and opened her. First his hand lingered, almost hovering above the pink petals, brushing them lightly with the tips of his fingers, and then he rotated his hand gently around but never into the tender and helpless leaves of her womanhood.

Her leg muscles relaxed.

"That's right. Just relax, Lydia. I have no intention of hurting you."

Her body was on fire. Her skin's fragrance—a scent of simmering perfume or perhaps mulled wine—was so tantalizing. Delicious. He let his tongue rest tenderly on the breast nearest his chest. Touching the tip of his tongue to the rising and lowering of that sweet swollen berry that had changed from a dusty pink hue to a tulip's springtime red; Grant toyed with it as perfectly as a trained musician would an antique violin. Her upper body rose and fell almost as if it wanted to dance with his hand, as if she were trying to imitate his body's rhythm as it would eventually move when they became one. She cooed and sighed deep in her throat as first her breasts rose and fell and then her hips reached upwards for him to take her then lowered in desperation. Like a cobra basking in the sun, unaware of the dangerous man close by, Lydia oscillated beside him as his fingers moved deeper and his rhythm turned staccato. He did not speak but let his hand speak of his prowess with women.

Suddenly, her body stiffened slightly, but not with an orgasmic finale, so he stopped for a minute. She clawed at his arms with her fingers, reaching her hands around his body so that she could dig her fingernails into his perspiring flesh. Her body's sexual undulations seduced him, and he lost control. His hand began again but with an altered course. His fingers fell deeper into her body, piercing her, making her ready for him. His hunger, his urgent need for her, overruled his stratagems. She wanted him to terminate his game, consummate their love, and find that wonderful climax for which she so desperately yearned; so he pulled away from her just at the moment when she would have found ecstasy.

"Why did you stop?" she cried with little breath to speak the words. She moved to her side and let her breast touch his chest. She kissed him hard on his lips, then bit them. "You must want me. Why do you hesitate?"

"Anything worth having, mistress, is worth waiting for. One should never rush love." He gazed into her eyes. "What do you want?" he said. "I am your slave and will only do as you request."

"I felt a rising...a wonderful terrible burning itching inside my..."

"Yes, I know."

"But there's more!" She kissed him hard on the lips again. It was all she could think of to get what she wanted.

"Yes, there's more," he said casually as if he were telling a child that there was one more piece of chocolate cake in the pantry.

Her lips trembled. "And you will give it to me, *now*!"

"Your command, mistress?" he replied coolly.

She looked down at the fur and played with it with her fingers. "Not a command, Grant."

"Then what?"

She shook her curls in desperation. "You must want it too."

He let his hand move to the back of her head, pulled her face towards his, and sealed her lips to his, pressing down very hard on her mouth, and forcing them open with his tongue.

He stopped all movement and took a breath. "Of course," he whispered into her ear. "I can't think of anything I want more."

Lydia moved her face away from his; she pushed him over on his back and began to run her hands across his chest. She found his nipples with her lips. "I can play, as well."

"Yes, of course."

"I'll make you mine."

"I'm already yours," he said smiling. He thought she was adorable when she tried to beat him at his own game. He closed his eyes and enjoyed her embraces. She hesitated when she reached his manhood.

"Still frightened, Lydia?"

"Maybe." She looked at him. "I want you."

"Yes?"

"I want you and...I must have you."

"I understand."

"Then why do you wait? What do you want from me?"

He sat up and pulled her roughly to his body but said nothing. He rested her back on the fur. "Allow me," he said and spread her legs. "Close your eyes. Relax."

"What are you doing? Oh, no, you can't do...don't go down there like that...oh, that's no good at all—*stop*—what do you mean by this?"

He couldn't answer her at that moment.

"Ah...no...that doesn't feel...wait...oh," she said, allowing her body to rest contentedly on the soft fur.

Again, Lydia allowed Grant to control her body. To love her. And just as he had done before, the moment she moved towards her climax, the moment he felt her soft skin harden and grow, he stopped.

She sat up quickly. "Tease me no longer!"

"Touch me," he said. "I want to be touched."

"I did. Was that not enough?"

"If you love me only that much, I am a slave, indeed, only fulfilling the wishes of my mistress and never once knowing of her true affection for me. You say you love me, but then you hesitate when I only want your kiss, your caress on...well...my body is on fire for you, Lydia, and only you can extinguish the heat of its flame."

Lydia was unsure of what to do but smart enough to know what he meant by wanting to be touched. There was a strained moment, and he thought she would never surrender to him or give him the satisfaction of doing his bidding just once. Would she please him as he had done for her? He rested his body on the fur, closed his eyes, and sighed happily.

"It is so soft, isn't it? The fur, I mean. It feels so good when it touches your naked skin. When you close your eyes, even the tiniest sensation on the skin becomes magnified."

He felt her tentatively trying to please him. So, he rewarded her with a deep moan of happiness. Would it give her pleasure to please him? Would she understand that making someone else feel joy was just as satisfying to the doctor as it was to the patient?

His eyes opened quickly. It had nothing to do with Lydia and everything in the world to do with life. You did find joy when you gave it to others. It was even better than gaining the prize. Other women had pleased him, and it was nothing but physical necessity, but, now, Lydia—playing the time period role of boss—was being taught the very lesson he needed to learn.

"Stop!"

"Did I do something wrong?"

"No, but I won't be able to..."

She rested her hand delicately on her chest, leaned over to him, opened her mouth, and kissed him. Her lips were hot. Her body was inflamed. Lydia was not like any woman he'd ever loved. Her eroticism was shocking, and he credited himself with staying in control this long. Was it just that she was a woman born in a more barbaric time period, or was it simply Lydia's personality? He'd remembered the way she'd tried to fight him in the small arena of the ludus. He reached out to her, cupped her face in his hand, and returned her passionate embrace with a softer more penetrating kiss.

"Please. I beg you to cease this torture and give me joy."

Those were the words Grant needed to hear. He pulled her underneath him, flat on the fur, smiled at her and said, "No more games." Then, moving on top of her, he angled his sword in a parallel line with the target. His skin was burning; his desire for her a heady, wonderful aggravation that needed a cure. His thighs moved with a dancer's grace as he separated hers. His arms—holding almost all his weight—held her upper body, pulling it into his dangerous blaze. He would consume her until she could no longer breathe from ecstasy.

Grant was tender even in his lust for her, however. He knew that the first few minutes would not be pleasant for Lydia. "Look at me. That's right look right into my eyes."

Her dark eyelashes fluttered open. She smiled up at him. A smile to steal a man's soul. She trusted him.

He moved his manhood into her satiny softness.

She cried out in pain. "Is it going to be like that? Is it going to hurt like that?" she said.

"No, but I wanted you to look at me and see how much I love you and how very brave you are. Brave enough not to be afraid of love. Lydia, it isn't the physical part that's frightening." She closed her eyes to ease the pain. "Look into my eyes. Do you see what lies behind them?"

She cooed, "Pretty dark eyes." She closed her eyes, arched her back, and let her body fall into the rhythm of his hips as he moved in and out of her at a very cautious pace.

"Yes, but look deeper. What do you see?"

She stared at him, kissed him, and let the tears fall. "Yes, I see. Grant. Loves me. Take me now, I can no longer endure patiently."

Grant rocked from one position to another, putting his body weight first on his hips, and then on his arms. He was the master conductor of the symphony they were creating with their passion. He'd never known a woman with so much fire. It took her a minute to get used to being entered by a man; she did not allow the first dart of pain to keep her from enjoying their lovemaking. His hips thrust deeper and deeper. His toes dug into the fur to help him push further into her luscious body. He rocked his abdomen, closed his eyes, and lost himself in her. There was no more need to overpower her. She was his heaven now. An angel he didn't deserve, but had somehow earned on this trip.

Grant lost himself in her. Moving deeper into her, he cuddled her face close to his and let the tears fill his eyes. His heart ached in his chest. His breathing became increasingly more difficult. He kissed her neck, shoulder, cheek, as he moved rapidly in and out of her. She clung to him. Her fingers digging into his back. He felt no pain. She was wonderful. Her head rolled backwards and to the side, so he freed one hand to brace it close to his. He touched her hair, feeling its smooth silky softness, and inhaling its perfume. The oil on her arms glistened like jewels. Her lips and tongue found his neck, and she kissed his skin reverently.

"You're so strong," she said not referring to his muscular stomach and arms in any way.

"Lydia?"

"Yes," she whispered into his ear.

"I love you!"

"I know. You told me. And I love you."

"No, that's not all. I have to tell you..." His body signaled that it was no longer going to react to his control, so he closed his eyes. "I would die for you, love."

She kissed his cheek as he released his life into hers.

The rocking began to slow, and she became frightened. "No, don't stop."

It was then that he realized that she had not been concentrating on her sensual needs but on his words. She didn't know how to let go. A problem he had overcome when he had declared his love for her.

He removed himself from her.

"No!" she screamed.

"Relax, love. I will not fail you." But, he could not lie to her. It would be a while before he could pleasure her, and he had been cruel not to let her have the joy when her body signaled for it. Cruel now that he realized that she had not danced with his rhythm.

"Come here," he said, motioning that she should lie in his arms.

She whimpered. "There's more."

"Yes, I'm sorry."

"But you teased me."

"And that was to make you all the more delighted, but I can't..."

"You must."

"Lydia, you don't understand men...we can't..."

Her hand darted to his manhood. "There's no point in that, Lydia," he said, closing his eyes and letting her massage him.

His eyes opened wide. My God! Her hands were soft and hard, quick and slow, loving and cruel, and his body reacted. Rode the wave with her determination to find happiness as if it were having the affair not him; as if it knew that Lydia was his soul mate and that life would spring from her body by mating with him; his dagger stiffened as if it had never loved.

"You see," she said, climbing onto his stomach.

"You are a wonder, mistress." He rolled her onto her back and entered her again.

This time he thought only of making her happy. His muscles controlled his thighs which helped him attain a gentle, almost nonexistent thrust against her tender, swollen pillow. He kissed her lips; she pushed him away with ferocity. She shook his hand away from her hair. He concentrated on her.

"You mustn't try so hard, love. It isn't something you can force." She bit his shoulder.

There was no taming the tigress beneath him. She held his buttocks in her hands and pinched in desperation. What if she didn't climax? What would he do then? She would attack him. If he came before her once again? He closed his eyes and soothed his libido, thinking only of pleasing her.

"Relax," he said to the panicky woman, but he could feel the rise of ardor in his own movements, and he would not be able to control that forever. By her generous manipulations his manhood had been brought back to life; his masculine pride had been enhanced, but he would not be able to please her. He knew it. It was pitch black outside the cave; they could not stay here any longer. It would be difficult to find their way home on horseback now. He would have to try to satisfy her another day.

The hunger grew with greedy anticipation of another rise to fulfillment. Like a demon possessed, his libido was grateful to find power and release after having been stimulated already by this woman. The blaze between his legs took hold of him in a way it never had before. He kissed her lips with tender sorrow for Lydia, the sweet goddess who had given him back his passion, would never know heaven in his arms tonight. He could feel her legs stiffen in an attempt to make her flesh obey her, could sense her stomach muscles tighten with anticipation and then relax in agonizing frustration. Her face was animated—first tightening her forehead in close victory, then relaxing in horrible defeat. And he could no longer wait.

He closed his eyes and quickened his pace. It was unfortunate that the very miracle she had created would end in her own bitter sacrifice. For to be able to stay in her, he had to remain aroused; and, paradoxically, that very stimulation would lead to his climax before hers. He closed his eyes and kissed her hard on the lips, cupped her face in his hand, and rested his cheek against hers. Pushing against the softness of the fur with his bare feet, Grant took hold of the situation in order to finalize the evening's lovemaking. He took both hands and placed them under the lower part of her back and raised her hips. It would feel so much better this way. Deeper.

She lifted her thighs to meet his. "Yes," he thought to himself, "place them high over my back, love."

As if she could read his thoughts, she did just as he wanted, and curled her arms around his neck to follow him to happiness.

He heard his own groan of impending release. Target. Determined attack. Thrust. To the very core of you, my dearest opponent.

"I love you," was the only thing he could think of to say at a time like this. She had given all of her love to him—unselfishly—and would not find any joy in it. And it was her first time. Vital to a woman's career with lovers. But, he could tell by the stress in her arms, in her whole anatomy, the way she clung to him for help—for salvation—that she was too tied up in the process to find freedom. Rocking with deliberate strides, he raced towards his goal.

Lydia cried out just as he pushed his abdomen one last time toward his goal to satiate his lust and become one with his love. "Grant!" she called.

They were riding the wave of passion together.

"Love!" he said to her as he embraced her tightly but let her body fall to the blanket of fur. His body was saturated with perspiration.

"Oh, love." She held him close to her breasts, kissing him on the forehead, cheeks, and lips. "Never did I dream..."

"Nor I, I can assure you."

"You never..."

"Not until I met you."

They snuggled close to each other on the fur, keeping the cool breeze at bay by combining the fever of their bodies.

"Time has stopped," she said suddenly.

"What do you mean?"

"How could there have been a *before* without you?"

"I know what you mean," he answered truthfully.

"How could there ever have been stars in the heavens, peach colored moons, or the ebb and flow of the sea before you entered my life."

"There wasn't."

She rolled onto her side and stared into his eyes. "What do you mean?"

"I mean that if you are dead to love; you must be dead to life. Finding love defines existence. Defines life. Puts the whole world into perspective." He smiled at his own words.

"There is no other world but the one we've just created, is there?" she said kissing him.

He combed her hair with his hand, kissed the top of her head, and then maneuvered it onto his chest so that she could relax and enjoy her body's new sensations. He closed his eyes to fight back his tears, wiping them away with the back of his free hand. He couldn't let her see him like that. She wouldn't understand that the pain in his chest was gone forever; that her love had healed him.

Chapter Twenty-One

There never was such a sky nor such a sun as the one that brightened the morning after Grant and Lydia shared their love in the cave. Grant awakened from a deep sleep refreshed, invigorated, happy, and wearing the most wonderful smile of his life on his lean, tanned face. He went to the well and drew water, pouring it into a bucket. He took it back to the twins' villa and bathed privately with oil and cool water. He washed letting the water pour over his head and cleansing the grime from his face. He even splashed some fragrant oil over his face and chest. He was a new man and wanted to feel like one.

Lydia's keen sense of direction had helped them find their way home in the dark of night. He had walked her to the patio outside her room and kissed her good night. He could not share her room. Not yet. The twins would be suspicious if he were not in his cot when they woke the next morning.

He did have early morning plans, however, and before the household came to eat their 'breakfast', he sauntered over to Lydia's patio to see what was going on with his lady.

Lydia was awake and being bathed by Diana. His lover's back

was to him, but Diana saw him and smiled. He gave her a wink, and her grin widened. She allowed her mistress to climb from the water and onto the massage table, and when Lydia's face was turned to the wall, she left the room. Grant tiptoed over to the fragrance jars and opened one, sniffed at its scent, and de-cided it was the sweetest perfume, and the best one for Lydia. He tugged at the cloth that covered her back and poured the oil onto her skin. Gently, he maneuvered his hands across her back. She noticed the heavy touch and turned.

"Relax, mistress, allow me," he said.

She grinned and rested her head on the rolled cloth while he massaged her back, legs, arms, thighs, and buttocks.

"Roll over."

She did so and kept the towel around her body.

"Oh, that will never do," he said.

She was in his arms in a second. The towel dropped as she clung to him. She wanted him again.

"I wanted to awaken with you by my side this morning," she said. "Wanted you to give me a good morning kiss. I miss you already, and we've only been separated for a few hours."

Diana brought breakfast for two into the room and placed the food on the patio table. "My lady will need food," she said with a kittenish smirk—obviously Diana was happy for them. She would tell Theodosus the very moment she had a chance.

Lydia stood before him and let the towel drop. "My mistress will catch cold," he said, then took her in his arms.

"Not with your arms to hold me and keep me warm." She kissed him.

He looked at the delightful display of food set on the table. "Hungry?" he asked.

"Famished. For your kisses."

"That I will give you aplenty." He reached for her white dancer's tunic and loincloth of white silk and allowed her to dress herself while he poured cool water into goblets for them. She joined him on the patio.

They watched the sky fill with the morning light as they ate a meal of sweet white bread and fruit.

"Is it just me or is the sky a rosier hue than it was yesterday," she said, leaning into his arms and resting her back and head on his chest. The two, like spoons in a drawer, held each other while they ate. He placed sweet pieces of fruit in her mouth, and she cuddled close to him.

"Everything seems more alive today, Lydia. My head seems clear of its usual morning ache, the air seems crisp and invigorating, and the dawn never looked so beautiful."

"Does that mean you're in love, Grant?" She turned her head to read his facial expressions.

He smirked and said, "I think so." And then he kissed her. "I am in love, Lydia. With my mistress, who holds my heart in her treasure chest along with the gold coins she found in the pirate's cave."

She giggled. "And I am your slave, Grant. For no one has ever made me as happy as you have. I was in love once before so I know this is real. I know that you have shown me what he never did—how to love. Not a girl's innocent idolatry, but a true, deep, mature woman's love. Encompassing all. In a way, I'm rather glad it turned out this way though I know that sounds awful. I don't think he could have loved me with such total admiration as you did last night. There can't be any man who can compare to you. I love you so much, and I thanked the goddess this morning for giving you to me."

He cradled her in his arms. "We could postpone practice today."

She giggled. "What would Milos say when you weren't there to teach the boys?"

"You're right. I should go." He pushed her away from his body. "No! Don't."

"But I must go. I can't leave Theodosus alone like that. But, afterwards, when I must do my lady's bidding, we can...ah....run to the sea."

"For a swim?"

"You should practice fighting on the rocky coast. It will teach you balance."

"Of course, you're right. And then..."

He perused the sky. "It looks like a mighty hot day. If you should seem exhausted, we could swim."

"I'll tell Diana took make us a large meal so that we can eat before we go. Do you know how to sail a ship?"

He shook his head. "Actually, I don't," he admitted.

"Well, I do. We'll sail to another spot, on the far side of the cove. No one can see us there."

"What about pirates, milady?"

She tilted her head up to meet his and said, "We're a match for any pirate, don't you think?"

"I pity them if they try," he said softly and then kissed her.

Grant and Theodosus challenged the boys to a fight with wooden weapons, real shields, and their uniforms. They gleefully asked Milos if it were all right. Theodosus gave Marcus a workout, but Grant allowed Lucius to give him a few good hits that increased the boy's ego immensely.

Theodosus whispered to him, "Grantus not eat this morning?"

"Oh, I ate all right," he said smirking.

"Lydia?"

"I'm in love."

"Yes, that's good, maybe."

"It's good all right, no maybes about it."

"But you slave. She no can be your wife."

"I think I'll take one day at a time with this. I have her heart, and she has taken mine. Right now, that's all I want." He looked at his friend. "I stopped worrying about everything last night. Magic, Theodosus. She is magic. She's placed my soul in her treasure chest and locked it with a golden key. I shall never have it again."

"Venus?"

"Okay, yeah, sure. Venus has done this to us, and she will have to work it out."

That thought struck him and after practice, he went to the garden and plucked two roses from the bush of pink flowers. He placed one in the open part of the water jug Venus held in her hands.

"Okay, it's not as if I believe in this stuff you understand, but, if you're some sort of guardian angel, please make this work because I only have so long, and I need some reassurance that all will go well. I've quite thinking; you're going to have to do it for Lydia and me from now on."

When Lydia came to the atrium, he handed her the second rose. She looked at it first and then at the one in Venus's jug. "She will note your sacrifice though it is a small one; she will grant you your heart's desire."

"I have only one desire. To stay with you forever."

Just then, Wainwright came into the atrium and gave Grant a quick look. The look was a reminder that he could not stay with Lydia. Grant ignored the look, took Lydia's hand in his, and set off for their run.

Grant and his new love raced to the beach, stripped off their clothes, tossed them into the ship, and then swam for fifteen minutes. He had no intention of keeping his hands off his lady. He grabbed her as soon as they surfaced and kissed her while running his hands over her fragrant, oiled, hot, wet body. She wiggled in his arms causing his manhood to stiffen.

"How often can we do this in one day?" she asked.

He slipped his erection inside her with no hesitation. She belonged to him now. "With you? You're the miracle woman; you tell me?" He pressed her body against his and pushed himself deep inside her. She hugged him and allowed her body to follow his rhythm. The water enhanced their lovemaking, acting as a third party—as if Venus herself was there to play servant and massage their bodies with her soothing waves while they made love.

He pulled her down into the water a bit so that he could move at a better angle, and she sighed contentedly against him. "Don't I have to do anything?"

"Just relax and let me please you."

Her body quivered with a spasm of satisfaction. "Oh..." she cried into the sky.

"Early morning is definitely your time, Lydia," he said, holding back his passion. He would need some reserve today. He had plans for that new spot Lydia had mentioned and the sailing ship. He slipped from her body and let the chill of the water end his desires.

"Happy?" he asked her.

She kissed him. "Oh, yes."

"Take me for a ride in that pretty ship, captain?" he said.

The sailing ship was bigger than Grant had first realized. There was a lot of room in its belly even if the deck looked as though it needed a crew of only four men. All in all, it would hold eight maybe nine if the trip was short and the weather good.

Lydia knew exactly what to do and moved around the anchor, sails, and wheel like a seasoned sailor.

"My father taught Helena and me how to work the ship so she and I could travel to any part of the coastline we wished. He loves this little boat. I guess he and my mother used to take short, midnight trips in her. He loved her so much."

"Those are good memories, Lydia. You're very lucky to have them. A father and mother happy and in love with two clever and pretty daughters to play with in the bright sunshine surrounding a heavenly villa. Your father was smart to bring your mother here. And it is very touching to think he would build his whole house around her love of flowers."

"The Athena." She looked at him while she moved the ship to the opposite side of the bay. "Named after the daughter of Zeus—goddess of war, music, art, and poetry. Quite a mix for one woman."

"Sounds like you."

Lydia blushed and carefully glided the ship to a small cove far way from any intruders' eyes.

"By the look of this abandoned cove, I'd say you have wicked plans, mistress."

She looked at the rose that she had brought with her. She'd tied it into her leather binding and worn it in her hair, taking it out only to swim with Grant. "My mother's rose." She smiled at him. "I have something for you, Grant. I hope you like it."

She reached into the small sack she had tied to her dress at the waist. He'd noticed it before and wondered why she needed it.

"A merchant came by our villa many years ago, and I had him make this during the week he stayed at our home." She took a cameo broach from her purse and held it lovingly in her hands. "It didn't take him long to make it." She handed it to Grant. He saw whose portrait was chiseled into it.

"It is a Roman tradition for a woman of wealth to give her lover a cameo with her likeness on it. I had it made, and planned to give it to my fiancé when he returned from war, but since he did not, I've kept it in my jewelry chest all this time. It doesn't belong there. It belongs in the hands of the man I love. Will you?"

Grant took the gift in his hands and marveled at the old tradition he thought was something born of the Victorian time period. "It's you!" he said and then cursed himself for such a stupid statement. "Of course it's her. Say something better than that," he told himself.

"I will cherish your gift as I do your love. For eternity."

She smiled and handed him the pouch so that he could tie the gift safely around his waist. "Don't lose it. Keep it right there in the waist pouch."

"I'll never lose it."

They had exchanged love gifts. A rose. And a portrait of Lydia.

She signaled for him to come into her arms by slowly taking down the shoulders of her gown and exposing her breasts. He took them into his hands lovingly and kissed them. Then she took the skirt section of her dress and tossed it aside exposing only the silk loincloth. She stood up and motioned that he should dive into the sea with her by untying that garment and tossing it close to the gown.

"You are a goddess...or a sea nymph bent on driving me wild with desire."

He took off his clothes, being sure to place the waist belt close to his skirt, and dove in after her. She swam to the cove and walked onto the beach.

"She's totally naked. If this was 2000, there'd be helicopters overhead snapping photos of her. I *love* time travel!" he said to himself.

As soon as he exited the water, he had his hands on her. "It's too rough on the beach."

"I don't care."

"Here in the sunlight?"

"Yes, in the sunshine, on the beach, now."

He dropped her to the sand with a trip, and pushed aside any rocks or pebbles that might hurt her back with his hands. Lydia laughed with delight. "No more teasing, Grant?"

"I have no intention of wasting a moment with you," he said, taking one breast in his mouth and sucking hard on its tip.

"I guess not," she said as her head rocked back on her shoulders. He let her back fall flat onto the sand.

He was ready to love her. She had achieved a climax so it was no longer a requirement to wait any longer. He moved her underneath his body. One hand on her neck to ease her head down, and the other separated her legs. "You are good at this, aren't you?"

He didn't answer her. His hands took hold of her heat while he kissed her breasts until the buds grew hard with passion. "I've had some practice, yes."

"Oh my!" she cried out happily. "You plan to teach me this as well."

"Absolutely. Right out here in the wind, the sun, the surf, and the sand. Hope none of your pirates decide to invade us right now."

His mouth reached for hers hungrily.

His manhood was in her again and taking its own pace as he had when he'd raced her that first day. First, he moved slowly, allowing her to be comfortable with his stride; then he forced her to keep up with his rhythm and pace. Lydia became wanton.

She thrashed her head back and forth moaning her total loss of control. Then she tried to move her abdomen up to match his thrusts, but was forced to keep still with one aggressive move of his hips. He pressed her body against the sand and pushed hard into her. "Not her first time," he said to himself. He lifted his torso when she relaxed so that she could squirm underneath him. He placed his hands under her back. He closed his eyes and lost himself in attaining his own pleasure.

"I love you," she whispered, but he ignored her words so intent was he on self-fulfillment. His hip movements were graceful, accomplished with the new strength they'd gained from all those races with Theodosus up the hill. His assault was based on all that he had learned about sizing up your opponent and taking advantage of their weaknesses. She was fooling no one. She needed him. She didn't have to say it in so many words; it was in her flesh, her eyes, her animal cries of joy and discovery. Lydia had lost her power to control him. He knew exactly how to make her happy, and she needed him as much as she needed food and water.

"Wait, I can't keep up," she stammered.

He ignored her. His body was in a feverish state, his manhood alive and hungry, his mind in desperate need to burst with an invigorating release of tension and stress, and his heart was rhythmically drumming a staccato crescendo for the symphony of sensations flooding his being. His taut legs and chiseled abdomen burned so hot; they shimmered with perspiration and her moistness. His focus remained on achieving the mind-bending explosion he'd had the night before. Her erotic cry earlier was running circles in his head. He wanted that too. Freedom was close. It curled up his spine, shortened his breath, made his thigh muscles quiver, tingled to the very tips of his toes, and shot through his temples. He smiled contentedly, rested on her chest and stomach for only a second, let himself drop from her body, and then rolled to her side.

Lydia was on him like a panther who had just outrun her prey. It was a little too late now to remember that she was only twenty-one. Her body slid across his. Flirting with his warm skin, her hands massaged his chest and arms. The erect tips of her breasts skimmed seductively across his. She let her fingers tease his hardened muscles all the way down his stomach and over his abdomen until they rested on his manhood.

"Oh, Lydia, let me rest a moment."

"Venus, give him strength," she said loudly and leaned over to kiss him hard on the lips.

"Bad girl. Very bad girl," he whimpered but found his libido suddenly alive. "Do you have a direct line or something?" he said, and then realized that she would have no idea what that meant.

She caressed him back to the proper size, and then climbed on him. "If you are so tired then..." she said sitting on him, "...oh...that's nice....I have no problem leading the way, love."

And she did. Her hands embraced his chest as she rode him to her own satisfaction. Her scream was loud enough to wake the gods from their midmorning nap.

"Can I die now?" he said and chuckled.

She released his manhood and settled on his stomach, then rolled to his side and fell asleep.

He turned over to gaze at her. "Lovely, lovely, mistress of my heart. My life is yours," he said and then slept with his face close to hers.

Chapter Twenty-Two

"It was all worth it, Bruce," said Grant to Wainwright the next morning. "The trip was worth every penny I paid and then some. I'm glad it didn't work out the way I planned it. I would have been a married emperor/warrior and would never have met Lydia."

"Time Travelers, Inc. is pleased that you're pleased," said Wainwright. "I'm enjoying the trip as well, if you know what I mean. I'm even thinking that Diana and Theodosus might never have had the life they have now if we hadn't come along. Theodosus would have met Diana, but she would have been given to another man just as she was given to you first. They would never have been brought to this home."

"Oh, I don't know."

"It was your pairing with him, and your determination to be successful at the ludus that made him an impressive fighter. One who would catch Milos's eye. Helena probably would have still lost her husband, and the boys would have still yearned for chariots and swords, but Theodosus would have probably died in the arena."

"I think I like this time travel business."

"Well, it has its ups and downs, Grant, just like anything else; but so far, it seems to be a positive endeavor."

"How's the 'other' guy in your head?"

"Quite passive lately. No complaints. Very dormant which happens to stable individuals when you become one with them. Most personalities just return to a peaceful state and experience life along with you, hoping that you won't get them into serious trouble."

"I might like to try that when I get over this trip...but..."

"What do you want to know—as if I couldn't guess."

"What will become of Lydia when I leave suddenly? And more important, what will become of me without her?"

"The down side of time travel."

"Can I come back?"

"Yes, of course, you can, on the next solstice. But, you have to make a clear decision about that when you are completely away from the time period. You have to realize that if you choose to visit her twice a year, your relationship with her, and the lies you will have to perpetuate to keep doing this, might change both of your lives for better or worse. She might wonder why her husband—lover—can't stay with her all year. What happened to her slave? Would you be punished when you return? Would she be suspicious as to why you are leaving them and then returning? Will her life in 200 A.D. be harmed by the whole scenario of a half-time mate?"

"We could leave here?"

"A decision you should not be making without her permission. What if she doesn't want to leave her sister, father, nephews? What if she wants a whole and happy life?"

He looked at Wainwright and smiled. "She has no life without me, and I have no life without her. No matter where we are or what we are doing; we belong together."

"Are you sure of that?"

"As sure as I am that there's a sun in the sky. I don't like the thought that she will be without me to protect her. She asked me not to leave her, and she has issues with being abandoned because of her fiance''s death. She might think that if I go away from her; I might not return."

"You may have hit upon an idea. You could tell her that you are going to run away to fight with the emperor so that you can earn your freedom."

"But I just told you that she would be frightened if I did that. You have no idea how upset she is over his death; how my intervention in her life has changed all that. She's happy now, and so am I."

"This is a problem."

"What about that slot transfer thing? Could I be one of those?"

"We wouldn't exactly know that for a year. You come home for one year to evaluate the situation with a clear head. Once you make that decision, there is no returning. You'd have to give up your own life as a businessman. If you came back, and she was married or dead, what then? No changing your course."

"She would wait."

"For what—whom? Are you going to tell here that you'll be back in a year?"

"I suppose I could tell her that I am going away for one year to seek...my fortune, freedom, honor, whatever, and that I will be back in one year; but that if I am not back by June 201 A.D. to forget me."

"The stuff of romance novels, but with an element of incredible emotional risk."

"I love her. I am sworn to protect her with my life. Nothing else matters. I need her in my future."

"And if you are *not* a slot transfer, then what?"

"How am I supposed to live without her?"

Wainwright smiled. "Look, don't worry about it, okay? Let the time mechanism work its magic. My alter ego has been teaching me to let the whole thing flow. Don't think about the worst that can happen, think about how much you love each other. The rest will take care of itself."

"A rather fatalistic attitude for such a logical person, Bruce."

"I am learning that logic is a waste of *time*. The water pours from the hills to the sea; the clouds come and go with the breeze; the birds build their nests every year in the same location; and the sun rises and sets on its own. People need to realize that humans are a part of nature as much as the trees and the plants. I'm not saying that we shouldn't toil, have goals, seek pleasure where we can; but there's a point where we try too hard, and if we let go of our grip just a little bit, and have just an ounce of faith, everything falls into its proper spot."

Grant stared at Wainwright. "Good Lord, he's taken over."

Wainwright arched his eyebrow. "What are you talking about?"

"What you just said. That isn't something I would have ever expected the founder of Time Travelers, Inc. to say. C'est la vie? Que sera sera? That philosopher has your mind in a whirl."

Wainwright smiled and looked into the sky. "Well, I don't mind. He's given me a libido to die for."

"Thea?"

"Oh, my heaven, if the Cooper brothers could see me now."

"You and Thea?"

"She's beautiful. Inside and out. Weaving is her specialty. She made this new toga for me. The palla is her own design."

"She's artistic then?"

"She doesn't care about numbers or alphabets. She just wants to make me happy."

"And what will happen when you leave?"

"I might put Rome on the list of return engagements. Next client that wants to go..."

"Like me? Would you come back with me?"

"Sure. Here's a thought. If you are a slot transfer, you won't be able to go back in for one full year. We'll try to come back at Christmas time. If I go and you stay, then we'll know that you're a slot transfer. I could come back to see the boys and Thea and check out the situation with Lydia. I'll tell her that you are coming back if she's pinning for you, but if she's married and pregnant or something, I won't say a word."

"That sounds like a plan. Well," he looked at the twins advancing towards Theodosus and Milos with their uniforms, "I had better get back to work. You've eased my mind."

Wainwright walked away mumbling, "Que sera sera?"

Lydia wanted to work out on the beach, and fighting wasn't the only program she had in mind for the afternoon. She saddled their horses—he had his own white horse that she had given him as a gift—attached two saddlebags of food and wine and their practice equipment on the hind end of both horses, and told Diana not to expect them for the rest of the day.

"Milos might not like my missing the afternoon session with the twins."

She tossed her free curls to the wind. "I don't care what Milos wants. I am half-mistress of this estate, and my needs supersede his," she said before kicking her horse into a run.

He shook his head as he watched her get a head start on him. "I love you!" he called to her as he climbed into the saddle—or rather a facsimile thereof—and raced after her. "Like Anthony following Cleopatra, I have a whole new appreciation for powerful, determined women. Letting them lead the way isn't always a bad thing."

Lydia took the food and wine into the cave and returned in her fighting togs. "I'm ready." And she meant for practice. She had not given up on her goal to be a gladiator.

"I intend to give you a tough workout," he said, placing his helmet on his head and taking his shield and sword.

"That's what I want," she said.

She began with fast short parries to his head. He countered quickly shaking off his slumberous morning mood. She was very alert and alive today, and he knew that this was a good indication of what lie in store for him later. He would overpower her now as well as then. What a challenge she was and how wonderful to have a physical rather than a mental workout with such a noble opponent. His thighs tightened and helped him hold the lead as he batted at her furiously. She held her shield up to ward off his attack then backed away.

"No more tripping games, mistress," he thought to himself, "it's weak strategy. Fight me!"

Grant pushed towards her body with short, quick, almost vicious thrusts. She used only her shield to ward off his blows, darted away from him to catch her breath, then whirled around him so fast that he was caught completely off guard. She tried to drive her sword into his back, but he parried with his own sword, and blocked her body from getting too close to his with his shield. He turned towards her. She hadn't noticed that her footing was unbalanced on the pebbles, so he pushed her backwards with a furious attack aimed at her head. She hated anything coming towards her face and recoiled involuntarily being careful not to fall. He moved in for the kill; her shield went to cover her face; he lunged his sword into her stomach. She fell to her knees to indicate that he had made a fatal move on her.

"Yield!" he said as he pointed his fake sword at her head.

"I yield," she said and removed her helmet. "Now what will you do with me?"

"Let me see," he said not allowing her to move while he thought. "You are my prisoner now."

"I am?" she said smiling.

"I am the pirate who claims you as my prize. My prisoner will rise and do as I say."

Her dark eyes glimmered with the fun of role playing. "Yes, I must do as you wish for my very life is in your hands."

"Indeed, and don't you forget it, *slave*."

"What would you have me do, Captain Tyrell?"

"First, I want you to go to the cave and prepare me a delicious meal for I am hungry."

"I will have an advantage when you get drunk on the wine and will use that moment to escape," she warned him.

He smiled. "Just do as I say."

She ran off delighted with the game. She placed the fur wrap she'd brought with her on the floor of the cave to make a table for the bowls and food. He sauntered over to his horse, took something from the tack, and casually strolled to the mouth of the cave.

"I have done as you asked, Captain Tyrell."

He tossed the workout gear to the ground. "Take off that equipment!" he ordered.

She did as he said. She wore only her short gown tied at the shoulders now, and her sandals. He took a strap he had wound around the handle of his sword—the same one that had tied the saddlebag to his horse—and motioned for her to come to him.

"Kneel, prisoner."

His mood seemed odd to her, and she displayed an expression of apprehension on her pretty face.

"Give me your hands," he demanded.

She offered them to him. He tied the leather strap around her wrists but did not tie them tightly enough to keep her from moving her hands. "Now you won't escape and I can eat in peace."

"But I'm hungry!" she said as Lydia.

He bit into a grape. "As a pirate captain, I should think I wouldn't care about *your* needs."

She sat on the cave floor and sadly watched him eat the fruit and chicken the family cook had prepared the way Lydia had requested.

After he'd eaten one or two grapes, he took a cloth that had been used to cover the food, and walked over to his 'prisoner'.

"I don't like your looking at me while I eat. It bothers my digestion." He took the cloth and covered her eyes with it, tying it tightly at the back of her head.

"Grant?" she said weakly.

He kissed her. "Hush, prisoner, I will do as I please with you."

He took a chicken breast and pulled one section from it and carefully placed it in her mouth. She ate the white meat and smiled. "More?" she asked.

"I suppose I must keep you alive to work my ship, mustn't I?"

"Yes, I am good with sailing ships."

"So I've heard," he said, placing a grape between her lips and watching her bite down on it.

"Would you like some wine?"

"Yes, please," she said respectfully.

"You know if you don't do as I ask; I could throw you overboard when we leave this cove."

"I will do my best to please you, captain."

"Well," he fought to think of how Douglas Fairbanks might speak in a pirate movie, "you do seem to be a pretty wench, at that."

She didn't say anything for she was drinking the wine offered to her by her 'captor'.

"Taste some more of this chicken. I need you to keep up your strength. You will steer my course for the Athena, and I will lie on her deck and enjoy this delicious wine."

"I'll need my hands free to do that."

"I'll get her out to the sea first, then I'll untie your hands and take the blindfold off you so that you can direct our course. No sudden moves though, or I'll tie you to the mast and feed you to the sea serpents when we get far out to sea."

She took hold of the chicken with her white teeth and ate it hungrily.

"Poor wench, you are hungry, aren't you?"

"Ah...I attacked you for your food," she improvised.

"I see."

"I haven't eaten for...days," she said grinning.

"Well, I must admit your tale does move my heart, but never seek to run from me."

"Oh," she swallowed another grape, "I wouldn't want to incur the wrath of such a notorious pirate."

"Try this," he said not disclosing that he was placing soft white bread in her mouth. She sniffed at it and then opened her mouth to take it.

"Now, I must tell you that I've heard stories about captains who have become so enamored with beautiful wenches— such as yourself—that they have lost their hearts to these vixens only to be overpowered and murdered by them whilst they slept."

"Oh, I would never do such a thing."

"You wouldn't?" he said, kissing her lips.

"Never!"

"Very well. I'll take you to the ship now. Take my arm, and I'll guide you."

He took her out of the cave, across the beach, into the water and pushed her up onto the deck of the Athena.

"Sit there until I get my ship into the water." He did what he saw Lydia do the time before, drifting the tiny sailboat onto the course she'd used the time before.

"All right," he called to her, "you can steer our course now, prisoner." He untied her hands and took off the blindfold. She was in his arms immediately and kissing him delightedly.

"Now, now, prisoner, I realize that you're grateful that I didn't kill you as I had planned to do when you attacked me, but don't let my softness give you hope that I am not a bloodthirsty villain who will kill..."

he kissed her hard on the lips and touched her breast with his free hand, "you if I am so provoked."

"Oh, I hope I can provoke you," she said, giggling at the change in the meaning of his words.

"Set our course for that island over there," he said, pointing to their lovers' nest.

"Yes, captain," she said and sprang to the task.

They dropped anchor off the shore of their hidden cove. "Would you like to swim?" he asked.

"Whatever you wish," she said, stripping off her clothes and dropping them with little concern to the deck, and then diving into the cool water. He followed her. It was a beautiful day filled with bright glorious sunshine and no clouds in the sky.

Grant swam under her and grabbed her legs. Holding her in his arms, he allowed his manhood to touch her thigh.

"Captain of my heart," she said softly and kissed him gently on the lips.

"I love you, Lydia," he said as he slipped his body into hers.

"And I love you!" she said, curling her legs around his hips so that he could enter her. The water splashed against their skin and relaxed their muscles so that they could become one. She held onto him while he moved his hips in the water until he climaxed. Lydia hugged him as he let her abdomen drop—so that her legs could swing free.

He picked her up in his arms and carried her back to the beach and let her make love to him.

When they were finished, Lydia sat next to him and watched his face as he lay contentedly on the sand. "This is true happiness, isn't it?"

"Yes."

"And nothing on the earth can compare to it."

"Nothing."

"Do other people find love as we have?"

"I suppose your father and mother did. Probably."

"I can't think of anything but you, Grant. When I try to fall asleep at night, I see your face and stay awake to watch you in my vision. Then when I finally do fall asleep, I see you in my dreams."

"I have the same ailment."

She laughed. "I suppose we had better get back to the cave before small animals devour our feast."

She scampered into the waves, headed briskly for the ship, and climbed aboard.

"Lydia..." he said, rising from the water and climbing aboard the Athena, "if I should ever leave..." He wrestled trying to put his dry clothes on his wet body as she was doing. He put his waist belt that held her cameo around his midsection and tied it.

She placed her finger to his lips the same way she had when she'd warned him about Zeus's anger. "You won't. Don't ever say that, Grant. Do you have my cameo?"

He showed her that it was safe in the waist pouch. "As long as you have my cameo, we are pledged for eternity. You must never lose it, or Venus will not protect us. As long as it is with you, and your vision is in my dreams, we are bound together just as the leather straps tied my wrists. We are each other's slave, Grant. No one can break us apart. The ties may not be visible to the outside world, but we know they are there. We know we belong together."

He cupped her face in his hands. "My lady. Mistress of my heart."

"And my captain, the pirate who stole mine."

They embraced, and then she weighed anchor and headed for the safe cove near the villa.

As they brought the ship to rest among the rocks, they heard a voice from above the cliffs. It was Marcus waving to them.

"What's he saying?" she said. "I can't make it out."

"I think he said something about your father."

Marcus cried louder, "Lydia, come quickly, grandfather is

home!"

She was so excited; she half rolled, half fell from the sailing ship and hurried to gather their picnic supplies and workout equipment.

"Hurry, Grant," she said breathlessly, "my father's finally home."

Grant did as she wished and ran for his horse so that he could keep up with her. Somehow the idea of meeting her father brought an unsettling pang of fear into his heart, and he had no idea why. He had a feeling that nothing would be the same now that the head of the household had come home to take command of the estate.

Chapter Twenty-Three

Lydia chose to greet her father by coming into the atrium by way of the garden. Grant nonchalantly followed her until he realized that he was a slave and not privy to family discussion. Still, he wanted to see the man whom they had spoken so highly of—the man who had loved his wife so much he had ordered statues and portraits painted of his beloved, gardens to be planted by their love bed—so he stayed back but in earshot of the conversation.

The picture of the familial homecoming was perfect except for Marcus Flavius Antonious's mood. Lydia's father looked like the sort of man who had once been a soldier but had given it up to farm and be a businessman with aspirations to be more than that in the high social circle he planned to enter. He had a face that looked like a perfect model for a statue—handsome. He was all business with no intention of showing his grief before strangers. His hair, worn in the fashion of the day with tight curls placed in exact spots on his broad forehead, was brown with flecks of gray at the temples. Slightly receding hairline. Long eyebrows filled with gray. Long mouth to match the eyebrows. Wide but not unattractive nose. Mustache and beard with flecks of gray swimming in them. Broad chest with a wide neck. Short arms and small but strong-looking hands. About five-five in height and his weight was approximately 200 pounds, although it was very difficult for Grant to guess at that because the line of his toga was wide enough to cover a Volkswagen. Once in awhile, Grant glimpsed the man's sandals which appeared to be brown, leather, and tied with leather straps at his calves. It wasn't the way the man looked that both impressed and frightened Grant. It was Marcus's attitude. Brash and rough, he ordered food with quick, tempered commands. His dark eyes were piercing and almost cruel as he inspected the new 'staff' members he hadn't ordered. The expression on Marcus's face was not a happy one. He was hot, dirty, dusty, hungry, and his clothes were disheveled and muddy.

"Trouble on the road, Father?" said his oldest daughter, hugging him with obvious affection if not a slight air of detachment.

Wainwright was sitting in one of the round-backed chairs near the doorway to his room in the atrium of the house while Lucius flanked him on the right.

"How's the new tutor working out?" he asked.

Before Helena could answer, he scowled at Theodosus and Diana and said, "Why are there so many slaves in the atrium today?"

"Socrates is a gem, Father, and...well...there have been quite a few changes since you left me in charge weeks ago."

Milos stood behind Helena and in front of the boys and their tutor. His hands clenched; it looked like there might be a battle, and if there was one, he intended to win it. Master Antonious gave him a perfunctory quick glance and then glared at Helena. Grant wondered if her father knew of her relationship with the retired gladiator.

Diana stood by Lydia's doorway with Theodosus behind her. Thea was nowhere. Marcus came running from the courtyard after letting one of the slaves have the reins of his horse—the same servant who had taken Grant's and Lydia's horses—and then went to his tutor instead of his grandfather. The action told a story all its own. The way both boys stood beside Wainwright was a credit to the time traveler. Finally, Marcus sat at his teacher's feet and curled his knees to his chest securing them with his arms. Lucius stood solidly beside Wainwright and placed his hand protectively on his instructor's shoulder. Wainwright was trying to look comfortable, but Grant could tell by Wainwright's tight lipped, locked-jaw expression that he was concerned with what might take place today.

"That poor excuse for a horse fell down in a muddy ditch—wasn't injured, thank the gods. That storm we had washed over the roads, and they're a mess. Tell Thea to hurry with that food. We'll eat in the garden. Tell those slaves to get out of here. I haven't a clue what you mean by allowing Milos of Rome into our atrium."

Grant thought the fireworks were about to begin, and he had no intention of leaving Milos right now. Neither did Theodosus.

"Milos is a free man, Father."

"Yes, yes, I know, but he has no business in my house."

"He has every right to be in this house, Father, he's my lover."

"Oh, now that's supposed to please me, Helena? What's he doing here besides satisfying your enormous appetite for men?"

Grant grinned. But Lydia looked concerned. A quick look towards Wainwright reminded Grant that Marcus Flavius Anto- ious had just insulted his daughter in front of her sons.

"Thank Zeus I have one daughter with sense in her head. Come her, Lydia, my child, and kiss me."

She did as she was told and accepted the kiss on her cheek, and the squeeze that came with it.

"Milos is instructing the twins in gladiatorial skills."

The man looked somewhat impressed. "Really? I thought they would have outgrown that by this birthday. By the way, the hounds I promised are tied to a tree in the front of the house, and I suggest you look to their needs. Twin hounds," he said to Helena, "identical! It wasn't easy, but I found them in Rome."

Marcus stood up. "Thank you, Grandfather. We'll be back when the food is here."

"Ha! just like good healthy boys." He glanced at Wainwright. "My friend said that you were the best tutor in Greece and Rome combined."

Wainwright said, "Thank you. I do my best."

"These two look like gladiators," he said, pointing to Theodosus and Grant. "They look strong and healthy enough. Are you breeding them?"

"They are helping train Marcus and Lucius."

"Really? Nice. Just as long as Lydia keeps her hands out of all the silly sword play. Don't think I missed your performances while we ate our supper. 'I'm not hungry' was your reply whenever I asked why you weren't eating with Helena and the boys. You were playing with their swords at a man's game. Poor lost girl. My love."

It was obvious whom Daddy favored. Perhaps that would not last for long.

Lydia gave a nervous look towards Grant.

"But enough of that. We'll talk later. I'm famished."

The food was brought and Thea and the other slaves hastily set up tables and moved chairs so that they could eat in the garden. It was an enjoyable spot for the reunion because the day was lovely. Cool breezes now quieted the usual waves of summertime heat in Rome, and it struck Grant that it would be August back in New York. Time was passing far too quickly for him. He wanted to freeze it so that he could be with Lydia forever. Like Brigadoon, he could just go away with her to 'Forever Rome', live and love inside a special time vault, and never say farewell. An ache stretched across his chest. The trip was moving too swiftly.

They had a good meal of fish, fruit, and sweet bread. Of course, Lydia and Grant were not very hungry, so they stayed close to each other and tried not to look in love.

"Well, boys, what do you think of the dogs?"

"They are brave and...well...cute pups. We'll take good care of them. Thank you, Grandfather."

"And the household, Helena? Is it well?"

"I have kept things running smoothly, and Milos has helped me manage the slaves and the harvest. I couldn't have done that without him." She grabbed Milos's hand and Master Antonious noticed.

"Your mother loved the garden so much. And I loved her so much." As if he had a new thought he said, "Socrates, I would not have the boys miss their afternoon lessons. Take them inside. I'll call for a report on their progress later."

He wanted them out of the way for a reason, there was no

mistaking that.

"Helena, you need to take a husband again."

"I have a husband."

"No, I mean a man of position and power. You know you can't marry a slave free or no."

Helena's jaw tightened, and the timbre of her voice rose with anger. "I have no need of any man but Milos and with him will I stay."

"Don't take that tone with me, girl. You have a house, nay two, in Rome and can sell them and move here if you wish."

"You know how I love it here," she answered.

"As long as you get rid of Milos and the two gladiators."

"But the boys," she said her voice trembling with emotion.

"If you want them to learn these arts, take them back to Rome. They should be spending all their time studying and choosing their careers. You indulge them too much."

Milos spoke, "Helena is a good mother and loves her sons. How can it hurt them to learn how to fight? They may enter the military soon."

"I am sure you taught them many things that will be useful for them to know, and if you want them to continue in this, go back to Rome."

"Why the sudden change, Father?" Helena asked. "Why does it concern you if the boys are attentive to their studies and growing up to be fine men with the gladiators help? You have said often that education and physical exercise are meant to be taught together. Good for the body—good for the brain."

"Yes, well things have changed in my life too. I am seek- ing a position on the Senate."

"Why, Father?" said Lydia nervously. "We're so happy here in the country, and if you enter the Senate; you will need to go to Rome often, and we will miss you so."

"It's not that far to Rome, Lydia," he answered.

"I know but I hate it so."

"Well, you won't after I tell you the good news. I have an 'in' who can get me that seat in the Senate. That's why appearances are so important, Helena. No one must know that I allow my daughter to have a slave lover."

Lydia looked pale, and Grant was feeling nauseous.

"I am more than a lover to Helena; I am a husband.'

"Only in the bed not by marriage contract."

"I would have that done but she resists."

"And with good reason, Milos. A freed slave cannot marry a highborn woman of Rome. Especially now that her father might attain wealth and political advancement. She would be called a whore, and I a whore master by everyone in Rome. We have a grand reputation in society now. Helena has had two husbands and born two sons. She has done everything according to the standards of our empire to give herself credit in the people's eyes. She cannot parade her sons through the city streets with a husband/slave. I won't allow it. And since she is my heir, she has to listen to me."

"Not necessarily, Father." said Helena. "I have my own business, and Grant, one of the gladiators, was once a businessman who lost his wealth to treachery. I could continue or sell my two husbands' businesses and one house and have plenty to live on without your help."

"But you would ruin *our* reputation."

Helena's lips pressed together, and her forehead wrinkled with determination. She had learned much in the last few years and wouldn't let anyone order her around. "I will have my way in this. I will marry Milos of Rome, and you will not stop me."

"Then your inheritance is forsaken, and all goes to Lydia."

"I will not destroy my newfound happiness, nor that of my sons, to please your political ambitions. Milos, Theodosus, Grant, Diana, Thea, Socrates, and myself will leave this home at once. For all those are of *my* house, and I will not destroy my domestic contentment for your ill-founded goals. Why do you need to go to the Senate? Why can't we just live happily here at the villa where no eyes can see our business?"

"Because my fiancé wants me to have a high political standing."

Lydia could no longer hold back the tears. "Oh, Father. What about Mother? You said that you would never marry again so you could keep her alive forever in our home."

"I am a lonely man."

"Who will become lonelier if he alienates his daughters and his grandsons."

"I need a woman to bring laughter into my life."

"You said that the twins brought you all the joys you needed in this world," said Helena.

"I am growing old with no sons of my own. She may give me some yet. I grieve for your mother and Lydia's fine fiancé. Life is so very short, Helena, and this woman is young and beautiful and..."

"Wants a rich husband," said Lydia.

"Now don't you start, girl. I have no intention of marrying yet. There are many things to take care of first before that date. I need to have a Senate position, or she will not marry me. And I need both of my daughters in good domestic households with wealthy husbands."

"I do not wish to marry again. I'd rather join the cult of Isis before I'd marry for prestige instead of love," Helena declared.

Grant wanted to hug Helena for her courage for she was angering her father and close to pushing the button that could get them all sold into slavery or disinherited.

"Then leave immediately; that will rid my house of many useless slaves too."

Lydia spoke, "You are wrong to do this, Father. This house has been so much happier since Helena, the boys, and the new slaves have come."

"Don't worry, Lydia, let her go. I have good news for you as well."

Grant's heart stopped in his chest.

"The man who wants to help me into this Senate seat has agreed to take you as his wife even though you were once pledged to another and are quite old."

"I have no need of a husband."

"Now don't you anger me as well. Cranus Tiberian Julian Seira."

"Is an old man."

"And a good catch."

"He's never been married before; he's forty some years old; and I've heard he takes male lovers," interjected Helena.

"Hearsay. He has agreed to get me a seat in the Senate with a signed contract of marriage to Lydia."

"I won't. I won't!" she screamed. "You can't make me marry a man I don't love."

"And one who may never give her the joy of children either," said Helena.

"You must have known this was coming, girl. We talked about you marrying and having a family before I left."

"I won't marry a man I don't love."

"You have no choice; you best do as I say."

"I can live with Helena and the boys. Since you have obviously lost your mind over this younger woman, no one will ever think poorly of me for leaving you."

"You will not do that, Lydia."

"And why not."

"Because you have no husband and no babies. You have no house of your own should something happen to Helena. And if you anger me, no way of surviving should this new wife bring me children. This man has so much money; he could buy me three times over. As you have already stated, he is very old. You would be taken care of forever should anything happen to me, him, or Helena."

"Then I will run away and be poor for the rest of my life." Lydia seemed to be heading for the rocky cliffs now and about to topple over her emotions.

"You don't mean that, Lydia, you've such a good life. Why would you want to throw it away?"

She hardly hesitated before she said, "I love another."

"Who?"

"I will not mention..."

"Oh, you don't need to. I've been watching the two of you as you've tried to look uninterested in each other. Just like your sister. I don't blame you; he's younger and far more handsome than any husband I could find for you. But it's over, Lydia. You will go to Rome tomorrow and meet your new husband."

"I will not! I will go with Grant and Helena, if she'll have me."

"Don't anger me. You will not embarrass me with my friend."

"You have lost your head to this woman and think only of yourself. How could you arrange such a contract with this man before asking me?"

"You were crying and grieving so for your lost fiancé that I thought it would bring you such joy in having a husband and some babies to love. He won't be home much, and the children will be such a blessing."

"If he ever makes love to her," said Helena.

Marcus Flavius scowled at his oldest.

Lydia hugged him and begged him, "Don't make me so unhappy, Father."

"I go and arrange a marriage between my beloved daughter and the richest man in Rome, and she falls in love with a slave from some ludus."

"I love, Grant, and he makes me happier than I have ever been in my whole life."

"Well, then I am sorry for that, Lydia. You know you cannot marry a slave, and have no choice but to marry a man who will keep you secure for the rest of your life. Do as your father says."

"I would rather be crucified!"

Grant moved to her side in a show of support. The waves of the sea were stirring from the storm.

Marcus Flavius's lips tightened in a grimace, and his eyes became sharp daggers. "Something I can arrange for your lover if you do not obey me."

"You are *not* my father!" she screamed.

"The prenuptial agreement was signed before I left for home."

"No!"

"You will inherit all the man has when he dies, and I have already told him how wealthy you will be upon my death. He's waiting for you to return with me. He is anticipating a grand feast that will encompass many community activities such as chariot races—he owns his own stable—and gladiatorial combats in honor of his long-awaited marriage. He's had no wife before you. The day you wed him, I will be accepted into the Senate. After that, my own lady and I will wed."

"Grant belongs to Helena's household; you cannot threaten him."

"I have friends who can pay high officials, and if you want to see your lover bleeding from a cross, or thrown into an arena for the amusement of your fiance''s friends, I suggest you pack for Rome now."

"If you hurt him..."

"None of that has to happen, child. Come now, Lydia, you must have known that sooner or later you would have to marry and have children. I understand your having this little infatuation, but it's over."

"I'm in love with Grant."

"Don't be ridiculous, Lydia, he's a slave. You could never marry him anyway. Now I have one daughter who has disgraced me, must I have another. Shall I rid the world of both of you and start fresh?"

Lydia said, "This woman is the daughter of evil who has so mesmerized you that you would hurt the daughters you hold so dear. You love those grandsons of yours as if they were your own sons. You have no need of any others. This house, a fine and noble tribute to love with my mother, has been filled with joy while Grant and

Theodosus, Diana and Milos brought smiles and wiped away our tears."

"But I need a little happiness as well, Lydia. And Claudia, an intelligent woman like Helena, and a beautiful woman like you and your mother, wishes to give me some life healing joy. Besides..."

"I don't want to hear about Claudia," said Lydia.

"The physician I saw in Rome has told me that I shall not have many more days on this earth."

"What?" said his daughter, her voice showing obvious concern.

"I had a small attack, nothing serious, and I didn't want to tell you about it, but this argument has made me weary, and I fear another attack. The physician thinks that marriage would heal me, that healthy exercise—the sort a young woman might give me—would allow me to live longer."

"Father!"

"So I won't be around much longer, Lydia. I need to know that you are safe. I don't want to hurt your lover, but you must obey me, or I will have no choice but to have Grant arrested and killed. Let us have no further words on the subject. You were foolish to allow yourself this delusion. Cruel to let Grant believe anything would come of it."

"May I speak?" said Grant.

"No, you may not. Leave me now, both of you, I am weary and wish to rest from my travels. Follow your mistress to Rome. Helena is packing. Go and help her. You do not belong with my daughter despite what she has told you."

"Who will run the estate now that Helena is going?"

"There are slaves I can trust to handle the harvest. I will not be gone long. Claudia and I will return eventually."

The tone of Lydia's voiced turned cold. "I would rather see this house in flames than to have another woman lie in my mother's bed."

Master Antonious rose from his chair and slapped his daughter's cheek making it turn bright red. She held back her tears and soothed her face. "How dare you speak so to me."

"I speak so to my father who has died and whose spirit abides in my heart still. But for this demon who has come back from Rome, who calls himself my father, I will say nothing more save this...for Grant's life, I will marry this man, not for you; for you are not worthy of the title father, and so I shall never speak to you again for as long as I live."

"Lydia! Love!"

It was too late. Lydia had turned her back on him forever.

Chapter Twenty-Three

Wainwright intercepted Grant's rush to catch Lydia as she fled in tears to her room.

"I have to go to her. What a total bastard!" Grant exclaimed.

Wainwright stopped him and turned him around to face him, and so that he could see his expression and hear his muffled voice. "Okay, I understand, he's probably having some sort of mid-Roman life crisis; but before you speak with her, you need to think. Her future not yours depends on it."

Grant stared at Wainwright. "What do you mean? I wouldn't hurt her for the world."

"You might have already done that."

"How?"

"She would not have carried on to quite such a traumatic degree if you weren't in the picture. I mean about marrying the dork. What I'm saying is that she wouldn't have wanted to marry him, but she might not have gone ballistic about the idea as she just did."

Grant stood quietly and listened to the time traveler.

Wainwright continued, "You will be leaving her soon. Very soon by my calculations. Only a month and say a week from now, the equinox will hit."

"But you said there were ways to come back."

"Yes, I did, and there are. But before you get everyone crucified, disinherited, and thrown into the arena for hungry lions to eat as a midmorning snack; you need to acknowledge the fact that Lydia might be better off in her time period being with the old dork, who could leave her a rich widow when he dies thereby giving her a chance to have a new life...should you make the decision in your lifetime to stay in 2000 or to go to 1216 next solstice. You aren't thinking rationally right now, and I can appreciate all that. But, you need to be sure that what you are doing is for her best interests before you ruin her life forever with promises you can't keep. If you truly love her, then be selfless right now, and be sure you're thinking about her lifelong happiness not just how to have a satisfying conclusion to your summer romance—if that's all it is. And you may not even understand how you truly feel about her until you get back home and have a chance to think it over."

"You're a wise man, Wainwright, but..."

"Just think before you open your mouth."

"But, I do love her."

"And she loves you too, I'm sure."

"She shouldn't have to live a half-life with a man she detests."

"But this is Rome 200 A.D., and it's their custom to marry their daughters to men of prestige and wealth...not to slaves free or not as you have just witnessed with Milos and Helena."

Grant spied the statue of Venus. Her eyelids, turned away, looking at the water flowing from the jug, seemed disinterested in the lovers' plight. "I thought you were on our side," he whispered to the statue.

"What were you going to tell her?"

"To flee with me to Greece. We could go on that sailboat and get out of here."

"And she would either be abandoned in a boat without you come late September, left all alone in some city in Greece where she knows no one, with no money, and with no roof over her head to give her security. She'd be open to being attacked by thieves or pirates, or hunted down and disciplined by her father at a time when you would be nowhere to protect her...do you get the picture?"

"It's starting to come into focus."

"Lest I remind you that you are a slave in these parts. Do you want to test our time travel theory that you can't die in another time period unless it's your time to go in yours by facing a crucifixion?"

"Ah...no."

"Then think about all that before you place her in jeopardy. I care about her as much as I care about you, Grant. We are tourists, in essence, and the local time and location can be altered on a small scale if we mingle with it. You have touched her heart and sacrificed your own. Is this a summer fling that you'll get over when you get back behind your desk in New York, or is this the sort of love that hurdles all obstacles?"

"I understand. I might hurt her if I take her out of the life cycle that I have inadvertently altered with my visit and love for her."

"Hey, I'm not telling you what to do...I am advising you that's all."

"The woman of my heart has just had hers broken into tiny pieces. I have to go to her. I'll heed your words, Wain-wright, but I can't tell her that I'm cool with her marrying another man because I'll kill him if he touches her. And as far as that woman is concerned, a sailboat to anywhere would be better than a passport to unhappiness."

"Just making sure that's all. I feel somewhat responsible for what happens."

"You're a good man, Wainwright."

"We're here to experience the past not destroy families and risk our own lives as well as others for a whim. But, Grant, if Lydia is no whim, and you are sure of it with your whole being, then you can visit her twice a year and may even be a slot transfer. That would be the time to get her away from the dork and promise her the moon. Just be cautious about hurting her, making her father any angrier—say to the point of hurting Theodosus, Diana, Helena, the boys, and Thea. I am a Greek tutor who will still be here when I leave this shared space in time. I can't get Socrates into hot water with this family either."

"Have to go."

"Good luck."

Lydia was in Diana's arms, and they were both crying. Theodosus didn't seem to know what to do or say and stood quietly by the archway to the slave's room.

"Diana, you can't leave me. Oh, I shall be so utterly alone."

"I won't go with Helena; if you buy me from her I can stay with you, mistress."

"I wouldn't keep you from Theodosus. You have such a great chance at happiness together in Helena's townhouse."

"You could visit us. Or Cranus might die."

This only made Lydia cry more.

Grant said, "Leave us now."

Diana stared at him, and Lydia shook her head that it was all right to leave her with the man she loved. He sat beside her on the bed.

"I love you, Lydia..."

"And I can't live without you. Oh, how can Venus be so cruel as to tear us apart like this."

"I don't want to leave you either; I can't even imagine that man touching you."

"I'll kill him if he tries."

He held her in his arms and cuddled her close to his chest. "I could take you away from here."

"They would only hunt us down and crucify you for running away. We could never be happy like that."

"If we went to Narbonensis then to Aquitania...maybe all the way to Britannia..."

"Which would cause us to travel over the...the..."

"I know. The Alps Maritimae. But, surely, the emperor has roads through there by now."

She buried her head in his chest and sobbed.

"Think of something. I'm too upset to think straight."

He thought of Helena's surprise when he was no longer in the house at the end of September to teach the boys warfare, and how Theodosus and Milos would be shocked to see that he had gone without taking Lydia with him. What would they think of him then? Would she track him down? Maybe he should get Lydia out of Rome and in a safe place before he left. Far away from her father, sister, nephews, Diana, Thea. He sighed. Wainwright was right.

"Lydia, I am a slave. I want you to be my wife forever but how can that be? I have nothing. I don't even own myself."

"We'll escape."

"We are a tough pair of warriors, but are we tough enough to ward off the Roman army? I am sure your father and fiancé won't put up with me taking you away from Rome."

"You want me to love this man?"

"Of course not. I want you to love me with all your heart for the rest of your life." He took out the cameo from his waistband pouch. "I have this forever to keep you in my heart. But, I can never give you the life you can have with him." That phrase had meanings on several levels. "As long as we both shall live, love, we have each other in our hearts and minds and souls. He can't own your heart, Lydia, for you have promised it to me."

"Yes, and no other woman can take me from your heart either."

He suddenly saw the truth in her comment. No other woman would ever match Lydia on any plane. "I will never have another woman in my life, Lydia. I will be celibate rather than let another touch me." He meant it too.

"I cannot make such a promise, Grant. He will expect me to

have babies."

"I know." He hugged her tighter and kissed her. "It is a cruel fate that brings us together to have such brief joy and then tosses it away so easily. I am yours, Lydia, for the rest of my life."

"And I am yours. Those are the only marriage vows we need make. We can't change our circumstance, but we can hold onto our love for eternity. You have my cameo which is my gift of everlasting love to you."

"I have nothing to give you."

"You don't have to give me anything but this..." she said and kissed him. "For I am *your* slave forever. We are married in the eyes of the goddess who respects the commitment of our hearts over a contract made by men. You are the man I chose to be my husband; you must know that." She looked into his eyes and held his face between her open palms. "You were my first time. That special, sweet moment only a husband should share with his wife on their wedding night. In Venus's eyes, we are one in spirit."

"I'll take your portrait with me to the end of all time."

"More than that, love. You take my heart. It has flown from my chest and resides in yours forever."

"Lydia," he cried. "I love you so. You've changed my life. I'm not the same man I was two months ago. Believe it!"

Grant's heart was broken. That tender, wonderful ache in his chest that he'd come to know as his newfound sense of compassion; that tickle of affection he'd never felt before he traveled to 200 A.D. was gone. His smile faded. Tears streamed from his eyes and settled on his cheeks and lips. "I can't live without you."

Lydia entwined her arms around his neck and cradled him against her body. *"Never leave me!"*

He took her into his arms and embraced her. Would it be the last time?

Chapter Twenty-Four

The household of Marcus Flavius Antonious was gradually dismantled in the next few days. The warm domestic happiness that had surrounded it before the businessman/farmer/would-be senator came home from his adventures in Rome was being stripped away with each bundle laid upon the caravans. Helena spoke with her sister insisting that Lydia disobey their father and come to live with them. Lydia, holding back her tears as well as her pride, reminded her that their father's wrath could endanger everyone's safety. Sadly, Lydia did not have the ability to make the same bold choice that her sister had.

Helena had inherited a business, property, and a great amount of wealth from her deceased husbands, but Lydia could not live as an orphan if her father disowned her, and a husband was necessary for the young woman if their father intended to marry again.

Theodosus and Grant helped the twins pack. The boys said little; they knew how heartbroken Grant was, and there was nothing anyone could say that would soothe him. Wainwright and Thea worked to the end of exhaustion to get the manuscripts and their few personal items ready to be moved. Milos left Helena to take care of packing their belongings while he made the horses ready for their one day ride to Rome. Helena's servants readied their caravan, and Diana helped Lydia pack hers. Because wealthy Romans shifted constantly between houses, and they didn't have much that would travel with them anyway, moving day proceeded expeditiously—exactly as the father of the house wanted it to.

"You will ride with us to Rome?" Grant asked Lydia.

She couldn't make eye contact with Grant. "My father will take me to my new husband after Helena and the boys have departed. His new slave, Printax, gives me his messages for I will not speak with him. Helena has told me that I can stay with her, but I hardly think she would like our father to make good his threat to crucify you and Milos. I'm sure he would find some miserable excuse to blame Theodosus, as well, for your actions. He's lost his mind."

"I'll work on a plan to save you."

She held his face between her hands and looked into his eyes. "How? There's nothing you can do. And even if you could, it will be too late for me." The meaning of those last seven words was obvious. Her new husband would have consummated their marriage before Grant could devise a rescue. The wealthiest man in Rome, save the emperor, would have the power to destroy Grant with one casual wave of his hand.

Helena had broken the rules of feminine decency by refusing to remarry a nobleman, and she could get away with it because she was as rich as her father. In the next few years, however, Helena would need to leave Rome for her indiscretion would eventually plummet her place in Roman society. Gladiators were all fine for sport and girlish crushes, but grown women did not marry them, even if they were free men. Not unless there was something mentally wrong with them. She would be given the same respect as a prostitute. Helena had loved a slave and brought him to her bed instead of marrying again and honoring herself and her family by bearing a third child. The social embarrassment was proving to be too much for their father and was no doubt his rationale for wedding a young woman of high social standing who was equal in age, if not younger, than his own daughter. Helena would either leave Rome, come to her senses by ridding herself of the ex-gladiator, or be conveniently disposed of. Her sons would lead the way to a new future for the Antonious family by making good marriage contracts—marrying girls in their proper social circle. Providing no one learned the truth about their true father.

Lydia's transgression of falling victim to amour with her tutor/slave could be forgiven as something stemming from her grief. They'd say that she was out of her mind with sorrow over the loss of her fiancé. She and Grant had loved far from the city's gossips. If she married this nobleman, no one would think ill of her father or learn of her actions. If her new husband, by legal contract, ever heard about her passion for her slave; Grant would be secretly assassinated or led to a long, slow, agonizing death by crucifixion on a trumped-up crime.

It was easy to have someone murdered in the Roman Empire. Any allegation could prove useful in sending a man, or woman, to death by fire, crucifixion, beheading before thousands of witnesses in the arena, or by being torn limb-from-limb by wild beasts for the noontime delight of the Roman citizens. To make the Romans cheer for someone's destruction, however, a good motive for the victim's death needed to be assigned to them by way of a proper crime. Any crime would do, but treason, religious infractions, and adultery were generally considered unsurpassed as reasons for execution. The horrific sacrifice of newly converted Christians, slaves, women, and small helpless children were the very oxygen that kept the fire of the Republic alive. Its flame would consume Lydia, Milos, Theodosus,

Diana, Thea, even Socrates, and Helena if its dark eye singled them out.   Grant felt like his hands were tied. Wainwright warned him to play the role as it was written and not act as he wished. The hero's task of rescuing the princess from the horrible ogre would result in the death of his new friends. Grant couldn't be that selfish. So it was Lydia's happiness alone that would be sacrificed to keep her sister, her nephews, and the slaves she'd grown such an affection for, alive. The equestrian families married their own. Their wives had to bear three children—one needed to be male—to remain virtuous in a society that allowed men to lie with prostitutes and to murder their wives if they too took lovers. Though Marcus Flavius had loved his beautiful wife, she was gone now; and she had left him with two wayward daughters and no son. Their father was inserting himself into the heart of city life now that his beloved wife was gone. He had a right to a new family with a new woman. He had a right to do what he willed with his headstrong daughters. He had the right to free or kill any slave he owned. Marcus Flavius Antonious was the only one in the family who had the right to do anything he wished with his bloodline.

That is why Grant could do nothing. That is why Helena ran away from the country villa she loved. It was why she would sell all she had and leave Rome as soon as she could, with her sons, Milos, the tutor, and the four slaves in tow. Lydia had nothing save a slave's oath of eternal love in her heart. It would

be something to cling to in the long hours, months, and years of imprisonment she would have to endure with a man she did not love, and who was old enough to be her father. Everyone in Rome would be told that Lydia had agreed to marry him with a full heart, because no one must ever know that she had given her virginity to a...slave.

The small caravan of disgruntled travelers left the villa with no word of farewell except to the slaves of whome they had grown fond and to Lydia. Grant took one last look at the woman he had spent a lifetime searching for, and, with thoughts as depressing as a man could have, rode the horse she had given him to Rome.

Theodosus and Diana watched Grant closely. Helena and Milos spoke in whispered voices so that Marcus and Lucius could not hear them. The boys looked forlorn as if they had no idea why their grandfather would treat any of them in this cruel manner. Wainwright looked at Thea and tried to soothe her sobbing with words of encouragement. It was beyond the travelers wisdom to make anyone feel better about leaving a happy home.

"He'll be sorry," said Helena loud enough for Grant to hear her. "When she leaves him flat for a younger man, and he has no one to comfort him in his old age; he'll be sorry. And I won't come to him then. He's thrown me out and crushed Lydia. I'll not forgive him for hurting my sister. She had awakened from her grief and was joyful again—smiling and obviously in love with the slave—and now she is lost."

Grant heard those words above the horses' hooves and focused on everything Helena said.

Milos squinted at the path ahead as his hushed words reached his lover's ears. "It doesn't have to be this way. We could start fresh elsewhere. We don't have to go back to Rome," said Milos.

"The boys have a future there."

"They have a future wherever they go. Do you want them to live a life like you and Lydia? Do you want them to fall in love with a woman of their own choosing only to be told they can't marry her."

"It is the only way for them to survive and be successful in Rome. All is Rome."

He turned in his saddle to look at her. "Not necessarily," he said.

"I will not lose you again," she said and patted his hand.

"I have no intention of leaving your side either. Or my sons."

"Hush then. They'll hear you."

"What if they do? I love them. They have learned so much in the last month about the art of fighting. I am very proud of them; I want the world to know that they are mine. I can't do that in Rome."

Helena's voice softened. "Where do you suppose we would go?"

"I'll ask Socrates; he might have a good idea. He's very smart about many strange and unusual things as well as maps."

"I'm glad he's with us. I was so afraid father would sell him."

Grant was astonished at her words. Sell Wainwright after he had just found him?

"Slaves! Buy and sell them like cattle. Helena, haven't you had enough of it? I gave you my heart. You never had to pay for my love. Why do you Romans insist on living in such terrible pain?"

"It isn't pain for the men."

"The Equestrian clan, no. But not all men live so richly, Helena, and I swear they will all perish for this evil."

"You are Roman."

"I was born in Rome as a slave of slaves. But, even as a free man who may own land, a business, and marry another...slave, I am not a citizen of Rome. I would burn the whole city if I had a chance."

Helena stopped her horse and looked at him. He slowed his steed so that he could look at her. "Do you honestly think there is a world that is not Rome where we could live?" she asked.

"The emperor is a brave conqueror but will go the way of all the rest. Sooner or later, men will not allow this Roman world to rule. There are many slaves who would revolt against the empire."

"And how would they succeed?"

"Attack the heart of the Roman Empire—its city. Burn it to the ground. Septimius is never home. The Senate can do nothing; they are old men."

Helena kicked her horse into movement. "We would have nothing, Milos. No house, no money, no security."

"On the contrary, love, we would have the world. For you and me and the boys...Theodosus, Diana, Grant, and Lydia. We would make a world all our own. One free to love, with no hatred, no violence. Pure and basic. It would be everything you   have always wanted."

"And that is?"

"A family. You lost that when your mother died, and your father began his grand ambitions."

"To risk our lives for that?"

"Yes, Helena. To be free to live the way you wish is worth everything."

"What would you do?"

"I would begin by freeing those gladiators who will die in the arena this week. The rest would follow."

"I am afraid. Something could happen to you."

"Helena, you love a free man—once a gladiator—who was destined to be carnage for sport in the grand arena. A fighter who knows only two things, how to fight and how to die. I had nothing to live for until you came along. I knew nothing about love and desire. I never dared to hope for a family, or a name, a house, or a family. I never felt real pride until the boys came along. I would risk my life for a free and good future for us all."

Milos turned in his saddle again to look at Grant. He smiled for he knew that Grant had heard all that he had just said. "And to see Lydia smile again."

"Let us not speak of this right now," Helena warned. "I will ponder your words, my love. I cannot bear to see my sister's heart broken like this."

"Do not ponder long. Lydia will be a bride very soon; your father will marry his young lady who might bear him sons who will inherit all he has; and very soon the boys will wed according to the dictates of society rather than their hearts. You know as well as I that it will happen if the grandsons of Marcus Flavius Antonious enter Roman society. You will have no choice but to play the part of the dutiful Roman mother. The whole world thinks your sons belong to a businessman who never touched you. Choose. Life with me. Or life in Rome."

"You would leave me?" she said.

"Do you honestly think I could watch the gladiators die in that arena without doing something about it?"

"What would I do?"

He turned in his saddle once more to look at her. "Wait."

"Well, I suppose I have waited twelve years to find you again," she said with a brave smile, "I don't suppose it will hurt to wait a little more."

"I will handle everything, Helena. I will do it for our sons and our future together. Rome will not allow you to stay with me, and you know that."

Milos rode ahead of the caravan, and the twins, anxious for a chance to race their horses and the dogs, followed him. Grant stared for a moment at the reins in his hands and then, for some odd reason, decided to turn in his saddle to regard Theodosus and Diana. Theodosus had heard and understood. His eyes were filled with the same bitterness and anger he had once worn on the road to Capua when he was chained to the man ahead of him. Theodosus had mastered enough Latin to comprehend sedition, and he was ready to kill for it.

As they traveled to Rome, Grant took note of the coastline whenever he could. He thought of Lydia and their wonderful days of lovemaking in the sunshine of their little cove. About noontime, when they were planning to stop and eat, he noticed a young woman, possibly a slave girl by the look of her clothes, standing on the shore. In her hands was a crying newborn whose hands reached into the air around it futilely searching for its mother. The slave girl tried to quiet the baby's wailing by rocking the child in her arms and singing. The bizarrity of the scene entranced Grant. The girl knelt down onto the sand, tightly wrapped the infant in its new blanket, and placed it in a small basket that had been sitting beside her on the sand. Then, weeping from the heart, she placed the tiny basket with the crying child into the sea. The water took the little bundle of screaming life away from the shore while the young woman watched forlornly, wiping tears from her cheeks. Diana suddenly stopped her horse to run to the beach and save the child, but Theodosus deterred her. "You must not prevent a slave's duty to her mistress," he said with true bitterness. "Better for the girl child to die now than suffer the same fate as Lydia."

The gentle waves enveloped the cradle, muffling the baby's cries, and the slave girl walked up the mountain side to her master's house.

Chapter Twenty-Five

Helena's home was not as spacious as the villa by the sea, but what it lacked in size, it more than made up for by the grandeur of its interior design. She had created two households in one by moving the rich decor of her first home into her second husband's estate. It was a city home rather like a townhouse by today's standards. Though the rooms were not large, the house had a second floor. Planning to live at her father's villa, Helena had sold many of her slaves before the move but not the house. She had no intention of giving up anything she owned unless she was sure her father wanted her to become the lady of *his* home which, based upon his recent actions, he obviously did not. Milos and Helena spoke quietly in her bedroom, and Grant watched for hopeful signs of the rebellion that would free Lydia from her loveless marriage. He loved Lydia, and he wanted her to have a wonderful life, but though he knew that he might not be a part of that life; he intended to do all that he could to rescue Lydia and the people he now called friends.

"I can't wait like this," he told Wainwright.

Wainwright seemed bitter for some reason. "You have no choice."

"I will just leave then and find her on my own. You can't stop me from doing all I can to save her. I was an idiot not to force her to follow me...anywhere. Why did I listen to you?"

Wainwright grabbed Grant's shoulder with both hands and spun him around so that he could look at him. "Because I was right, and you know it. Hindsight is always twenty-twenty, as they say; you can look back now and claim the hero's role for your imagination's sake without remembering the danger we were in."

"I can't stand the thought of her being unhappy."

"That's important."

Grant gave the time traveler a puzzled look. "What do you mean?"

"Sometimes separation shows us how much we really feel for someone. Maybe you needed to know that you couldn't live without her. Maybe that's part of all this."

"We've been apart for five days now. I can't sleep at night and think about her every minute of the day."

"Is it because she is with another man?"

Grant stared at his hands and wiped the dirt of the day's work from them. "No, Bruce, it's because I miss her. I miss all the things she said and did. Her imagination and her stories about pirates, ships, treasure. How free she was in that little cove of ours. How she stood on the boat and let the wind blow her hair around her face. And her smile. A pure and happy almost childlike smile of total joy and independence. And her insatiable need for me to touch her, to teach her, to love her. I would give my life for her."

Wainwright smiled. "Then find her, and while you're doing that, remind yourself about the risk you're taking. For both of you."

"I can't do this alone. Did you hear Milos and Helena while we were riding?"

"No, I couldn't quite make out what they were saying."

"We may be reliving the story of Spartacus soon. If we do, I get to be Tony Curtis."

"I don't think he was in Spartacus," said Wainwright. "I also might remind you of the climax of that story."

Grant grinned. "Will you be there for me if we have trouble?"

"I'm your tour guide. Your safety is my utmost concern, after all. Whatever you need me to do, I'll be there."

Grant looked away. "How long do we have?"

"Not long."

"Damn."

Milos and Helena had made some sort of decision and called Theodosus, Grant, Thea, and Diana into the atrium to discuss the plan to free the gladiators and Lydia. It was a complex plot and involved relaying messages to Lydia provided they found her. Speaking with the gladiators would be easy for a seasoned fighter like Milos. So, they told the boys little except that they should discover their aunt's new home. Like amateur detectives, the twins scrambled to help. They admitted not caring much for their grandfather's cruel plans. It took some searching on their part—and some chariot rides around the city—to find their Aunt Lydia in such a huge city like Rome, but find her they did. She was soon to be married to Cranus Tiberian Julian Seira and would live in his mountainside home near Rome.

"He has *so* much money, Mother, it would make you swoon to see they way he lives," said Marcus, munching on bread and figs while he told his tale.

Lucius remarked enviously, "He owns the Blues, Mother! The Blues mind you."

Even Milos gave a low whistle at that piece of information.

Lucius continued, "Empress Julia, herself, brings her sons to watch the chariot races and personally chooses *his* faction to praise. She sits beside him in his box, they say, which is an odd picture if you don't mind my saying so. Her sons wave blue banners and scream, 'Felix Populus Veneti!' They stay *all* day; they even watch the boring parade before the races."

Milos shook his head and said, "Sounds like Cranus wants to be more than a friend to his empress. Geta and Caracella must have grown since I left Rome."

"As old as Marcus and I, I should think," declared Marcus.

"Have you heard anything about the emperor?" asked their mother, apparently changing the subject but cautiously digging for more information that would make a difference to Milos's plan. For a mighty warrior/emperor home from the wars could silence their goals with his infamous army.

"It's said that he is returning; that he marches towards the city; and all of Rome is bursting with excitement save perhaps Cranus," ventured Lucius.

Wainwright noted his pupil's expression. "Why, Lucius, what have you noted?"

"It seems that Cranus is possibly the most important man in all of Rome right now. Julia seeks his wisdom on certain issues they say. He is Equestrian, of course, a businessman, and a senator. He really does have enough power to place grandfather in a senator's seat."

"Why hasn't he married Lydia? What's he waiting for?" asked Grant. The room went silent, and everyone stared at him. "Just wondering," he added.

Milos smiled. "Yes, Lucius, why hasn't he married Lydia? I should have thought that would have happened immediately."

"He's waiting for the Feast of Venus."

"But that's not for several weeks," said Helena.

Marcus spoke, "They say Cranus plans to celebrate for an entire week. He will be hosting chariot races and has invited some rather big names in the Equestrian world to gather there. He has also rented the Colosseum for an entire day of battle with some of the top names in the fighting world, and has even sent for wild animals for a hunt. He has sent personal invitations to everyone who's a name in society including grandfather and *his* new wife."

Helena cut him off, "You mean father has already married?"

Lucius answered, "Marcus thinks she looks younger than Aunt Lydia."

"Aunt Lydia remains quiet according to what the servants told us, is dutiful, but remains aloof to her fiancé. They say Cranus is only marrying her to silence the rumors that he wants Septimius dead so that he can take over Rome."

Helena said, "But what would happen to Julia, Geta, and Caracella if Cranus were the emperor?"

Milos said, "He charms her to win favor and a place by her side, then if something happens to Septimius, he would probably attempt the role of substitute emperor, benevolent stepfather, and provide solace to the new widow. For a while. Lydia would be in great danger should Cranus wish to marry Julia and rule Rome. He would divorce Aunt Lydia or simply have her killed. The lives of the emperor's sons would also be in peril. Caracella's age could be a big factor in Cranus's plans. He's older than his brother; and, if he has the mind and fight of his father, and thinks that Cranus had his father murdered—not to mention being upset that he has taken his mother as a wife, would defeat Cranus. If Cranus wished to begin a new regime, then he would kill Julia, Geta, and Caracella and have his new wife, Lydia, deified.

Playing fortuneteller is a difficult task."

"Nice work, boys," said Wainwright in the put-upon, aged, wizened voice of a sage.

"When is the actual wedding?" said Milos.

"The actual feast day, I guess."

Wainwright whispered to Grant, "September 26, 200 A.D. We may be gone."

"Even more reason to stop it. We can't be killed; Lydia and Septimius can."

"Does Septimius plan to be home in time for the feast?" asked Helena.

"Who knows? He sends runners with messages to the empress daily."

"He loves her so," said Helena.

Marcus interrupted. "I think Caracella and Geta are too young to rule, and Julia is, after all, just a woman, and though all of Rome speaks of her in the most glowing terms; she is no match for this Cranus should he decide to usurp Septimius's authority."

Milos laughed, "Septimius defines courage with his every move. From what I've heard in the barracks of the arena, he has spies all over the city to bring him news and to protect Julia and her sons. But, he has been gone from Rome too long."

"Surely his sons have learned how to fight...just like us," said Lucius.

Marcus said, "I could beat Geta. He looks sweet in the face."

"Are we going to rescue Aunt Lydia?" Lucius remarked suddenly.

Helena took a moment before saying, "Whatever gave you that idea?"

Marcus said, "He's been eavesdropping on the two of you, if you must know."

"That's a lie," retorted Lucius.

"No, it's not. We've heard a great deal. Did you plan to leave us out of it, Mother? *Father?*"

The sound of the word shocked the adults into silence.

"You know then?" said Milos.

"Do you think we are stupid? Mother's hand mirror showed us the proof even if you tried to hide it. We certainly don't look like Denius; he was so small and not very strong. Were you planning to keep it a secret? We've been guessing at the puzzle since we met you at the ludus."

"I thought it would...be better...for your future if..." said Helena. "We wanted to protect you from the knowledge that your father was a slave."

"That's funny. Marcus and I have wondered how we could be Denius's son for years.

"You're not angry?" said Milos vainly trying to hide his excitement.

The boys grinned. "We respect you above all other men. Why should we not be proud of a man who is the most famous gladiator of the past ten years?" said Marcus.

"You'll help us free Lydia?" said Wainwright, changing his thoughts about interfering with the past rather quickly.

"It is a dangerous undertaking?" cautioned Milos.

"Would you fight without us? Are we such poor fighters? Have we learned nothing at all in the past weeks? Are you suggesting that we are better to sing songs than conquer evil?" asked Marcus.

Milos hugged the boy and said, "I cannot think of anyone whom I would rather fight beside. Theodosus and Grant will be with us; we have already spoken of what we plan to do. We will need you to run messages to Lydia. She should not know a thing until it is time. She might give away her excitement."

"My sister is so emotional. If I go to her, Cranus might become overly suspicious, but if her darling nephews visit...and they mention how fond they are of chariots, horses, and how they are big fans of the Blues..." said Helena.

"They could calm her fears," said Grant. "Perfect. I am ready to fight, Milos. Use me in any way you wish."

"Then you will be Lydia's protector when the time comes."

"My life is hers," said Grant.

"Then we are of one mind now?" said Milos.

Grant shook his head and said, "And if the time comes, Milos, Cranus is mine!"

Milos placed his hand on Grant's shoulder. "He is yours. My word."

Chapter Twenty-Six

Marcus and Lucius conveyed messages to Lydia for two days, and Grant listened intently to all they told them about her condition and spirit. They didn't have much time. The races were the next day, and the games the day after that.

No one minded Milos volunteering his expertise in the training camp beside the Colosseum. The lanista welcomed an old comrade in arms. So, Milos spent much of his time 'teaching' the already conditioned gladiators some new techniques he said he'd learned from the ludus in Capua. No one seemed to hinder him, and he whispered the news of rebellion with each man until the news was spread all through the barracks. The break was to be on the day of the games.

Helena and Wainwright fussed over the real estate deal to sell the villa; the tutor proved useful in gaining the best price for Helena who also used his math skills to get the best price for her personal belongings as well. It would appear to the curious neighbors that Helena must have had enough of Rome, or that she was going back to take care of her father's estate while Antonious stayed in Rome to live there with his new wife. No one asked many questions because Helena had beautiful items for sale at a great price.

Grant and Theodosus exercised with the twins while Milos spent most of his time at the gladiator's training camp where he not only taught skill work to the hapless fighters, but plotted treason with them. Helena gave the two men money to purchase weapons. To make sure no one caught on, they 'spread the wealth' and shopped at several different locations around the hills of Rome. The twins accompanied them so that no one would be suspicious about slaves buying swords.

The empty house became the headquarters for the rebels. They would only be able to take what they could wear on their backs. Helena, Diana, and Thea shopped for warm wool pants, tunics, cloaks, and solid footwear for the entire army of slaves. The route through the mountains would be hard and long, and the weather would be dismal, and the temperature freezing before they were finished with their travels. The women decided that everyone would wear layers of clothing which might prove heavy at first but a lifesaver later.

To make sure that the citizens of Rome noticed nothing unusual, Helena decided to attend the festivities that honored Venus and her sister's marriage. She visited Lydia and her fiancé once before the holiday at the Circus Maximus and gave them a wedding gift—a beautiful wooden chest with gold brackets. The chest also had a false bottom that held traveling clothes and boots that Lydia would soon need. Helena revealed nothing about the plans or the secrets of the chest when she visited. It was Marcus and Lucius who confided to their aunt later that day that the chest had something hidden inside it that Lydia would need *before* she married Cranus.

Helena, her sons, and her slaves attended the parade that always started the day at the races. Though the boys grumbled that it was a "overrated attempt to place some sort of religious significance to a sport," Helena calmed them by telling them that Aunt Lydia would be on a special cart as she was the magistrate's fiancé and the reason for the huge expense. Grant was anxious to view everything...especially Lydia.

Carts similar to floats decorated with flowers and statues, some of which were guided by children, horses, dancers, priests, and consuls, assembled in a march that started at the Capitol, crossed to the Forum, passed the Vicus Tuscus and the Velabrum, and ended at the Circus Maximus. The lengthy route allowed everyone in Rome to participate in the adoration of the gods and goddesses; but more importantly, to view the hero of the races...the magistrate who had orchestrated the races to celebrate the Feast of Venus. Cranus, who rode in his own gilded chariot, was a small man of average height of—five feet-four inches—who weighed little more than one hundred and forty pounds and wore the exact same costume Grant had planned to wear himself on the trip to Rome—a purple toga. This one was embroidered with gold palm trim. In one hand, he held an ivory scepter. On the top of this staff was an eagle with its wings spread. A slave who stood behind him held a golden crown over Cranus's head.

"Doesn't think too much of himself, does he?" Grant mumbled to Wainwright. "So where's Lydia?"

"Patience," was Wainwright's whispered reply.

Young boys riding their horses or walking beside the chariot waved to the crowd who applauded them as the defenders of the Roman Empire. Then came the statues of the gods and goddesses, who were not easily recognizable as they all looked alike. Other statues, which were symbols rather than actual figures, were escorted by cart or litters to the Circus by priests. One chariot was driven by youths whose claim to fame was the simple fact that both their parents were alive. The busts of the emperors who had been deified, and certain women who had attained honor in Rome rode on a double-decker style chariot.

Troupes of musicians and dancers performed between the corteges, carts, and horses. One leader directed the dance troupes. The dancers were dressed in red tunics with garish sashes of many colors tied around their waists, and wore plumed hats to imitate Roman warriors. This group danced to the music of flutes and lyres, while the audience tossed rose petals and floral bouquets into the streets. Following them was a troupe of satyrs who comically parodied the first troupes' movements by gyrating their goat-skinned posteriors towards the crowd. Incense filled the air, and the priests who walked beside the carts tossed white powder into the crowd.

"Cocaine?" said Wainwright sneezing.

"I'm getting lightheaded," admitted Grant.

Then came Lydia's cart. Dressed like a goddess herself in a fine, pure white toga embroidered in gold, Lydia wore a small but impressive gold crown on her head. Her long dark hair was pulled into a hairstyle that duplicated the way Helena and the Empress of Rome wore theirs. Someone had placed dark liner on her eyes and red paint on her cheeks. Grant wanted to take a cloth and wipe the makeup from her perfect face the moment he saw it. It took away from her natural beauty. He wanted to pull the crown from her head, the heavy gold bracelets from her wrists, and the golden loop earring that were dangling almost to her shoulders from her ears, and let that long, lustrous hair of hers drop to her shoulders—the way it had when they had practiced warfare.

Everyone performing in the parade waved to the crowd and smiled at the passersby except Lydia who did not move from the grim charade. She did, however, spy Grant. The twinkle in her brown eyes and the crease in her pretty forehead, told him how much she still loved him, and how unhappy she was. She had not forgotten him, and he touched the cameo she'd given him, which he still carried in the pouch around his waist to remind himself of the girl he'd lost at the villa.

Grant heard Helena gasp, "They've turned her into a cheap statue. Look at my beautiful sister. Zeus curse the man!"

Just then the statue of Venus, that had been pulled on the cart behind Lydia's litter, began to shake. The head of the lovely goddess tilted its stone curls in Grant's direction.

Marcus cried, "She gives you a favor, Grantus."

"What do you mean?"

Lucius explained, "Whatever you wish for will be granted to you by the goddess whose feast we celebrate—Venus. It is believed that if any of the statues fall or weave in your direction for any number of reasons, that particular deity is telling you to make a wish, and that they will grant you your heart's desire."

Grant pulled from his pouch the portrait of Lydia and stared at it.

"Do you hear me, Venus? I wish to be with Lydia forever. Give me my heart's desire." After he had said the words, he felt a tinge of embarrassment.

"Silly," he thought. "A childish idea." But, Venus stopped shaking and seemed to smile at him...or at least he thought she did.

"The heat of the sun must be too much for me today," he thought to himself.

No horses faltered. No children dropped the reins of their carts. No statues fell or broke. Not one dancer tripped. No false notes were played on the instruments. The pompa, or parade, marched most of the morning down the streets of Rome in perfect precision and without a hitch. It was an omen, but neither Grant nor Wainwright understood that this was an important sign from the goddess.

Helena had reserved seats. As an aristocrat, she could afford top priority box seats close to the empress who sat with her two sons near Cranus and Lydia.

Grant took everything in and whispered to Wainwright quietly behind all the fanfare. For a moment, he forgot about Lydia and overthrowing the Roman Empire and became the time traveler once again with the unique ability to see 200 A.D. up close and personal. He smirked at the thought that the whole activity mirrored the Rose Bowl. "Mind giving me a lock on all this," said Grant to Wainwright.

"I'll do the best I can," said the historian.

"The procession of 'Mardi Gras floats' is coming onto the field through the oppidum—that arched gateway made of gray and pink granite surrounded by white marble over there. The parade will head passed the oval shaped racetrack which is two long tracks of sand angled on the side by those tiers. This place seats about 300,000 people if filled to capacity. The columned box positioned on two towers rests over the carceres where Cranus will sit since he probably has given himself the unique duty of naming himself president of the races. Kind of cute since he owns a faction; but, hey, it's his party."

"Like a press box?"

"I guess you could look at it that way. All important decisions about the race are made there, and the race begins when the president drops a white cloth called a mappa onto the sand."

Wainwright pointed as he spoke, "See the carceres? That's where the horses come from. The seats are arranged so that the privileged have the best box seats while the slaves sit far away from the track in rows of benches that have no marking to determine any particular seat. The slaves are just as excited as if they had the best seats in the house; though, because all of Rome comes to the races at the Circus Maximus. The household of Helena of Rome sits in the podium area which is reserved for the upper class. She had to have paid a pretty price to have all of us sit with her."

Grant noticed that the crowd was sitting so close together that if someone spilled a goblet of wine, it would fall on several heads. The good citizens of Rome seemed to be enjoying this closeness as he noted several persons fondling one another's erogenous zones in clear view of anyone who might be interested in watching...which they weren't.

"What's up with the fondling stuff?" he asked.

"Oh, this is an excellent place to pick up women. A lot of these folks could care less about who wins the race, but they have to be 'seen' so to speak; and, of course, there's always the chance that you might get laid. A meaningful wink, a seductive nod, and one could leave the area and hurry down to a local town- house a friend might own near the Circus and have some fun...be back before the end of the game...who would know?"

"Sweet."

"The arena is made of wood. See the booths over there?"

"I noticed. What's going on there? They selling hot dogs and beer?"

"Not exactly. Merchants set up booths on race day and sell," he stopped to chuckle, "souvenir items such as red, white, blue, and green banners; there are prostitutes selling their wares; and those in the weird clothes are astrologers who are doing good business selling 'tips' to any person wanting to bet on a faction. The stables are behind the arena, but I don't know whether you can see all that from here."

"The statues? What gods do they represent?"

"Well, the beige one placed on the altar in the center of the arena is obviously Venus whose feast, or holiday, we're celebrating. The one on this end is Ceres, the god of grain; and the one on the other end is Consus, the god of, well, Hell."

"We're celebrating Satan?"

"The god Consus rules over the races at the Circus Maximus because it was built on a mundus. The Romans believe that there are little mundus, or ah...mundi... tiny portals all over the world that open occasionally to allow the dead to communicate with us. Consus opens the portals three times a year and the dead get to come out of Hell and mingle with the living."

Grant interrupted, "Portals, Bruce?'

Wainwright smiled and looked at Grant. "Yeah, little portals all over the ...world. Just a coincidence? They believed it as far back as Rome—before Christ's birth."

Grant shook his head. "Why didn't I let you do my research for me? You know more than that professor I paid all that money to."

"I offered."

"I know."

"You didn't know me and was unaware of how extensive my research has been. My father and I did a great deal before he died, and I have followed his tradition of scientific investigation. By the way, you're the first person I've ever told that to."

"Our secret?"

"Please. The god who watches over the gladiatorial games is Saturn. So it's a big deal for them to make this valley, that holds an all-powerful mundus, into a place for racing horses."

"This isn't as cruel as the ...games?"

"Oh, no, this should be quite exciting. They train the horses for this sport for years before they're allowed to run. The men who drive the chariots are trained in a ludus sort of place just like the gladiators are trained for combat. Only the very wealthy have the cash to support a faction. The colors by the way are important. People will root for their favorite, but it is considered unwise to root too vigorously against the emperor's color. Since the emperor is sort of out-of-town, the races will be more evenly divided which should make them more interesting to watch. Of course, the president of the games just happens to own the finest color in all of Rome—the favored Blues. The Blues have ruled at the games for years. The people will go nuts in a few minutes. Did you see the Latin graffiti on the walls along the streets?"

"So that's what 'Up with the Blues' meant. I wondered."

Lydia was smiling at the empress and her sons and chatting amicably with a woman obviously lonely and in need of a friend. She looked Grant's way. A sign passed between them, but just about the time he was beginning to understand the signal, Cranus handed her a goblet of wine and kissed her cheek. Grant's fingers tightened into a ball.

Wainwright took out a banner that he'd hidden under his palla.

"So," said Grant, "we should..."

"Root, root, root for the Blue team!"

Grant took a blue banner that Marcus had given him— that he'd folded into the tiniest ball he could then rolled into his belt—and waved it towards the field. "If they don't win, it's a shame..." he sang.

Grant nudged Wainwright and whispered, "Will there be someone coming by soon with popcorn, nachos, hot dogs, peanuts, and 'beer-here'?"

"Nah!" Wainwright said and then tilted his head to give his friend a secret smile. "They do that at the Colosseum!"

The two time travelers laughed, and Helena gave them a stern look.

The Circus Maximus looked like a Rose Bowl half-time show at this very moment. The carts stopped and were placed into specific positions so that it looked like little altars all around the hemisphere base, the spina, which divided the racetrack lengthwise but stopped by the edge of the sand so that the chariots could make good turns. In the center of the spina was a stand that held seven wooden eggs parallel to seven wooden dolphins—who spouted water into a basin. There was a ladder close to the stand.

"What's the ladder for?" asked Grant.

"Oh, when a lap is concluded, an egg is taken away and a dolphin's position changed so that the drivers and the spectators can determine what lap it is."

"Like a scoreboard?"

"Trust me, when this thing gets going, you won't know 'who's on first' so to speak. See the men down there. No, there, see the four men in the white, blue, green, and red outfits?"

"Yes, I see them now."

"Each missus, or round, will have four contestants. Those men are in the first missus."

Grant watched as four colored balls were tossed into a double-handled urn that had a rod going through it which connected it to two uprights. The urn was overturned. Below the urn were four bowls, and the colored balls plopped one at a time into a bowl.

"The ball in the first bowl will get the inside track, or the spot by the rails. An enviable position, indeed," said Wainwright.

"The worse spot would be the lane by the stands that has a more dangerous turn?"

"Exactly."

The drivers went to their chariots pulled by—for this particular race—four horses, and drove their horses to the carcer, or horse-box that was immediately closed by a gate once the horses and chariots were secure. The horses pawed at the ground, whinnied with excitement, and stamped with beastly impatience. They were more than ready for the race, and the drivers had a chore in keeping them still.

"Are they going to play 'My Old Kentucky Home'?" asked Grant, and Wainwright smiled. "Enjoying your trip, Grant?"

"Right now, it's pretty damn exciting!"

Just then Cranus stood holding the white mappa.

Lucius sighed, "*Finally!*"

Marcus agreed with, "Why do they make us sit through that idiotic parade to get to this?"

All speaking and cheering stopped.

"There will be twelve races today," Cranus proclaimed.

Grant's smile faded. "Twelve?"

"A day at the races, Grant."

Then Wainwright looked over at Helena and said, "Probably won't stay for the whole program. Helena looks bored already although she *is* enjoying some polite conversation with Empress Julia and Lydia."

Cranus continued, "They will be dedicated to the goddess Venus whose likeness we do honor on the center altar. She has given me a wonderful gift. My soon-to-be wife, Lydia of the House of Marcus Flavius Antonious, who sits beside me with his new wife, Claudia."

Grant hadn't noticed Lydia's father before, and when Marcus stood to be recognized, Grant could just barely make him out.

"Tomorrow, I ask all of you to join me in the Colosseum for a day of great entertainment."

Theodosus, who was sitting next to Diana, gave an audible grunt of disapproval. "And the death of many men!" he said. Diana nudged him to be quiet.

"We will begin with a hunt followed by the battles of fifty or more gladiators—the finest Rome has to offer."

The crowd cheered, and Cranus waved for them to be still. "When the sun is at its highest point in the sky, I will wed my beloved bride before her father, our Empress, Julia, and her sons, as well as all of my good friends in Rome. A joyous event, to be sure. As a special gift to Saturn and Venus, forty nonbelievers will be offered to the great, wild beasts that I have specifically ordered from Africa for this occasion."

The crowd went wild with excitement; the horses almost burst from their posts at the tumultuous clamor.

"May Venus and Saturn honor my new wife with immediate

fertility." Cranus motioned that Lydia should stand beside him. The audience applauded. Then Cranus kissed Lydia's hand, and she tried to smile for the crowd's sake but she nervously looked towards Grant whose jaw was locked and rigid.

"The man is dead!" said Grant.

"Take it easy. All in good time," said Wainwright.

"By nonbelievers I assume he means Christians."

"Of course," said Wainwright who turned suddenly pale after the remark.

"Where's Thea?" Wainwright asked too loudly.

"She was with us at the parade, why?"

"She's a Christian. She told me in absolute secrecy back at the villa, and I've said nothing to anyone. I haven't seen her since we sat down."

Wainwright turned to Lucius. "Master Lucius, have you any idea where Thea went?"

"I haven't seen her since the stupid parade. She didn't take a seat with us. She wouldn't run away would she, Socrates?"

"No, Master Lucius, but she might have gone to one of 'those' meetings."

"She's a Christian?" asked Marcus who had overheard.

"It's her secret, and I promised not to tell anyone about it; but if Cranus plans on killing 'nonbelievers' he might be raiding that meeting right now."

"You have my permission to leave to find her. Do you know where she might have gone?" Marcus said.

Wainwright was more emotional than Grant had ever seen him. "She didn't tell me much, but I think I have a good idea where they are," he said, knowing where the history books would have placed the Christian meeting halls in Rome.

Marcus and Lucius exchanged a look. Then Marcus said, "Do you want us to go with you?"

"But you'll miss the races..."

"But *you* haven't learned how to fight."

Wainwright shook a worried head. "I would appreciate that, yes."

"We'll tell Mother that we'll return soon, but that we asked you to take us to the stables so that we could see the horses and talk to the drivers. Missing one or two races is no trouble, and she won't guess where we're really headed."

Wainwright said, "Normally I would not allow you to lie to your mother, but under the circumstances..."

"Do you want me to go with you?" asked Grant.

"Lydia will be frightened if we all leave. You keep an eye on her. I have all I need. The finest pupils a tutor could ever have."

Wainwright and the boys paused near Helena and Milos—who understood immediately that their words were a lie—did not detain them from leaving their seats.

Grant was alone, sitting beside Diana and Theodosus whose sour mood was not lifted by the dropping of the mappa, the opening of the gates, nor the excitement that would normally occur in anyone at the beginning of a race.

Grant whispered to Diana, "Thea may be in danger. She's left us to go to a ..."

"She follows the sign of the fish?"

"How did you know?"

"I caught her drawing the symbol of the fish in the sand one day. Haven't you noticed the small, silver, fish symbol she wears on the leather strap around her neck?"

As usual, Diana's curious eyes had examined every detail of the people she had met at the villa.

"She told me that she worshipped the Christian God and that man who was crucified. There are many believers in Rome. They meet in the burial caves not far from here. I'll bet that's where she is. She left about halfway through the parade. No one else noticed?"

"If there are so many who follow Christ, why do they still

persecute His followers?"

"Romans are allowed to honor many gods, to worship as diverse an array as they please, but they find the worship of *one* god, at the elimination of all Roman gods, to be treasonous. The Christian cult has been around a long time, and Cranus is a butcher to do such a thing in our modern world."

"They must be rounding up the nonbelievers right now for tomorrow's executions," said Grant.

Diana whispered something to Theodosus.

Theodosus turned to Grant. "We need act soon. No more wait. I tell Milos. Watch Diana. I follow twins. They no ready for big fight. Socrates no good fighter."

Diana and Grant gave each other a worried look and watched as Theodosus motioned to Milos that there was trouble, and that he would have to leave the Circus. Milos shook his head that he understood and whispered something to Helena who gave a pretend smile and a worried look towards the vacant seats where her sons had waved their blue banner only seconds before; then she smiled again as if nothing were more troublesome than the fact that the Blues had darted out of the blocks way too fast.

Grant watched Lydia who caught her sister's worried expression and then glanced Grant's way.

"I need to speak with Lydia. When and where, Diana?"

"The race looks bad for the Blues right now because they can't possibly hold this lead. But...it will be a long day. I'd pick the fifth race and the fifth lap. That should give Socrates, Theodosus, and the boys time to make their way through the city. No one on the streets now anyway. A good time to look for Thea."

"She might need a restroom break by then."

"What?" said Diana puzzled.

Grant stared at Lydia until she recognized that he had a message for her, then pointed to himself, then to her, and then to the street outside the nearest of the twelve gates. She shook her head that she understood that they were to meet there. Then he held up his right hand so that his fingers were extended, closed them once she saw them, and then opened his palm again. Five—five. She shook her head and resumed watching the race. Cranus was standing and screaming to his charioteer while pretending to pull on the horses' reins. A faction of Blue fans stood, and—taking their banners in their hands—waved their bodies and their banners of blue simultaneously to the left and then to the right while chanting, "Felix Populus Veneti!" In response to their group cheer, several priests, attending to the altars and who stood next to Consus's huge image, reached into large jars and threw white powder into the 'bleachers'. The ivory cloud cascaded like a veil over the happy but disgruntled Blue supporters.

Chapter Twenty-Seven

Out of four races, the Blues only won three, and one could see that Cranus was trying hard to conceal his ire. The fifth race would be close, and that was exactly what Grant wanted. He now understood the wisdom of Diana's words. When the fifth egg was dropped from the architrave, the race—which lasted seven laps—took on a grotesquely suspenseful hue. The horses' mouths spewed white foam from exhaustion, heat, and sweat. A cloud of dust and sand flew around and behind the chariots—the ones still in the game. The charioteers stood with one leg leaning to the back of the chariot, and the other leg's muscles stretched taut to hold tightly onto the reins while trying to direct the wheels. Not only did they have to make sure they didn't fall over at the turns, but they were forever turning around to see what was going on with their rivals behind them. One White charioteer deliberately, and at great personal risk to himself, drove his chariot directly into his opponent's wheels in an attempt to overturn his rival while not harming his horses. There were no rules in the Circus

Maximus. Win at all costs was their eternal slogan.

The crowd screamed at every turn that one of the factions was going too near the boundary mark, or wailed when one faction was smacking the face of an opponent with his leather whip, or trying to 'shipwreck' the faction they supported. After all, the small, fragile, wooden box used as a chariot could not survive much of an assault and would explode into dust after breaking its overheated axle. Splinters would fly, and the horses would fall head over heels into the sand. If the charioteer saw disaster, he would use his dagger to cut the reins that he had tied around his waist before the start of the race. This quick maneuver would save himself and the horses. If the reins were not cut fast enough, the poor driver was thrown headfirst before his own cart, and the horses would drag him around the arena. Many a tale was told of the driver who fell from his chariot when the post gates first opened, but his horses and his chariot went on to win the race. Coaches shouted instructions to the drivers from the sidelines cueing the driver to speed up or advance cautiously; and a 200 A.D. pit crew was always ready to aid their own faction when in need. If the 'shipwreck'—as the Romans called it—was simply a turned over but undamaged cart, and the horses could be easily pulled from the track, the contestant was hurriedly dragged from his chariot to safety. While the 'pit crew' resurrected the man's animals and cart, the driver was given a special drink made from the dung of a wild boar that was supposed to invigorate him. Thus restored, the driver would return to the race.

During the fourth lap, a Green faction driver was violently whipping a Blue contestant about the face with his horse whip, and Cranus was livid as were most of the Blue fans. Empress Julia simply smiled with her lips tightly held together as if she wanted to hide her teeth; but Caracella was beside himself with anger at the abuse of his favorite, and Geta cried for retribution. The three fans hardly noticed Lydia excusing herself from her box seat. She looked at Grant who left at the same time.

They were under the gate, in the shadows, when they met.

"Come over to a safe place," whispered Grant, and he   took her into a neglected tent that had been the booth of Uba Ten-aden, the mystic astrologer.

"I won't risk getting you into any trouble," said Grant.

"I don't care anymore," she said, grasping him in her arms and holding him so tightly he thought he might lose his senses.

"You miss me?" he asked with a smile.

"How could I not miss the man I love?" She pulled away from his body so that she could look at him.

"You look pretty in those clothes, Lydia," Grant said for lack of any other words. His throat was closed with emotion, and his tongue was swollen in his mouth. He was lucky to be able to say anything.

"I hate him! I hate these clothes. I hate everything about this charade. Get me out of here," she said.

"In good time. Hopefully before tomorrow night."

"You speak the truth? The twins told me some of your plans but not all," she said.

"Well, that's because you're so emotional and might get over excited..." he said unable to finish his sentence with her lips pressed against his. He gasped for air. "I missed you too. Oh, baby, did I ever," he said and pulled her into his arms.

"I'm supposed to marry him tomorrow...and he's going to kill innocent people because of..."

"I know all about that. We have others to be concerned about as well as ourselves. Thea has run off to be with her Christian friends without realizing the danger. They're rounding up the 'nonbelievers' to be lunch for the wild beasts."

"Socrates?"

"Theodosus and Socrates and the boys have gone to find her. Socrates has a good idea where to look. Did you get the clothes Helena sent you?"

"Yes, but when do I wear them?"

"I'd say tomorrow would be a good idea. Say that you're cold and uncomfortable sitting at the Colosseum for so long in the wind or something."

"All right. Will we leave then?"

He looked at her for some time. "I sure hope so because I will kill that man if he touches you tomorrow night. Now, Lydia, you're going to have to be a good actress, and pretend you're happy for all our sakes. At some point tomorrow night, someone will come for you."

"Where are we going?"

"I think we'll be taking the high ground."

"Will we be going near the villa?"

"I would say there's a good chance we'll be close, why?"

"Because I have some gold pieces I'd like to take with me that might help later."

He smiled at her childlike fascination with her fairy tales. "Now, Lydia, there weren't any pirates around that cove."

She seemed astonished that he didn't believe her. "Yes, there were! My story was not imagined. I only hesitated telling you about them because I wasn't sure if you would believe me and try to take the coins. They have Julius Caesar's image on them."

"Are you serious?"

"There's just enough to help out without being way to cumbersome to carry."

"Well all right, if you think you can carry them all the across the Alps."

"It will be just us, won't it?"

"I can say no more on that score. Look. You need to go back to your box before you're missed."

There was a loud, fanatical cheer. "The Blues must have won after all," he said. "Cranus will be looking for you."

"Do you still have my cameo?"

"I will never lose it."

She began to walk away cautiously, checking to see whether

there was anyone watching outside the booth, when he called her back.

"Lydia, wait!"

She looked back at him appearing to be puzzled by his words. His throat relaxed a bit so that he could whisper, "I love you! I've never said that to any woman before. You *are* my life now. May Venus watch over both of us."

He saw the tears in her eyes. "And I love you too," she said and was gone.

Bent over with emotion, Grant could hold back the anguish no more and allowed the tears to fall. More emotion than a lifetime of triumphs. More meaning than anything he'd ever dreamed he could achieve. A reason to live. A heart renewed by love and ready to break. He had found her and would have to leave her behind to return to New York. His head was twisted with ideas of freeing her and spinning with thoughts of how he might see her again before he left at the end of September. So much more than he bargained for when he had purchased his ticket for the solstice. More than he'd planned on gaining when he had purchased the fibulae and the purple toga. Friends to die   for. A woman to love. Lives to care about. And people who truly needed him, and who looked to him for support and comfort. Not admiring him for what he could *get* for them, but for whom he was, and what he stood for. Friendship. Love. Courage. Honor. Tenacity. Pride. He just had to stay with her. With all of them. He couldn't go back to New York and be who he was; he liked the man he'd become so much more.

As he was putting himself in the proper mind set to be the slave of Helena of Rome, the curtain in front of the booth flew open. Standing before Grant, was Cranus and two of his men.

"Yes, this is the slave who tried to rape my fiancé by luring her into this booth while she was stretching her legs between races. I saw him pull her in here."

"That's not true. I would never hurt Lydia."

"A gladiator by build, a slave by dress, and a perfect match for our finest fighter in the arena tomorrow. Seize him and take him to the barracks. Lock him into one of the cells lest he try to escape. He will make good show tomorrow at the games."

Cranus moved closer to Grant. "Win and you'll be given sailing passage from Rome; lose and you'll be given passage to the underworld. Take him."

The guards pulled Grant from the booth and 'escorted' him to the barracks that lay beneath the Roman Colosseum.

Chapter Twenty-Eight

Once again Grant Tyrell found himself a criminal of Rome and locked in a cell awaiting whatever fate Cranus administered. From what he had witnessed so far on the trip, he'd have to say that he had no hope of a reprieve. In the darkness and the peacefulness of the night, he wondered if she had fallen prey to Cranus's wrath. Had Cranus found them embracing? Was he the type of man who would hurt his lady as well as her lover? The man would not give the public a chance to whisper about the old man's foolishness in taking a young wife. That his new woman loved another and preferred him to her marriage contract. Far too embarrassing. Grant would have to fight his way out of the arena, and if possible, take Lydia, his friends, and Wainwright with him—if he were given a chance to win his freedom as Cranus had promised. He would have to fight to the death in the arena, and he would just have to win. Now all he had to do was find everyone else.

He heard mumblings, sighings, laughing, and crying in the barracks. Grant peered from the small opening in the door to see down the hallway. Torches burned brightly there, and he could smell soiled clothing, ointments, salves, oil, and sweat. A man laughed after he sighed with pleasure, and then there was a woman's giggle. Obviously, some gladiator was taking his 'take joy now for tomorrow we die' principle to a happy conclusion. One woman let out a wail of passion. Grant couldn't tell what the men were talking about in the other cell, but the crying and praying must be from the Christians who were gathered together in one massive holding cell.

A lion paced, grumbled disapproval at not being allowed any food, and panted from thirst. An elephant stomped in his cage. He could hear the thin legs and tiny feet of dozens of deer rustling in their pen. A tiger gave a low grumble of warning to anyone who came near his cage. Several rhinos banged against the door of their enclosure. He could hear someone sharpening a sword on stone. Another man hummed a song Grant had never heard before. The Christians picked up a 200 A.D. version of some hymn from an ancient time before the Roman Empire. All waiting. Most of the creatures understood that they were trapped and in danger; but only the humans realized that they were locked in for the night so that they could not escape from being tomorrow's entertainment.

Grant took a chance. "Hey, does anyone know the tutor, Socrates?"

A voice from the Christian holding cell called back. "Is that you, Grantus?"

"Thea? Socrates and the twins as well as Theodosus came to find you before you were taken from your church...ah...group meeting."

"He did?" she called back in Latin. "I never saw him. We were taken shortly after the parade. He came to find me? Oh, I hope he's all right."

"I don't know. I tried to speak with Lydia, but Cranus imprisoned me on a trumped up charge of rape."

"Oh, Grant, I have ruined all our plans."

Another voice called, "Is that you, Grantus? I am one who trained with you in Capua."

Grant couldn't recognize the voice, but the man had to be someone he had seen every morning at breakfast at the ludus.

"Yes, I am Grantus. Thracian warrior, Milos's pupil."

"Milos?" said another voice from a closer cell. "We are awaiting his call to arms."

"It will come soon. Say no more—the guards," warned another.

"Humph, I sharpen my blade to cut Roman throats. There are fifty Christians who will be slaughtered tomorrow, and we can do nothing until it is our turn."

"Thea?" cried Grant.

"I am not afraid; my Lord guides me to be with Him. My people are not afraid."

"Why did you run off like that, Thea?"

"My father lives here and hides in the tombs for fear of being discovered as a Christian priest."

"How did you ever end up at the villa, then?"

"Just because my father is a man of God does not mean that I am free from slavery. He earned his freedom over the course of many years of labor with Marcus Flavius Antonious; I have not. I thought I could see him and left Socrates when he was busy looking at the parade. I didn't plan on being very long and would have returned, but Cranus has plans for a grand sacrifice to please Venus so that she will give his wife a child. Poor Lydia. Her fate is worse than mine."

"Something will happen; Socrates will come for you."

"I would like to see him again, but understand that whatever is the will of God shall be my plight. Heaven awaits me. I will pray for you to escape." Her voice was calm, controlled, and completely void of fear.

"You're not afraid?" He tried to get as close to the opening as he could hear her miniature voice.

"No, are you? I saw the way you fought as a trainer at the villa. I seriously doubt that you shall lose tomorrow. Don't be afraid for me. Save Lydia. I go to a happy place where I will be free; where I will find love and peace. Lydia is the one who will be enslaved, and it is not a just fate for one who has been kind to others."

"I think Socrates is fond of you, Thea. He told me how much you mean to him."

"I did my best to please him. He cannot help it that his knowledge does not guide him towards the truth."

Grant waited to hear if another voice would call his name, but none did.

The creaking sound of gates opening, bread and water being dropped onto a filthy floor, and water splashing onto stones, was the cacophony that awakened Grant Tyrell from his relatively peaceful sleep. He'd had dreams that still haunted him in those early morning hours. Dreams of Lydia in danger, Wainwright being killed by slashing swords, and Theodosus on a cross. The nightmares swirled in his mind. How could he escape his fate? And where were the people whom he loved?

Chapter Twenty-Nine

All of Rome was anxious for the games to begin. They had
heard that there would be a hunt in the morning, the execution of many
Christians around noon, gladiatorial fights with experienced, reputable,
and seasoned veterans in the afternoon, and the trial by combat of a
slave accused of attempting to rape Cranus's chosen bride. The good
citizens of Rome, as well as many foreigners, flocked to the famous city.
Advertisements were placed along the roadsides. Rich man and
peasant alike searched in vain for lodging in the already crowded city.

They camped in tents on the streets and along the roadside—some of them being crushed and killed by the masses.

Merchants rejoiced. The games were good for business. They made their sales quickly, however, for once the spectacle in the arena began, no one was in the streets. The streets were silenced, and the only sound one could hear at all, was the occasional burst of applause made by the huge crowd. The audience bought a libelous numerarius—program—that displayed the names of the gladiators who would fight but did not tell the ticket holder who would fight whom. So, the spectators spent much of their time discussing who Cranus might have chosen to fight the champions. Naturally, they wanted to bet on the outcome of any and all combats and did so while the events of the day progressed.

The customer did not have to randomly select a seat either. They had a counter—or ticket—that told them which tier, row, and numbered seat, their 'tribe' would be that day. Some even told whether the spectator would be staying for just one particular show—one-day pass—or a multio-day—multi-day game pass. To make finding the reserved seat easier, the level was inscribed above the entrance way so that one did not stumble around the amphitheater all day trying to find the correct spot. If the audience member really got lost, there were ushers at the foot of the stairways to help them find their group and seat. In all, it would be a grand day, one no man—even if he were a slave—would miss.

In a shallow valley that had been drained by the Flavian architects, built upon the remains of what once was the Golden House of Nero, stood a four level, pure white stadium-style, egg shaped structure. It had been constructed with a careful blending of eighty columns created in Doric, Ionic, and Corinthian design. Open arcades dimmed the brilliance of the bright, white travertine brought seventeen miles from the quarries in Tiber for the creation of this structure that could seat over 60,000 people. The amphitheater was built on levels and looked like a giant, white wedding cake. Pillars, statues of gods and emperors decorated the windows of the edifice. Naturally, there was a podium just for the emperor, or whoever would be sponsoring the games, to sit. There was no bad seat in the house.

The audience was protected. The three-foot podium was surrounded by a solid wall that had a smooth surface that prevented any claws or feet to get a good foothold. Commodus, Emperor of Rome for only a short time, and who preceded Septimius Severus, had once enjoyed competing as a gladiator so much that he had a gate built in the wall surrounding his box and steps leading to it so that he could enter from his kingly throne and participate in the games. He always won—one way or another.

There were rollers on the floor of the arena that moved from time to time to keep the animals off-balance, and, just in case that was not a determent, a long net was strung over the top of the wall so that even the spriest cat could not spring onto the people.

The animals were let out of the cellar and into their cages by a pulley system that opened the doors of their cells. There were hidden traps around the arena floor that could be opened when it pleased the guards. Unable to turn back, the wild beasts sprang on anyone who was near the door.

The animals were starved half to death so that they would give a good performance. Those animals who seemed frightened by all the noise, or bewildered by the commotion, were encouraged to leave the cage: a man would set fire to hay and toss it into their cages, or toss a blazing dummy at them to entice them to chase it, or goad them with poles and sticks to anger them into combat. The animals would eventually rush into the arena where they would attack another animal for food or be killed by a hunter. Some animals were left alive to feast on condemned men and women, and some of the animals, such as the elephants, tigers, lions, and even bulls, were used to perform circus tricks. These tricks would range from kissing a tamer, to imitating the gladiators, dancing, or walking a tightrope. Everything to please a diverse crowd.

Two staircases were used for the audience to climb to their seats. Each tier was reserved for a special class of citizen ranging from a pedestal and seats surrounding it for the emperor and the senators, to front row seats for the knights, second row seats for the tribunes and citizens, faraway and high rows at the top of the amphitheater for the raggedly dressed poor, and a specially covered wooden section way at the very top for women.

Mixed between the statues and grandness of the pillars lurked gigolos, bald headed men with greasy hands heavily laden with gem covered rings and shiny, gold jewelry, wigged old gents, and those who dyed their hair blonde for fashion—their togas were white and their hearts coal black.

Half-veiled women came to the Colosseum in their own private litters that were drawn by muscle bound slaves. These ladies, whose hair had been intricately designed by several slaves who were clever at changing the lady's hair color from black to blonde, came from a variety of foreign lands. They were draped with expensive jewelry; their faces stained with more rouge than their cheeks could sensibly hold. Dressed in clothes made of the finest materials and patterns, these 'ladies' came for only two reasons—to see everyone and have everyone see them. Vulgarity of dress was not allowed, however, and the Colosseum, unlike the Circus Maximus, was not the place for an assignation.

Irregardless of their station or their fashion, their place in society, or their place on the tiers; everyone came for one thing—to see carnage. They brought food and wine and sometimes purchased refreshments from vendors. It was a long day, and they needed to eat while they were waiting for the next act. The steadfast Christians, the strong and handsome gladiators, as well as the noble and wild beasts of Africa, would be degraded, defiled, and led to their deaths so that these citizens of Rome might be properly entertained. Neither slave nor senator missed the hunts, the executions, or the man-to-man combats. They came expecting to see bold fighters, and beautiful creatures die in the most hideous style of execution the president of the games could direct.

When the sun rose high above the Colosseum, Grant and Thea were awakened by the sound of guards in the hallway. Show time was upon them. No one gave them food or water; there was little point in wasting it. Grant heard the Christians praying and tried to catch Thea's attention, but his focus was drawn to a voice that sounded like Cranus.

"Citizens of Rome, welcome! I have orchestrated these games for your amusement so that you may celebrate my happy wedding day."

"Some happy wedding day. Marry a woman who doesn't love you, and kill a bunch of innocent people," mumbled Grant.

One of the guards in the hall said, "Well! A gift to us from Cranus. Wine! I never thought I'd see you again. I thought you had been sold to a lanista in Capua. Look everyone. A gift from the president of the games."

"Free wine for all the people of Rome who enjoy this day with my beloved bride, Lydia, and myself," Grant heard Cranus say.

"So that's what's going on; Cranus is giving ten thousand people wine. He must have money. Probably watered-down wine, I'll bet," thought Grant to himself.

"We begin the festivities with a hunt. To our deified Empress Julia and her sons Caracella and Geta, we dedicate this hunt to you."

As if a hurricane had rushed through the halls, the pulleys were cranked to open the cage doors, and the animals ran wildly towards what they thought was freedom. They shrieked with a deafening sound of hunger and fear as they stampeded into the arena. The crowd applauded fiercely, and though Grant could not make out the action taking place; he could guess from the roaring and high-pitched cries, the odor of blood, and the cheers from the audience, that a wild show was being performed.

A guard came to open Grant's cell door. "We have to put you in another cell; the program has just been changed. You're on after the trained animals do their tricks."

Grant thought to himself, "Tough act to follow."

The guard took him down the suddenly quiet hallway. "Here's your gear," he said, handing Grant the familiar Thracian outfit, a sword, shield, and boots. "You'll fight the champion. My bet's on him. He's never lost in five years." He had a sinister smile on his face when he said, "And I have a feeling someone doesn't like you. I'd stay away from his sword tip if I were you."

Grant could see some of what was going on from a small window in the door of his holding cell. He was in awe at how many people actually sat in this huge arena. "Just like the Super Bowl," he said out loud.

He could see the men on horses charging after the helpless animals as one by one they tried to escape, or proudly fought back only to lose to the huntsman's spear. The arena was filled with movement and spectacle. When the whole spectacle was completed, the slaughtered animals were taken to the sides of the arena where, later, they would be auctioned for their meat.

One by one, the majestic beasts were brought from their cages. Happily, no one was planning on hunting them. It was time to demonstrate a different side of the wild creatures. Lions and tigers became docile at the hands of their trainers and performed to the delight of the Roman audience. Elephants accomplished incredible tricks and danced for the crowd who applauded.

Grant wondered where Lydia was sitting. He scanned what little of the Colosseum he could until he noticed the podium for the first time. Julia sat at the center of the podium surrounded by her sons. Cranus had dared to place himself at her side. Lydia sat next to him. He couldn't decipher her expression at first glance, but he could see that she was dressed in a heavy garment much like the one he had told her to wear. "Have some faith, girl. I'm not going to let this guy beat me."

The animals were led back to their cages. Cranus rose and spoke, "Ladies and gentlemen, citizens of Rome. In one hour I shall make this beautiful woman, Lydia, of the household of Marcus Flavius

Antonious, my wife. But, before I may do this, I must avenge her honor."

The crowd was silenced by his words.

"Yesterday, at the Circus Maximus, when Lydia went to find some refreshment, a criminal, who desired her beauty, tried to harm her. Luckily, I found her and saved her from this vicious and humiliating attack and apprehended the brute. He has been trained as a gladiator in a ludus in Capua. Before we allow the animals their meal of scheming Christians, we will pit Grantus Tyrellius, of the household of Helena of Rome, against a worthy opponent, Claudius of Verona."

There was a squeal of delight from the audience.

"This guy must be one of the favorites. Well, I guess they'll lose their money when I beat him."

Claudius, dressed in fine, Thracian attire, waltzed around the circumference of the Colosseum. Everyone shouted with delight. Especially the women.

Grant spoke with himself, "Okay, so he's a studmuffin in Thracian shorts. But in this corner, we have the giant dude from 2000 A.D., Grantus Tyrellius, who's seen more martial arts movies than you can sneeze at."

"This battle will be to the death. I have promised the criminal his freedom and safe passage out of Rome if he wins; but if he loses, Claudius shall execute him on the spot. His head will be my gift to my soon-to-be wife."

Grant saw Lydia slump in her seat. Grant could feel the adrenalin pumping into his blood. He was hungry from fasting and ready to kill anyone for Lydia's sake. He had no idea how he would fare after the combat, and he didn't care. "I am a time traveler, and you can't hurt me," he chanted to himself. "Right?" he said as the door to his cell opened. "Right!"

The Thracian opponent wasted no time in smashing his sword over Grant's head while Grant tried to make eye contact with Lydia. As soon as he hit the dirt, he was up. His whole focus was on his enemy.

The crowd went wild with excitement, and he assumed that they were not cheering the so-called rapist.

"I got to get a better PR man," Grant said and smiled, as he rushed the gladiator with five rapid-fire thrusts. The man stumbled. "Yeah, that's right. Come on, I'm ready for you, Mr. Known-World Class Pro!"

The man shook off his defeat quickly. He took his time, like a hunter might when he has a lion cornered. Not wasting the advantage, Grant hurled his shield into the man's mask, and pushed him backwards and onto his back, thus choking the air from his lungs.

The crowd turned. Suddenly, they were cheering for Grant. "The fans are fickle," he said to the surprised man. "But what the heck, come on up and let's spar."

He allowed the man to rise to his feet while he took the time to turn his face towards the crowd to find Lydia. He saw her. She looked anxious and frightened but hopeful. That was all the encouragement he needed.

"Oh, you think so, do you?" he said to the gladiator who had decided to sneak up on Grant while he was working the crowd. Grant spun around and smashed his knee into the man's face thus tossing him again to the ground. "Get that passport ready, Cranus, only make it for two, because the lass and your ass are mine when this is done."

The fighter stood up and swung his sword into Grant's stomach. The point of the sword scraped Grant, making contact, and cutting Grant.

"Ouch," he said while turning his torso away just in time to prevent a serious injury. He had a very small flesh wound, but it bled badly just the same, and could have been misconstrued as being worse than it was. The crowd loved it; this was true entertainment. Two worthy opponents, death, an angry fiancé, and the lady, all playing out in front of him.

"Sorry," said the gladiator.

The word stunned Grant. "What did you say?"

"I say sorry, Grantus, I no mean so close."

It was Theodosus. The Thracian helmet had completely masked his friend's face.

"What are you doing?"

"Cause 'diversion' Socrates say. Now shut up, and make people happy, yes? Fight close to Lydia."

Grant came in close, and the two fighters locked swords. They moved and swayed in and out and the crowd, guessing that they were in the final death throws screamed the name of the man they thought would be victorious.

"Talk to me," Grant gasped into Theodosus's ear.

"We take Lydia. Socrates make good plan. Look like you go down in front of Cranus and Lydia. Now."

Grant pulled away from Theodosus and went down hard. Theodosus leaped on top of him and pressed his sword to Grant's throat. "Marcus and Lucius are by Caracella and Geta. Hold them with daggers. Julia and Cranus no stop us. Helena has horses. Diana give guards bad wine. Makes them sleep. Milos free gladiators; Socrates free Christian. They need time. Many of us—more of them. Socrates's plan work good, or we all die."

Grant kicked Theodosus away and jumped into the air to escape his opponent, then he swirled around and placed his shield in front of himself and pointed his sword to Theodosus. "Then let's give them the show of their lives."

All eyes stared at the two fighters while thirty Christians filled carts with the hay used for the animals' bedding, and slowly moved those carts into the exit archways, thus blocking the two staircases and the one leading from the podium that Cranus and the empress's guards would utilize. Meanwhile, the slaves and gladiators were handed swords and daggers by Socrates as they exited their cells. They hurried to the exits and waited. Grant spied the boys who were just behind the two princes. No one was watching them or the stairways and exits. The drama to save a woman's honor by the handsome hero gladiator as he attempted to kill the evil but strong criminal was far too entertaining.

"Get close to Lydia. I win now."

"Hell too." Grant knocked Theodosus down. "Socrates needs time."

"Crowd get restless," said Theodosus. "Start to notice things. We work while animals fight in hunt."

"In that case, I take a dive." Grant rushed next to the podium, and Theodosus moved in for the kill. He pointed his sword towards Cranus.

"What are you waiting for? Kill him."

The sword pointing at the president was the signal to the rebels to make their move. Marcus and Lucius placed their swords into the backs of the emperor's sons, then placed daggers at the boys' throats, and Julia screamed with fear. Cranus made an attempt to move. "No move or the emperor's sons die. I kill you."

Grant rose, and the crowd began to boo. He moved to Lydia and motioned for her to come to him. She surprised him by pulling a sword from under the heavy clothes she had worn, and leveling her weapon in front of herself to make sure that no one came near her or tried to stop her from escaping.

"Grantus, go to trap door of animal cage," Theodosus said while staring only at his adversaries. One of the trap doors in the sand of the arena that had been used for a lion's sudden entrance, opened.

Lydia ran down the small flight of steps that led to the arena, turned to make sure the boys were all right and that no one was about to follow her, and ran to Grant through the gate in the wall. Grant took Lydia to the trapdoor. He turned to watch Theodosus. Suddenly, fire shot from every exit and the good citizens of Rome realized that they could not escape the circular arena. The two staircases were then ignited with four carts of burning hay. The twins took the boys hostage and pushed them down the stairway just before that cart was rolled in to block any escape from the podium or any attack from the guards.

Theodosus ran to the open door. "Quick. Run through the tunnel."

Lydia, Grant, and Theodosus smiled at Milos who pushed them aside just in time to allow every beast there was left alive in the pit of the Colosseum to rush passed them and onto the grounds. The animals had been starved so that they would be ravenous for Christian meat. Right now, the beasts could care less what brand of theological doctrine dinner observed. They would be frightened by the fire; Milos would stop a retreat to the cages by closing and locking the trap doors. Cowering at the center of the arena, the animals would wait for the fires to die down before running; the crowd would not venture into the arena to escape; and when the fires did dwindle, the guards would be sleeping and unable to secure the beasts.

Lydia hugged Grant tightly, and he held her so close to his chest that he could feel her heart pounding against his naked skin.

Milos stopped anymore affection between the two lovers by saying, "We don't have much time and miles to travel to the mountains before all of Rome is on the hunt for us. Helena and I will take the path to the mountains with the Christians and the slaves and gladiators. I doubt that we'll be pursued there. The twins will meet us later. They'll keep the princes hostage to make sure we get out of the city, then leave them where they can be found. They'll use their new chariot so they can make it to the road at the same time we do. Everything depends on timing. And we will not all go the same route. Socrates suggests we confuse our trail."

Socrates/Wainwright came around the corner of the cells with Thea in tow. They were both filthy and smiling.

Milos continued, "Socrates and Thea, Lydia, Theodosus, you, and Diana will head for the villa and the boat. Helena says you have gold there?"

"Yes," stammered Lydia

"Good, then you will have enough money to get a new start."

"We'll never see you or my sister again?" asked Lydia.

Milos showed pity. The girl had been through a great deal. "Who knows? We may all meet again," he said, hugging her.

"Enough talking," Milos shouted to all of them. "The fire and the beasts will only keep them at bay for so long. The guards will not sleep forever, eh, Diana? Let's go!"

Helena waited with the horses. She smiled at Lydia as the woman climbed onto Marcus's horse's back. "I love you, sister!" Lydia said.

"And I you, Lydia." Helena reached for Milo's hand, and then the former gladiator called to his people.

"*Follow me to freedom!*" he shouted.

While the fires burned wildly into the tiers of the Colosseum; the spectators begged for mercy; Julia cried for her sons; Cranus screamed empty threats of murderous revenge; a chariot with two boys, two horses, and two happy pups raced around the corner of a Roman street; five horses danced along the coast as they headed towards the sea; and Milos—with the love of his life by his side—led their new army of slaves, Christians, and gladiators over the mountains of Rome to freedom.

Chapter Thirty

Grant hugged Lydia protectively to his body as he raced their horse to the villa. Helena had purchased the horses weeks ago, choosing only thoroughbreds full of fire and energy. They would be at the villa in no time. A quick check to see whether anyone was following proved that Wainwright's plan had been foolproof. Grant made a mental note to compliment the time traveler when they made it back to New York. Something told him that the equinox would be coming very soon. It stood to reason that the feast of Venus would correspond to the natural heavenly change of the seasons.

The fast pace of their flight brought them to the villa in a matter of hours. While Lydia ran to retrieve her gold, the riders gave their steeds some food and water. They would have a short run to the ship.

Grant pulled Wainwright aside. "Nice job, Bruce, now how to we get out of this one?"

"We say goodbye to everyone at the ship. Tell them that we're going to ride on the road because the ship will be too heavy and unsafe if we are all on it. That you and I will meet them in Greece; that we'll 'cover their tracks' for them. Meet at Athens. That they should wait no more than ninety days before traveling from that spot, but that if they appear to be in danger they're to go south, and we'll catch up to them."

Grant fought back his tears. "But we won't, will we?"

Wainwright placed his hand on Grant's shoulder. "We won't know that for some time. If you don't go back in December, it will probably mean that you're a slot transfer and will be able to come to Lydia in June and stay forever. Of course, you will also never come back to your own time period then as well. If you do fly on the December solstice, then it will mean that you are only a general transfer, and that you can visit her twice a year if you wish. One way or another, friend, you can see her again. You'll have some time to think it over."

"But how will I know where she is or if she's safe?"

Wainwright smiled and pointed to the pouch at Grant's waist.

"Easy. You'll have the cameo with you. Just come to the cabin and hold onto that portrait of her, and if it's meant to be you'll go right to her—wherever that may be."

"And if I am a slot transfer, and go to be with her forever, and she's been killed or something; I can never go back home, can I?"

"The risk you'll have to take. I seriously doubt that a slot transfer, who's meant to stay and change time in another period of history, would have that happen to him or her."

Grant stared at Wainwright. "I said that I would die for her."

"If you mean it, then your choice is an easy one."

Lydia came back to him, her face blushing from the excitement, her hands filled with two bags of gold coins with Julius Caesar's face on them, and a smile that would eclipse the heavens.

He cupped her face in his hands. "Beauty, what I wouldn't do for you."

Lydia kissed the palm of his hand and smiled at him. "I love you," she said.

"And I you," he said truthfully.

"You swore that you would never leave me," she said, and Grant noted that it almost seemed as if she'd been eavesdropping on their conversation, but, of course, she couldn't have been.

"Venus has been kind to us," Lydia said.

"And she's going to have to keep up the good work."

Theodosus whistled. "No time for love now," he said grinning. "We go."

They took to their horses and headed for the familiar route to the coast. Wainwright told them the plan to leave them on their own. It didn't go over well at first, but Theodosus promised to take care of the women, and Lydia said that she could handle the sailboat by herself. Thea gave Wainwright a kiss and then handed him a small metal emblem of a fish. The one that she always wore around her neck. The little Christian's eyes welled with tears; she clung to Wainwright for a second before entering the boat.

"It was on a necklace that I wore around my neck, but the guards broke it when they took us. I managed to keep the symbol safe, and you will have to replace the tie. I might have died save for you. What a gift from God you are to me!"

Wainwright was amazed, and his cheeks burned beet red. He just stood there, unable to say anything, staring first at the fish and then at the girl.

Wainwright coughed. "Thea...I may never...I mean, I might not..."

She placed her hand on his lips. "Don't say another word. God will be with both of us. His love is forever. We will see each other again; I just know it."

With tears streaming down her cheeks, Thea headed away from Wainwright and down the hill to the boat.

Lydia hugged Grant and then kissed him. "I will keep the memory of our little cove, and the love we shared here forever in my heart. We must be together again, Grant. Promise."

Grant stared at Lydia, his brave warrior, who was fighting hard to keep her emotions in check so that he would not think of her as being frightened or overly sentimental.

"Nothing can keep us apart," he said, meaning every word of the phrase.

Theodosus gripped Grant's arm in a brotherly tribute to all they had been through to protect the women they loved. "Grantus, good friend," he said. "Never have one like you...again. You be safe. We meet in Athens, yes? Brother."

"Brother," Grant said softly, almost reverently. "Yeah, you keep practicing your New York too."

Theodosus took Diana into his arms. "All Theodosus need is here," he said, patting her rounded belly.

"You're...with child?'

"I told you she haute. Have family. Free family now. Yes?"

"You'd better get going. Socrates and I have to get out of here, or they'll follow the horses right to you, and you need to get some wind in your sails—get out to sea."

"We stay together, yes?"

"Forever, man!"

Theodosus motioned for the women to go ahead of him. The women worked their way to the beach; Lydia opened the sails of her father's ship; and Theodosus weighed anchor.

"I can't do this!" said Grant with tears filling his eyes so much that he had to blink them away so that he could see Lydia wave to him.

"Don't forget your promise!" she shouted as the waves pushed the boat far from the coast, and the wind tossed her hair around her beautiful face as it simultaneously filled the sails of the Athena.

Grant's heart felt like stone.

"We've got to get out of here," Wainwright said, trying to hide his sniffling as he pushed Thea's gift into a pouch he had secured around his waist with a leather tie.

"Could we maybe ride close to the coast for a while?"

"To keep an eye on them? Sure. By my calculations, we should actually hit the equinox in less than twelve hours."

"Home," Grant said and physically shuddered.

The two Roman slaves lifted themselves onto the backs of their steeds and rode at a gallop along the coastline. The two riders could see the white sails of the tiny boat from the tall cliffs along the way. At one point in the journey, they hid from the army of Septimius Severus marching home from a long campaign.

"Which one is he?" asked Grant.

"The one in the front with the tough looking uniform and the white horse.

"But he's...."

"Yeah, Equestrian—began the African dynasty and..."

"Dark skinned!"

"Ah...yeah," said Wainwright.

Grant turned his head so that he could look at his new friend.

"That's why they laughed at me."

"I would suppose."

"Me standing there in that purple toga saying that I was the mighty, warrior emperor. You knew all along, didn't you?"

"I assumed I was correct in my research, yes."

"Was I really that much of an asshole?"

"We call it a donkey vortex at Time Travelers, Inc."

Chapter Thirty-One

The two men from the year 2000 A. D. were sleeping, hidden from all eyes, between two cypress trees when the special blend of season and time turned them from the route just outside Capua on the western side, to a cabin in Richfield Springs. Neither traveler noted the exact time, but the sensation of falling and spinning was obvious.

Jim Cooper screamed, "Is Celeste with you?"

Wainwright seemed puzzled by the question. "Why?" Then he shook his head. "She's not with us."

"She disappeared at the same time you two did, only no one knew she was sleeping in the master bedroom, or that she would be caught up in the time tunnel," said Sam.

Grant said, "I'm home. Disoriented but home. Bruce?"

"What happened to him?" asked Sam said, examining Grant's blood soaked slave's attire.

"He'll be all right. Just a small cut. Get the first aid kit. If Celeste has left our time zone, then we need to worry about her right now."

"We can take care of her, Wainwright. You go ahead and take Grant to Trudy's so that he can unwind, and you can have a look at that wound. Take the truck."

Wainwright stared at his clothes. "Ah, we can't go dressed like this. Better change. Where are our clothes?"

"We put them in here so that if she did come back tonight, she wouldn't be bumping into two Romans from New York," declared Sam. "Did things not go so well, Wainwright?"

Wainwright grinned and said, "Better than expected." He helped Grant on with his clothes. The wound on Grant's stomach needed attention, but for now they had to get out of the cabin. Celeste would, hopefully, return soon, and she and Jim needed to be alone.

Grant was on the edge of a nervous breakdown. He was not adjusting well to the sudden shift from one time period to the other. Medically speaking, the man was in shock. During the drive home, he spoke about how he felt.

"It's important to speak about how you feel, Grant. I may not have experienced what you're going through, but I've watched others deal with it. It's better you talk."

Grant's hands were shaking uncontrollably. "I'm lost. I'm in my own time period, but I feel abandoned."

"That's a good start."

"I need to ride, run, drink, eat, fight, love...with them. I had friends. I had the love of my life right in my arms only a day ago. And now it's gone. They're gone. They're..."

Wainwright coughed. "Yes, they are and have been for a long time."

Grant covered his face with his hands and sobbed in disbelief. He held nothing back. "There is no point in being here, Bruce."

"Run with that thought."

"I have no purpose here."

"You're a very important businessman who runs a solid and profitable company that employs hundreds of faithful staff members whose very livelihood depends on you."

"I'm..." he spoke as his words spilled forth. "Cranus. Marcus Flavius Antonious."

Wainwright said nothing.

"They're me. I'm them."

"You once were."

"But not now."

"No."

"Lydia?"

"Not just Lydia. Theodosus was your friend who fought by your side. Thea taught us both about courage and faith. Diana taught you how loving, loyal, and gifted a person could be in helping others. Milos had the wisdom of the world. Helena a love that cracked Roman society. And two young men..." Wainwright allowed the tears to stream down his face, "...who only wanted to laugh, play, and who took such joy in learning and living." He wiped his eyes with the back of his hands. "God, I miss them. I miss Thea. Her eyes. I miss the way Marcus used to test my knowledge constantly, and how I felt when I watched that chariot race to the coastline and thought that they would be killed."

Grant was in his own world of thoughts. "The way Lydia's hair flew into the wind. Did you see the way it flew around her face when she waved to me from the Athena? Her innocence. Her courage. Her trust."

"I'm not the man I was," said Grant finally.

"Nor am I," said Wainwright. "Nor am I."

"I want to get very drunk!"

"It's too early in the morning for that."

"How do I deal with this pain? This terrible grief."

"It's part of the whole process, and in a few days, maybe weeks, you'll start to think straight again. Stay with me for a week before you go back to New York City."

"I suppose I need to call my secretary and tell her I'm back."

"Sure."

Grant cried aloud in anguish. "I can't! Do you understand? I can't do this."

"Call her so that she knows you're back but tell her you need some more time off. You can think about what you want to do next. Cooperstown is a good place to heal."

"Sure," he said as Wainwright parked Sam's truck in front of the old, stone house.

They ambled into the lit hallway. "I'll show you to the guest bedroom and get some bandages."

During the next few days, Grant Tyrell roamed around Cooperstown in a state of agitation and uncertainty. It occasionally crossed his mind to end his life rather than live without his friends and without the woman he loved. Wainwright reminded him that he could travel again to be by her side with the help of the cabin portal and the small cameo Grant held onto as if it were his very lifeline.

"Do you think they made it to Greece?" he would mumble over and over again, and Wainwright would always say that they surely had because Theodosus would allow nothing to happen to his new wife and the other women.

"They'll wait for us, but we won't show," he'd tell Wainwright.

And Wainwright would answer, "They'll know what to do."

"But she'll think that I abandoned her."

"She would never believe that."

"Then they'll think we died."

"They might think that," the time traveler admitted.

Grant called his office, and when his secretary answered he asked her how her sister was doing. It was the first thing he said.

"She's in remission, sir."

"That's good. She have insurance?"

"No, why?"

"Send the bills to me."

There was a pause. A silence indicating disbelief. "Are you okay, Mr. Tyrell?"

"Very fine but a little tired from the long trip."

"Your Jacuzzi came."

Grant answered halfheartedly, "That's nice."

"They had to spend more money than originally expected. Some problem with the plumbing where the waterlines were or something."

"That's all right. Does it look nice?"

"It looks like...some sort of Roman bath. Just as you wanted, Mr. Tyrell. Everyone wants to try it out," she giggled. "You really mean that about my sister's bills?"

"You doubt my words?"

"Oh no, Mr. Tyrell."

"Ask my staff to meet me for a meeting Monday morning."

"You coming back after the weekend?"

"I'll be there bright and early Monday morning."

"Do you want me to make the usual arrangements with the barber and the manicurist?"

He looked at his broken, chapped fingers. Then he stared at his reflection in the mirror. He looked terrible, but he looked like Grantus Tyrellius not Mr. Tyrell. "I suppose you'd better do that. I'll see you Monday. Take care of your sister this weekend, okay."

"Sure, Mr. Tyrell."

Wainwright had overheard the conversation. "Time to get back to your life?"

"Time to get back to *his* life. Not mine, Bruce. That life is not mine."

A new silver chain that Wainwright had just begun wearing around his neck, with a silver emblem of a fish hooked onto it, escaped the collar of his shirt; and the sun ray that had just crept into the room via the open window, made it shimmer.

"Call me if you need me," the time traveler said.

"Will do."

On Sunday, Grant drove back to his apartment in downtown New York. He stared at the World Trade Center which loomed high above the city, outlined the city, and marked the majesty of a different empire. "New York sure looks pretty today!" And he smiled. "Mighty pretty."

His apartment had been maintained according to the list of expectations he'd left his housekeeper. "My villa by the ocean," he said, wiping away the tears.

He placed Lydia's cameo on the bedside table. "Good night my beauty."

Chapter Thirty-Two

Grant Tyrell pumped more 'iron' than he could have imagined possible that first morning as he worked out in his office suite. The sauna's steamy heat felt as delightful as a swim in the sea. The barber asked him where he'd been as he cut away the long shaggy 'do' Grant had brought home with him. The manicurist told him that he could never resurrect the serious damage with one treatment.

His secretary arrived early and brought him his coffee and breakfast from the lobby restaurant.

"Just as you like it, Mr. Tyrell," she said with a bright smile.

"That was very nice of you, thanks."

The three servants stood frozen in their place.

"Your...welcome, Mr. Tyrell."

Tyrell's staff buzzed with happy animated discussion; each vying for a good position as they bolted out of the starting blocks for a covetous spot in the 'chariot race' to win favor with the 'new' boss. Each trying to push passed the other in expressing his or her joy at the boss's return. All their words were a jumble. None of it made sense to Grant right now.

Grant waved his hand for them to sit down, and, one at a time, he listened to all they had to say. Business had been good, and there were many suggestions from his staff as to how to make an even better profit. Some employees should be let go because they were arriving late to work and wasting time at the office. Others were going on maternity leave and should be let go indefinitely and with no pay if they could wing that with the union. The union had tried to push for better conditions while Grant was away, but they had cleverly put them on hold until his return. Some women in the production area wanted them to put in a child day care section, and other impertinent employees dared to ask for better health care insurance.

"Give my secretary a raise," Grant mumbled. "Give everyone double what they made this year. By June first, we will have sold the business."

The men and women, who stood beside him at the podium, who had clambered for the death of those who were unproductive, and who had waited like hungry beasts to see whose blood would be spilled next, stared in disbelief at the man they felt sure was the finest businessman they had ever met.

"I'm leaving for Rome in June. I won't be coming back to the United States. I'm selling the business, and I want a nice profit so that everyone is happy and has enough to get them through until they find a new job."

He pushed aside the microphone and walked slowly back to his own office and shut the door. He sat behind his desk and looked around his office as if he were seeing it for the first and last time.

"I miss you, Lydia. I didn't abandon you, and I am not dead. Far from it. I have never felt more alive in my life. Just very lonely for you. I'm coming back. Wait for me. Can you hear me across time? None of this," he said, stretching his arms to the walls, "means anything without you. Do you hear me, Venus?" He smiled. "May Venus smile on both us. That's what you always wanted for us, isn't it, goddess? That love would bring us together."

Grant took the cameo out of his pocket. "Wainwright told me that you were my passport back. I *have* to be one of the ones who stays. I'm giving it all up for her."

Chapter Thirty-Three

There was no need for Grant to go to the cabin in December. He took a flight to Athens and walked to the oldest stone structure he could find, and waited there—dressed in a plain white toga and wearing leather sandals—on June 21, 2001.

At two in the morning, he flew to Greece. It was the year 201 A.D. The morning dawned orange and red in the Grecian sky. Septimius Severus was still the emperor of Rome. The marketplace opened for business with carts laden with goods. One cart was being pushed by a young woman with a tiny baby in a special sling over her back.

"Diana?"

"Grantus!" she screamed and ran into his arms.

"You waited? For me?"

"We wouldn't leave without you! Oh, I am so glad to see you! Where is Socrates?"

"Ah...well...he'll be coming along in a few months. Are you safe here?"

"We have a small farm. It isn't much. We used all Lydia's coins to purchase it."

"Well that will all change very soon. Where's my lady?"

Diana showed him the way, and he carried Theodosus's new

son, Lucius, for her so that she could hold her skirt up as she ran beside him.

"Lydia!" she screamed.

A young woman moved away from the door of a small stone house and turned her head when she heard her name. As soon as she saw Grant, Lydia began to run to him. He handed the baby boy to his mother and opened his arms for his lady. A sack, that he had been carrying with him, fell to the ground as he gathered her into his arms.

"I prayed to Venus," she said breathlessly as she kissed his lips. "Oh, I never slept for worrying about you."

"I tried to get back to you, but it was treacherous for us. Socrates...will follow in a few months."

"Oh, I almost gave up hope," she continued. "But something kept telling me to hold onto the dream that you would return to me."

"A promise is a promise."

Suddenly, New York seemed very far away. His only life was here.

"Did you bring me a gift?" she said like a spoiled child suddenly noticing the sack on the ground.

"Of course. I'm buying my freedom from you."

She grinned at his play. "You no longer wish to be my slave?"

"That is correct," he said seriously.

Her smile faded. "You want to be free from me?"

"I didn't say that. I no longer want to be a slave under any man's terms."

"Then I grant you your freedom gladly."

"You'll write up a legal document attesting to that fact?"

"Yes, of course," was her bewildered answer.

"I am no longer your slave, Lydia of the house of Marcus Flavius Antonious?"

"You are free from my house."

"Good. Then as a free man of...New York by the Sea of Atlantic, I hereby do solemnly ask you—with all my heart—to be my wife."

The childlike grin returned. "I accept gladly, Grantus Tyrellius, free man of New York, wherever that is. However," she said, waltzing back into his arms and looking into his eyes. "How will you ever pay for your freedom? *You* have no money?"

"On the contrary," he said, kicking the sack at his sandaled feet open. She stooped to look inside.

The sack contained one hundred rather old looking gold coins with the image of Julius Caesar.

The End of <u>Portrait of Lydia</u>

Next book in the series:

<u>Beneath the Wings of Isis</u>

Printed in the United States
222264BV00001B/7/A